Lisa's Gift

Mackenzie McKade

A Samhain Publishing, Ltd. publication.

Samhain Publishing, Ltd.
512 Forest Lake Drive
Warner Robins, GA 31093
www.samhainpublishing.com

Lisa's Gift
Copyright © 2007 by Mackenzie McKade
Print ISBN: 1-59998-643-4
Digital ISBN: 1-59998-497-0

Editing by Angela James
Cover by Scott Carpenter

First Samhain Publishing, Ltd. electronic publication: January 2007
First Samhain Publishing, Ltd. print publication: July 2007

Dedication

To my wonderful friends on Macsdreamscape's loop, especially Crystal Scott who kept me energized and alive with ideas. You gals are the best!

Chapter One

Coming home for some people is a journey down memory lane—for Jana Ryan it was a trip down nightmare alley.

Even the starless night seemed to reflect her sullen mood as she drove closer and closer to the one place she didn't want to be. But her doctor had said coming home would be therapeutic, a chance to face her demons, a chance to be free.

Yeah, the doctor has no idea what she's talking about. Jana jerked the steering wheel, swerving the car just in time to miss a pothole in the street.

Distance—now that's true medicine. Out of sight out of mind.

And she had put Arizona as far out of her mind as she could—until now.

Of course, that was a lie. So here she was returning to a place that held few good memories. At least there were some. She allowed herself a smile when she thought of her best friend, Lisa Calloway, the only person on earth she trusted.

Yet another memory tugged at her. Even after being gone for five years she still thought of him. *Nicolas.* Jana had been a total four-eyed geek when she was in high school and she'd had the worst crush on Nicolas Marchetti, who'd often visited one of his friends a few doors down from where she lived. She thought of him playing one-on-one basketball with his friend. All those muscles. That gorgeous dark hair and those blue eyes.

If she ran into him now that she was back, would he even recognize her? She doubted it. Nicolas had never known Jana existed.

She gave a heavy sigh, flipped the turn signal, and slowed to a stop at an intersection before taking a left that moved her closer to the past.

An oncoming car's headlights nearly blinded her as she made the turn down a street she remembered all too well. A light film of perspiration dampened her forehead.

The six-hour drive from San Diego to Chandler had put an ache in Jana's back and a frown on her face. It was nearing midnight and her vision was blurred. She steered her red Nissan into her best friend's driveway and stopped. Tension caused every muscle in her body to clench. With a quick swipe of her hand she brushed a strand of auburn hair from her face. Tired blue eyes flashed back at her in the rearview mirror. She checked her appearance and then reached for the door. It made a low moan as she pushed it open and crawled out of the car. Purse hanging from her wrist, she slammed the door shut, before moving around to the back of the vehicle to pop the trunk.

Like a magnet her gaze was pulled toward the old house she'd lived in. It stood ominously in the shadows of the dimly lit street.

Nighttime was always the worst behind those cold walls.

Jana gripped her suitcase handle and yanked. *Stuck.* Another try rendered the same result. The damn oversized bag didn't appear to be going anywhere. Bracing her feet, she put her shoulder into it and pulled. Nothing. Dragging in a breath of frustration, she released the suitcase and inhaled, catching the slight hint of cow manure coming from a mile or more away.

Another attempt at dislodging the suitcase only made it jam against the spare tire. *Damn.* No way was she giving up. With as much strength as she could muster, she pulled. The suitcase suddenly came loose and proceeded to drop firmly on her toes. Pain splintered through her feet.

"For the love of God." A long sigh pushed from between her thin lips. She inched her feet free, slammed the trunk closed, and plopped her purse atop the car. "Where is that key?" She crammed her hand into the purse, rummaging through it for the key Lisa had mailed her. Jana had told her friend she'd arrive close to midnight. Lisa had told her to let herself in and Lisa would see her in the morning.

Key found, suitcase in tow, she moved to the front door of the house that had been her sanctuary as a child. Her chest tightened. Night after night, she had pretended Cathy and Joe were her mother and father, Lisa her sister. But it was only a dream. Nothing stays the same. Lisa's parents had deeded their family home to their daughter before they retired and moved to Florida.

A hollow, empty sound pushed from Jana's lips.

She had never known her mother and father. When she was two years old, her mother dropped her off at the Child's Crisis Center and never came back. Hell, she didn't even know when her real birthday was.

Tears filled Jana's eyes and she scrubbed them away with the back of one hand. She hadn't cried since leaving five years ago. God she was tired. She sucked in another breath and pushed away all sentimental thoughts, slipped the key in the lock and opened the door.

The house was dark as she cautiously moved through it. She couldn't trust that a couch or chair might be in the same place that she remembered. The last thing she wanted to do was wake her friend. Bumping into a coffee table, pain exploded across her knee. She barely stifled a yelp of pain in an effort to remain quiet.

As she progressed down the hall she saw soft light spilling from the master bedroom onto the hardwood floor. The door was ajar.

A moan coming from the room had Jana's heart beating and had her walking toward the door in haste. Was something wrong with Lisa?

Oh, God. What if she was hurt?

Jana pushed the door open a couple of feet and looked in, ready to call out to her friend.

The sight froze her feet to the floor and the words in her throat.

Lisa was on her knees, her lips wrapped around the cock of the man Jana had always dreamed of.

Nicolas Marchetti.

Jana started to tremble.

The scene before her looked like it had been ripped from the pages of some erotic fantasy. Lisa was buck naked, wearing only black stiletto heels, and her hands were tied behind her back,

Nicolas's fingers were tangled in Lisa's short blonde hair. Their eyes were pinned on each other as his erection slipped in and out of her mouth. The expression of rapture on her friend's face as she took the equally naked man deep crushed Jana's heart like a fifty-pound boulder.

Another rock of emotion slammed atop her breasts when Nicolas whispered, "That's it, baby. You know how I like it."

Well shit! Could the fucking night get any worse?

The answer was yes, since her feet wouldn't move. It seemed her body wanted her to take in the entire humiliation, grind it into her chest that the one person she loved more than life itself was betraying her.

Ridiculous.

Nicolas had never belonged to Jana. She had no claim on him for God's sake. How could she even think that way?

Her body shook.

Lisa had known every one of Jana's childhood fantasies about Nicolas. Lisa and she had even acted out what Nicolas might do to Jana some day. Their innocent sexual explorations together, touching and experimenting, and the dirty magazines that Jana's foster father hid away from her foster mother, helped to fill in many of the answers to a young girl's questions about sex.

The boy and those magazines put some crazy ideas into her head.

A husky moan tore from Nicolas's throat as he thrust one final time into Lisa's mouth. His hips jerked against her face. As his grip on Lisa's head secured, fingers curling deeper in her hair, he stilled. Eyes dark, his facial features tight, a satisfied groan pushed from his full lips sending a series of heat waves rippling through Jana. Her nipples stung, peaking into tight nubs as moisture built between her thighs.

Damn. Damn. Damn. This was all Jana needed. Talk about conflicting emotions. The three A's she had come to know were all too familiar: Angry. Aroused. Alone.

Firm, defined muscles rippled down Nicolas's impressive chest—larger, sexier than Jana remembered. He had matured into a man—a delicious and sensual man.

She tried to look away, but couldn't.

Mackenzie McKade

Why can't that be me on my knees? Me making love to Nicolas Marchetti?

Of course, Jana's breasts weren't as rounded and firm as Lisa's implants—a Christmas gift her friend had given herself two years ago. Jana knew she had a pretty good body, but Lisa's—her naked form was exquisite. No wonder Nicolas was with her.

His grip on Lisa gentled as he began to stroke her hair almost as if he cherished her. A look of complete admiration heated his eyes. "You were wonderful tonight. I think a reward is in order." He assisted Lisa to her feet, took her into his arms and captured her lips in a kiss that could only be described as commanding, forceful.

Again warmth radiated through Jana's body. That was what she wanted—needed—a man to take control, someone to assume responsibility for making her happy if only for a moment, a night.

No, that was wrong.

Jana, you are responsible for your own happiness. The doctor's words continued to run through her head. *No one can give you what you can't give yourself. What you really need to learn is to trust someone other than Lisa. Until you do you'll never be happy.*

Okay. Maybe that damn doctor was right. Jana couldn't help thinking it would be wonderful to have someone to share things with, even relinquish control to when things got rough. Yeah. Let someone else worry about the details. Maybe even tell her what she needed, as long as she could take back the reins when she needed to.

Jana finally got her feet to move and it was none too soon as Nicolas and Lisa parted. Without hesitation Jana backed into the hallway, gripped her hand tighter on the handle of her

10

suitcase and tiptoed to the small room at the end of the hall that used to be Lisa's bedroom.

Heart pounding, she flipped on the light, shut the door, and then threw herself on the bed.

Talk about a hell of a homecoming. Not only was she exhausted, but her body felt as tense as a time bomb. Tick. Tick. Every minute that passed, muscles and tendons drew tighter as if she would explode from the emotions swirling inside her. To complicate things, after the scene with Lisa and Nicolas, Jana felt the need to reach for her trusty vibrator.

"Okay, girl, put the situation in perspective." She fought back tears that burned behind her weary eyelids. "You've had sexual relationships. Nicolas was never attracted to you. And Lisa wouldn't do this to deliberately hurt you. You're an adult. Suck it up." *But, dammit, Lisa knew I was coming. The least she could have done was hide it from me for a while. Like fifty years.*

Rational thought left Jana and she was twelve again, needing to be hugged, needing to cry on someone's shoulder. But there was no one to hold her. The house that had once been her sanctuary now felt like a box trapping her inside. She glanced around the bedroom. Had it always been this small?

Little had changed since Lisa moved from this room to her parents'. She still had the soft pink walls and her queen-size bed seemed to take up what room remained.

The knife in Jana's heart turned another degree. She and Lisa had slept together in this bed so many times. Lisa would hold Jana as she cried over yet another beating from the hands of her drunken foster father.

A single tear slid down her cheek. She swatted at the drop angrily, refusing to believe that she would cry—could cry. Inside she was as dry as the Sierra Desert. A strong wind could blow her away, because within she was simply an empty shell.

Jana fisted her hands and pummeled the bed.

Dammit! Lisa swore they'd be friends forever. The desperate cry in Jana's mind sounded childish. No, she wasn't a child anymore. She was an adult. She didn't need anyone—even Lisa. Yet the void in her chest proved she did. She needed her friend more than life itself.

With her finger and thumb, she applied pressure on the bridge of her nose and sucked in a ragged breath. No more tears, she wouldn't cry. She couldn't help but think returning to Arizona was a bad decision, even for the cushy job offer she'd received.

No. It wasn't; she just needed time to adjust. She was tired and taking everything out of context. She just needed a good night's sleep.

As she rolled off the bed, the door opened and the effervescent Lisa, wrapped in a short silky robe, bounded into the room and into Jana's arms.

"Jana, my God, you're a sight for sore eyes. Let me take a look at you." Lisa's picture-perfect face beamed as she held Jana at arm's length. "Gorgeous. You're gorgeous."

Jana tried to smile, an action that fell short of its mark. Yes, she would admit that she wasn't the scrawny girl she used to be. It had taken forever for her breasts to develop, but when they did, they matured into a nice set of 36Cs. Her jeans rode low on a set of now slender hips, and she was taller by two inches compared to Lisa's five-six. Jana had taken to letting her hair grow long, showing off the natural highlights in her auburn hair, and her blue eyes were no longer hidden by glasses. Laser surgery took care of that flaw.

"What's wrong?" Lisa furrowed her brows, but then they shot upward. "Oh, my God, tell me you didn't see—" She searched Jana's face. "You did." With her usual casual air she said, "Awkward moment." She paused briefly. "Okay, the moment's over."

Jana couldn't help smiling at her bubbly friend.

She drew Jana again into her arms. "I'm glad you're here. I can't wait for you to meet Nicolas. Do you remember Nicolas?"

As if her friend conjured Nicolas, he appeared. Wearing nothing but a pair of jeans, the top button undone, he filled the doorway looking three times as good as Jana remembered. That cocky grin and the twinkle of mischief in his eyes glowed with the knowledge of a man and not a boy.

By the male arrogance in the way he leaned against the doorjamb, she knew *he knew* Jana had seen what Lisa and he had been doing earlier.

A wavy lock of ebony hair fell across one sapphire eye and Jana couldn't help but want to sweep it aside, run her palm across the five o'clock shadow that was present on his square jaw. He wore his hair shorter than in the past, cropped at his neck, longer on the top falling across his forehead.

Lisa brushed her hand in his direction. "Nicolas, she's here."

He moved with the air of a predator, slow and sexy, stealing the air from the room as he stepped inside. "I see that." His tone was a deep mixture of sensuality and heat.

Jana couldn't think, couldn't breathe, and she couldn't remember when she'd ever been this close to him. Man, what she'd give to reach out and run her fingers through his light layer of chest hair and follow the dark line that traveled down his six-pack and disappeared into his pants.

Jana choked out, "Yes. Uh...yes, I remember Nicolas." She felt his eyes caress her body, stopping at her breasts, causing her nipples to harden into tight nubs that pushed against the cotton shirt she wore. Then his hot gaze moved across her hips and touched the apex of her thighs.

Well fuck! Moisture released from between her legs at the mere thought of what he must be thinking.

Damn man. She couldn't believe he was doing that in front of his girlfriend, Jana's best friend.

God, Jana was tired. She cocked a brow showing her disapproval.

Lisa laughed and strolled into his arms. She swatted him on the chest. "Stop teasing her." She snuggled close and glanced at Jana with a smile. "Nicolas has an insatiable appetite."

Jana's eyes widened. *TMI! Too much information.* More than she cared to hear. It seemed odd that Lisa was lackadaisical at Nicolas's obvious interest in another woman. Namely—*her!*

Lisa wrinkled her nose in her cutesy kind of way and she said, "I knew you would like her. Soon you'll love her as much as I do."

Okay, this was too awkward a situation. *Duh!* Didn't Lisa realize how it would affect Jana, catching her best friend with the man of her dreams? Or was Lisa just clueless—something totally out of character for Lisa? She was the most sensitive, loving individual Jana knew. "Come into the kitchen and I'll fix us a turkey sandwich," Lisa offered. Damn, but her friend fit perfectly in the curve of Nicolas's body. Her blonde hair was a striking contrast against his golden skin.

"Uh, Lisa, I'm not hungry. In fact, I'm dead tired. We can talk tomorrow." *Please, please let me get away from those penetrating eyes.* Nicolas had yet to release Jana from his sight. Although he held Lisa, he stared at Jana like he was indeed hungry and his focus was not on a turkey sandwich.

He smiled as if he knew of Jana's discomfort and only wanted to enhance it. He released Lisa and made a move toward the queen-size bed. "Ready for bed? I'm game."

Jana's jaw dropped, and she knew her eyes had taken on the size of saucers.

Lisa's smile faltered. She reached out and circled his biceps with her fingers. "Nicolas, not now." He just gave Lisa that mischievous grin Jana had seen so many times in him when they were younger.

Surely he didn't think he was going to jump from Lisa's bed to hers. The asinine idea caused a sudden flood of heat to consume Jana's cheeks.

Lisa gave Nicolas a pleading look. And then once again her smile returned. "Jana, I'm sorry. We need to let you get some sleep." Lisa slid her palm down Nicolas's arm, capturing his hand in hers before turning and leading him from the bedroom. Before she disappeared, she glanced over her shoulder. "We'll talk in the morning."

Alone again, Jana tried to decipher what just happened, but she was too tired, confused, and numb from the rush of emotion that had hit her when she arrived in Chandler. She was better off not even thinking about the situation between Nicolas and Lisa, which could only push her deeper into the solemn mood in which she found herself.

What she needed was a good cry. Her doctor said to cry was healthy, but Jana couldn't—wouldn't. She had shed too many tears as a child. It was time to be tough. Time to start living her life and rise above the past.

Tears were for children.

And it was time to get some sleep and forget what she had just experienced. Tomorrow she would wake and everything would be fine. She released a disgusted breath. Yeah, and when

Lisa woke up she'd be in Nicolas's strong embrace. Perhaps Jana would just climb in bed with the both of them. Wouldn't that surprise the hell out of everybody?

Instead she undressed, slipped on a different T-shirt and crawled into bed—alone.

Chapter Two

Nicolas pulled Lisa's naked body into the curve of his own as they lay in bed. He was hard again. The little minx in the room down the hall had stirred a fire inside him he hadn't expected. But evidently Lisa had. For several weeks she had teased him, tempting him with her friend's attributes. And she'd been right. The instant attraction had been there.

He nuzzled Lisa's neck. They were going to have a helluva time together. "Your friend isn't what I remember."

Lisa cast him a frown over her shoulder. "She isn't the same person." There was a bite to her words.

Usually her disobedience in the bedroom would result in a punishment, but Lisa hadn't been acting herself lately. For several months he had enjoyed her company and not once had she tested his authority, until a week ago.

He had been in-between submissive partners when he met her at a mutual acquaintance's cave party. At the time, something had been missing in his life. He just couldn't quite put his finger on it. And then she appeared from out of nowhere, sexy and accommodating and available.

"Hey, baby, I wasn't talking trash about her." His hand caressed Lisa's waist, following the swell of her hip. He could feel her tense beneath his touch. "It's just that I'd heard rumors about what she went through with the Carters. The old man was a mean bastard." Nicolas slipped his fingers between Lisa's thighs, seeking her heat.

She gripped his wrist. "Not now, Nicolas, please. I'm not feeling very well."

Warning bells went off in his head. She had never refused him, nor had she ever used her safe word during their playtime. But tonight after her friend's arrival she had turned cold, distant.

Or could it be something else?

Even though they had drawn up a contract that specified that when they entered the bedroom his rules applied, his pleasures were all that mattered, there was a time for the Master and slave role and this didn't appear to be one of them.

"Did I hurt you?" They had tried a new toy tonight, one with electricity that she had appeared to enjoy. Had he been wrong? Always careful, he had tried the violet wand on himself before their play session. There was a definite sting to the charge, but nothing she couldn't handle as long as he kept the voltage to its lowest point. He drew her closer into his embrace. "I'd never hurt you, Lisa. You'll tell me if I do?"

She rolled upon her back. Her eyes looked weary, still she managed a smile. "I know, Nicolas. I guess I have a lot on my mind."

Lisa scooted further away, closer to the edge of the bed, putting distance between them. Another thing she had never done before, especially since she knew he demanded his woman naked and close, easily accessible when he had the desire to touch her. In fact, many nights he had fallen asleep buried deep within Lisa's body. She was his to do with as he pleased and it pleased him to take her at any time.

"We need to take it slow with Jana. I don't think she's ever been introduced to this lifestyle." She shielded her eyes with her palm, as if the light made her head ache. "You do like her, don't you?"

Nicolas chuckled. Hell yes, he liked Jana. What man in his right mind wouldn't? His fucking hard-on was proof. She had a natural submissiveness about her that called to him. Not to mention she was a beauty. He loved a woman with auburn hair. Just the thought of what he would do to her made his testicles draw tight. "Will Jana be interested in joining our lifestyle, especially after what the bastard down the street did to her?"

Old man Carter had beaten Jana days before graduation. She had missed the special event, because she'd been hurt so badly she couldn't walk. He had scarred her in more places than her body. Her return to Arizona tonight was her first visit since the attack. Even though the son of a bitch had been incarcerated for his sins and Jana's foster mother had moved away, Lisa had told Nicolas she believed Jana's return to Chandler would have a negative effect on her.

Breaking away from that abusive family was the best thing that ever happened to her. The next was a four-year science scholarship at the University of Southern California, a chemical engineering degree and the job she landed with Medical Devices in Tempe, according to Lisa.

Nicolas couldn't believe the anger that surfaced within him. He enjoyed the BDSM lifestyle behind the bedroom door, but only when his partners were consensual. He'd never touch a woman against her wishes. And damn the son of a bitch who did.

And yet, from the scene he and Lisa had staged earlier, Nicolas thought that Jana just might be interested in their lifestyle. Lisa's friend had been frozen in place, her eyes wide with shock at first, quickly melting to arousal. He had smelled her desire. It called to him, begged him to take her. Control to a

Dom was everything, and it took everything he had not to demand that she sink to her knees and assist Lisa in pleasuring him.

Lisa's laugh was weak as she withdrew her palm from her eyes. "Oh, yeah. She'll join us. You have never seen a more inquisitive person than Jana. She and I explored each other's bodies on several occasions. Horny teenagers." Lisa chuckled, her laughter dying. "But she has a lot of baggage. The fucker did a job on her, so just in case, let's take it slow." Lisa yawned. The glow had disappeared from her face. How she could go from vibrant and alive to looking like she was desperate for rest and sleep he didn't know.

Females were strange. Their emotions flipped faster than a light switch. He loved them all the same. Within each one there was a beauty and it wasn't necessarily external. Young or old, they held a charm about them that had always fascinated him.

He drew in a breath, inhaling Lisa's soft, powdery scent and the smell of sex lingering in the room. Her silky skin, moans of pleasure, even her cries of pain were an aphrodisiac to his senses when they acted out scenes. His erection grew firmer and he wrapped his fingers around his engorged shaft. He could fuck her all night long, which was his right. He slowly moved his hand from his balls to the tip and back again as he glanced at her back. His hot gaze followed her delicate spine until it reached the small of her back where the swell of her ass began. He stroked again. She had a great ass. The thought made his testicles pulse. Her shoulders rose with each inhale. He could hear her soft breathing. She was asleep.

Nicolas tightened his jaw. He was not a man who did without. His grip on his erection tightened as he pumped faster. Yet, it was obvious that Lisa was troubled tonight. Forcing her to submit would see to his needs, but something told him her heart wouldn't be into the act and that was the beauty of the game. The thought sent sensation radiating down his cock. The intensity of a woman's eyes as she submitted, the hunger to please her Master, even the haze of desire as she released upon command, was power—pure adrenaline raging through his body.

The image of Lisa only nights before made him suck in a breath through clenched teeth, his hand sliding up and down his cock, his rhythm increasing as he pictured the scene. The sound of leather slapping against pale skin spanked a delightful pink. Chains pressed against flesh, restraining her wrists and ankles. There was nothing like a woman on her knees, her hands cuffed behind her, eagerly waiting for the moment he thrust into her hot, wet mouth.

His climax hit with such an impact it sent his hips off the bed. He groaned as a stream of come arced through the air. Twisting his head to the side, he barely dodged the flow that landed next to his ear on his pillow.

Well shit.

After chuckling about his near miss, he cleaned up the come with a tissue from the dresser next to the bed, turned his pillow over, then switched the lamp off and chased sleep that never came.

Lying there for roughly an hour, he thought of pulling Lisa against him. If she hadn't expressed not feeling well he would have done just that; instead he began to think about Lisa and Jana, drawing out scenarios of the three of them together.

He heard Lisa stir. She moved quietly as if not to disturb him; still, the bed squeaked when she rose. After grabbing a robe off the chair she slipped her arms through it, securing the sash around her waist. Her silhouette moved across the room and then disappeared through the open door.

The quickness in her movements gave him pause. She hadn't gone to the bathroom just off the master bedroom. Perhaps she was hungry. In fact, now that he thought about it, he could eat a sandwich or two.

Well, so much for sleeping. He scooted off the bed, stretching as he stood. He didn't bother to put on a robe, he liked being naked, liked the feel of air caressing his heated flesh. As he made his way down the hall and then entered the kitchen, he noticed the back door ajar. A door he had personally locked before turning in.

No lights were on throughout the house and Lisa was nowhere to be found.

A strange feeling crawled across his skin like a million tiny bugs. Then from outside he heard faint noises that grew louder as he got closer. Someone was weeping, crying as if her heart would break. When he opened the door wider he discovered it was Lisa.

She sat on the top step, her knees pressed against her chest, her arms hugging them closely. She rocked slowly. Strangled cries spilled from her lips in heavy sobs.

"Lisa?"

She startled as his hand rested on her shoulder. Her voice caught, short, gasping breaths as she fought to cease her sobbing. A none-too-delicate snort was the result.

She wiped frantically at her tears as if she could hide the fact she was hurting. Before tonight he'd never seen her cry and she'd never revealed any emotion other than wanting to please him.

For a man who knew exactly how to treat a woman, he had no idea whether to back off or take her into his arms. He listened to the crickets chirping and inhaled the night air that had the tinge of bug spray used to kill mosquitoes. Better just to get to the point.

"Baby, do we need to talk?" He braced himself for what could only be the ending of their relationship. It was all making sense. The way Lisa was reverting inwardly, pulling away from him.

Moonlight danced across her face when she glanced up at him. The clouds had thinned. Stars dotted the heavens.

"No." Her single word response left him more than baffled.

"No?" he repeated.

"No." She was gaining control of herself. She sniffled, chasing away the last of her tears.

Without hesitation, she let him draw her to her feet and into his embrace. Her powdery perfume teased his nose. She clung to him tighter than she ever had. He kissed her forehead tenderly, feeling the worry lines beneath his lips. "You can't tell me that was nothing." She began to tremble, but kept her tears in check. "Talk to me."

"It's nothing," she choked out. "I'm just worried about Jana." She looked up at him with moist eyes. "You do like her, don't you?"

He nodded. "Is that what this is all about?" Women could be ridiculous. She probably thought that if the threesome didn't work that things wouldn't work between him and Lisa, which bothered him on several fronts. First, although he looked forward to having two women in his bed it wasn't something that drove him. Ménages weren't new to him. One woman was enough for him. But the second point was that he never really got the impression Lisa wanted a "forever after" kind of relationship. Theirs up to now had only been an agreement of sexual fulfillment. He didn't know if he was ready to make a commitment of any kind.

Lisa began to laugh, but something in her flat tone lacked enthusiasm. In fact, she sounded more relieved than anything else. "You can put that skittish expression to rest. I'm not looking to tie you down." Her firm gaze met his. "Right? No ties between us. Just really good sex."

Nicolas would have been lying if he didn't admit her words lightened the weight on his chest. He stopped himself from releasing a thankful sigh. Instead he held her tighter. "Not just good sex, great sex."

She slid her body along his length, the sensation hardening his cock. "Then if we're in agreement, why don't we go back to bed and you can fuck me all night long?"

Now this was the woman he had gotten to know. Sexy, sensual and always ready for a good fucking. "What's your pleasure tonight?"

She gazed up in surprise. "You're handing me the reins? I can tie you up and spank you." A sparkle lit in her eyes as her palms stroked down his back and rested on his ass before she gave both cheeks a squeeze.

He chuckled. A Dom never completely handed a sub the reins. Lisa would only think she held them. "What do you have in mind?" He cupped the back of her head and pulled her inches away from his lips.

The light in her eyes suddenly died. "Nicolas, would you just hold me tonight? Maybe vanilla sex, slow and tender?" There was a tinge of desperation in her voice that chilled him.

Lisa must care deeply for Jana if she was this worried about her friend. He couldn't stop thinking that there was more to Lisa's mood shifts over the last week.

If she couldn't confide in him, something was lacking in their relationship. The beauty of BDSM was trust and clearly it was missing between them. She would let him do anything with her body, but she wasn't allowing him total control of her mind and soul.

Apparently Jana wasn't the only one in the house with emotional baggage. Hell, even he carried a sack or two around. Didn't everyone? He pushed thoughts of his father from his mind.

Come to think of it, Lisa really hadn't let him get any closer than sex, and he hadn't forced the issue, preferring things the way they were. During the day he ran the family restaurant, a classy Italian place called Marchetti's on Val Vista and Baseline, while Lisa went to her job as a registered nurse at Banner Health Services in Mesa. At night they would meet at either one's home and share their bodies, but never their personal thoughts, or discussions of their day. Their agreement was physical only, no emotional ties.

"Is that a yes?" she asked almost hesitantly.

"Anything you want tonight," he said, realizing that he didn't want a relationship void of emotion like his parents. Although he had shivered at the thought of commitment, what was a relationship without it? Perhaps there lay the true failure of all his previous attempts. How could he have a healthy relationship when a contract stood between him and his partner in the bedroom?

A marriage license had been his father's contract to treat Nicolas's mother badly.

Honestly, Nicolas didn't care for where this mental evaluation was heading.

What was he was looking for? A commitment? Maybe it was time to settle down. He gazed into Lisa's misty brown eyes.

Nahhh. Just a temporary moment of insanity.

He felt like laughing aloud at his wanderings. Neither he nor Lisa were right for the other. They were just filling a momentary void.

Yeah, that's what it is, temporary insanity. That could explain the instant attraction he felt for Lisa's friend. Or perhaps in this case it was acknowledging that he would be Master of both women—every man's fantasy.

All he needed was a good fuck and tomorrow he'd be back to his old self. He pressed his lips to Lisa's and she melted in his arms as he knew she would. She was pliable, easily bending to his will, but tonight was her night. If a slow, gentle loving was what she wanted, he would give it to her with pleasure.

But tomorrow night was his and he had several ideas for what he planned to do to Lisa and her redheaded friend.

Chapter Three

Warm water pelted Jana's face and chest. Steam fogged the shower glass, which only made her feel like she was still in a haze. Her face felt swollen and tight even though she hadn't cried. Her jaws ached as if she had spent the night clenching her teeth.

What had happened to, "You'll feel better in the morning"?

With a brush of her washcloth across her face, Jana came to the conclusion that most—if not all—aphorisms sucked.

But did that stop her from thinking of another and yet another?

Nooo...

Today is the first day of your life.

There's light at the end of the tunnel.

And the one that her doctor continuingly quoted by Alexander Chalmers, "The three grand essentials of happiness are: something to do, someone to love, and something to hope for."

Well she had two out of the three. She had something to do. She needed to find someplace else to live. And she had something to hope for. With a little luck she could get out of the house before Lisa and Nicolas rose.

Clearly she'd woken up on the wrong side of the bed. She hadn't had much sleep, troubled by old memories that she thought she'd put to rest. Seeing Lisa and Nicolas together had been a shock. None of it was impossible for her to work through. She just needed to sort it all out. A deep inhale and exhale released some of the tension. Everything would be okay. All she had to do was believe, because it was time for her to live and enjoy life.

With that last thought she shut off the water, opened the shower door, and grabbed a towel. She was just about to wrap it around her when the door to the bathroom opened and Nicolas, wearing a soft velour robe, filled the doorway. His brows shot up and his gaze flew to her exposed breasts.

She released a squeal of surprise as she fumbled with the towel, which she proceeded to drop. It seemed rather ridiculous to try to cover up since he had seen every inch of her body. As calmly as she could she bent and retrieved the towel, keeping her eyes on him. As she did, his gaze raised to meet hers, a devilish smile plastered on his handsome face.

After wrapping the towel securely around her, she pointed to the door. "Don't you know how to knock?" Even if the lock on the door was broken, he should have knocked.

"Yeah. But what's the fun in that? Look at what I would have missed." He casually leaned against the doorjamb and crossed his arms over his broad chest. "Nice. Real nice."

She snorted. The unladylike sound deepened his smile. Heart pounding, she squared her shoulders and lifted her chin. "Do you mind?" God, he was gorgeous, simply gorgeous.

And Lisa's she reminded herself.

"Not at all." Yet he made no attempt to step aside or to leave. Instead, his voice dropped several octaves. "Would you like me to dry you off?" Lord, but the sensuality in his tone made goose bumps rise across her skin.

Nervous laughter burst from her lips. "I don't think so." Just the thought of his strong hands roaming across her body made every hair stand on end.

He pushed away from the doorway and slowly straightened, taking a step toward her. With a cock of his head he furrowed his brows, looking at her strangely.

She double-checked the towel around her. "What?"

"Soap. In your hair." His sapphire eyes lit up as if they were blue fire under glass. A twitch teased the corner of his mouth as he restrained a smile. "What do you say we jump back into the shower? I'll rinse you off."

Jana felt her eyes widen. Nicolas was a rogue, a whoremonger. But a handsome whoremonger.

Lisa slipped into the bathroom next to him. Casually, he wrapped an arm around her, but continued to smile at Jana.

Argh... He knew this was awkward for Jana. Still, he persisted in teasing her.

"Oh, good. You're awake," Lisa said, snuggling close to Nicolas.

Oh good! I'm awake. Duh, Lisa, doesn't this appear out of the ordinary to you? I'm naked. Your boyfriend is standing in the bathroom ogling me.

Jana realized her mouth was hanging open as she snapped it shut. Lisa's gaze shot to Jana then to Nicolas.

Oh no. Here it comes. Jana had no idea how she was going to deal with this awkwardness.

Lisa cocked a brow. "What are you two up to?"

Heat flared across Jana's face like she had just gotten caught in a wildfire, or with a proverbial hand in the cookie jar.

She was just about to blurt the truth, when Nicolas said, "She still has soap in her hair. I offered to jump in the shower with her and help her rinse off."

Damn. Damn. Damn. If Jana could have crawled beneath the sink she would have. And that wasn't exactly a truth she was going to reveal.

"Great!" Lisa perked. "I haven't showered yet. We could make it a threesome." She undid the sash around her waist and let her robe slip down her naked body.

Holy shit!

Okay... Exactly what kind of relationship did Lisa have with Nicolas? Jana had always known that Lisa was promiscuous. Hell. Who was she to talk? Lisa and she had learned about sex together. Neither was unfamiliar with the other's body. But how was Jana supposed to deal with this situation?

"Wish I could, but I have some things I'd like to take care of this morning." *Wish I could!* She couldn't believe those words came out of her mouth.

Jana was certain she was losing her mind, because beneath her terry-towel her nipples were throbbing. Just the thought of soap-slicked bodies rubbing against each other was enough to set her blood boiling. Thank God she hadn't dried off. If she were lucky, the flood of moisture between her thighs could be passed off as excess water from her shower.

And that devilish man was grinning from ear to ear as if he knew it, too. What had she ever seen in him? Then he stooped to pick up Lisa's robe and his own robe parted, giving her a bird's eye view of what lay beneath it, reminding her exactly what she saw in him. He was gorgeous and apparently hung like a bull. Well, perhaps she was exaggerating a bit, but hot damn he was long and thick and fully erect. The image of that impressive cock sliding in and out of Lisa's mouth flashed in Jana's head.

Lisa was so lucky.

And that wasn't easy to say. It had taken years in therapy to delineate between what her foster father had done to her and what was a normal pattern of behavior for most men. Not all men were abusive. Not all men were untrustworthy.

Jana didn't have problems with sex. She enjoyed the touch of a man. She just didn't trust them or want any commitments with one.

Lisa's excitement faded as her face went blank. "Where are you going?"

Tension tightened the muscles across Jana's shoulders, making them feel as if she carried the world's woes. She wasn't ready to deal with this, but as her doctor said, *Don't put off the ugliness in your life. Face it head on. And most importantly, deal with it immediately.*

And for the most part that's exactly how Jana felt, except for now. She mustered the courage to say, "I thought I'd start looking for an apartment."

Lisa flinched at Jana's words as if she had slapped her across the face. "No," she whispered almost inaudibly. "No," she repeated louder this time. "You can't. I need you." Tears welled in her eyes.

Jana hugged the towel around her. She had never seen Lisa react so emotionally. For a moment there was silence. Lisa bit her bottom lip like she did when she was nervous or afraid.

"Tell you what," Nicolas interrupted as he draped the robe over Lisa's shoulders. "You two can discuss this over breakfast. My treat, I'll cook. What do you say?"

Lisa directed her teary eyes at Jana. "Please, don't leave. I need you here. I-I mean, I want you to stay." Something in Lisa's pleading voice made Jana pause. Lisa had lived alone for several years now. In fact, she had written Jana a few times and expressed her happiness in being free from her parents, although she loved them dearly and visited them frequently in Florida.

Perhaps she wasn't as happy with Nicolas as Jana had assumed. She had barely exchanged hellos with her friend, much less really talked. The last time they'd spoken it had been brief, because Lisa was heading out to a doctor's appointment. Even during those times Jana had picked up a note of unease in her friend's voice.

Then a shiver raked Jana's back. Could Lisa have fallen into an abusive situation? Just the thought made Jana cringe. The scene between Nicolas and Lisa that Jana had walked in on when she arrived last night made sense now.

"If you're hurting Lisa, I'll kill you." The threat in Jana's low and steady voice shocked her. Where the hell did that come from?

Lisa's palm covered her mouth. Her eyes bulged. The smirk on Nicolas's face died a sudden death. For a moment no one spoke.

Nicolas's stance went rigid. In a controlled and firm tone, he said, "I would never hurt Lisa, or any woman for that fact."

Not true. The fire in his eyes said given half the chance he'd strangle Jana for offending him. His neck turned scarlet red. She watched in horror as heat consumed his face. It was always at this point that her foster father had attacked.

Flashes of her foster father consumed Jana's imagination. She swung around, frantically looking for something to protect herself. She spotted the toilet brush and jerked it from its sheath. If she'd been in an old-time movie she might even have said, "En garde," as she struck a pose and lunged forward.

That's when everything went to hell. Both Lisa and Nicolas burst into laughter. Their reaction froze Jana and from out of the corner of her eye she saw her reflection in the mirror. The picture made her wince—a half-naked, crazed woman attacking a large man with a toilet brush.

Lisa pushed past Nicolas. "I'm sorry if I gave you the wrong impression." Her arms folded around Jana. "And I didn't mean to laugh." If that was true Jana thought Lisa would have stopped. Yet each word struggled to escape between bouts of laughter. "It's just—" She released Jana, stepped back and took one more look at Jana and her laughter deepened. "What I mean is—"

Nicolas was the first to regain his composure, but the heat from his face had not vanished nor had the stern look he gave her. Clearly he was still offended. With more authority in his voice than Jana was comfortable with he said, "Release Jana and get dressed." Lisa's arms immediately fell from around Jana. Although her friend continued to choke back her laughter, she complied with his demand, but not before perching on her tiptoes and giving Nicolas a quick kiss.

And then Jana was once again alone with Nicolas. For a moment he didn't speak. His hot gaze remained pinned on hers. If fact, she gave it right back at him. If she'd learned anything in therapy it was that she'd never back down from a man. She was in control—well, sort of. And she would die before another person took advantage of her like her foster father had done. Even if she had to use a toilet bowl brush, which she still held, to defend herself.

Jana was magnificent. After all she'd been through she was willing to protect her friend and herself. Her choice of weapons left much to be desired. With her auburn hair wet and wild, her body slick with moisture, the fire raging in her eyes, she could only be described as a wildcat. One he would enjoy taming.

Beneath his robe his erection, which had softened the minute she threatened to attack him with the toilet brush and threw him into hysterics, began to harden again. Something about this woman called to him. One minute she was a child in need of rescuing, and the next a strong woman hard as nails. And for some unknown reason, he wanted to be the one who brought the child and woman together to make a whole person.

He sensed she needed a firm but gentle hand. "Get dressed." His tone left no room for discussion.

Her brows shot up so fast he half expected them to touch her hairline. "Excuse me?"

He softened his voice. "Why don't you get dressed?" His mind and body were at war. What he wanted to say was, "I'm not accustomed to repeating myself. You can dress on your own or you can choose to have me do it for you." Just the thought drew his balls up close to his body. He wanted this woman, wanted to feel her beneath him as he spread her thighs and entered her warmth. Would she make soft mewling sounds as he invaded her body, her mind, her soul? Or would she scream, clawing his back as she reached orgasm? Would her eyes glow with fire as he strapped her to his bed or would they be clouded with desire? A spasm clenched his testicles, sending waves of fire down his shaft and a shiver through his body.

Damn, he had to stop thinking like this. She aroused him to the point that all he wanted was to take her down to the floor and fuck her until she screamed. And he wanted to hear his name on her sweet lips, which was the wrong thing to think about as his gaze lit upon her mouth, sending his thoughts into a spin. How would those pouty lips feel wrapped around his cock?

Her shoulders stiffened and her chin raised. With a huff, she tossed the toilet brush aside, shrugging by him as she exited the bathroom. Heavy steps sounded as she stomped down the hall and disappeared into her room.

A smirk of satisfaction rose in him. If he had her pegged right she was going to be a pleasurable submissive.

When this woman surrendered it would be a true surrender. And Nicolas wanted to be the man to whom she gave herself. All he needed was a plan.

What better way to accomplish his goal than seduction?

As he moved toward the kitchen, his mind was going a mile a minute. It was Friday; both he and Lisa had taken the day off, making this Labor Day holiday a four-day weekend so they could share it with Jana.

Out of the cupboard he retrieved a large skillet and a smaller one. The night before he had chopped up vegetables and precooked the meats for their omelets. All he needed was to throw it together and sauté the ingredients in butter. Yes, it would have been better to cook it fresh like he would in his restaurant, but while he had waited for Lisa to come home last night he had gotten antsy. Nothing calmed him like cooking. They'd had plans for dinner; breakfast was the only thing he could think to cook.

From the refrigerator he retrieved the fixings, including eggs, milk and cheese. As he cracked eggs and placed them in a bowl he thought about Jana and his plan of seduction. Lisa was wrong in taking it slow with her. She would respond better to shock. Her own body's needs would do the rest.

Mackenzie McKade

With a grin he slipped his robe off his shoulders, baring himself. Then he headed to the pantry, grabbed his apron off the hook, hung his robe in its place, and went back to work preparing breakfast.

Chapter Four

Holy shit! Jana almost swallowed her tongue when she entered the kitchen. She stopped so quickly she swayed. Nicolas stood facing the old gas stove she'd seen Lisa's mother stand before so many times. A myriad of familiar scents—bacon, watermelon, and biscuits—brought forth memories of home-cooked meals that had quieted Jana's hungry stomach as a child. But what widened her eyes was the fact that he wore nothing but a white apron tied around his neck and his waist. The impressive span of his back, the globes of his taut ass, and the definition of muscles and tendons streaming down his thighs and legs were magnificent. Well, there were also his strong arms and sculpted biceps that caught her eyes as he moved like an expert about the kitchen.

Beside him were three plates. Two of them had delicious-looking omelets covered in melted cheese. Steam rose and the most heavenly smell touched Jana's nose. From the skillet, he placed the last omelet on the remaining plate.

Out of the cupboard Nicolas retrieved a small can of seasoning. Lightly, he sprinkled a red powder atop the omelets. Paprika, Jana guessed.

"Take a seat. Breakfast will be ready in a minute." Nicolas covered one of the plates with a silver dome.

This was just too weird. *I'm out of here.* She pivoted on the ball of one foot and ran right into Lisa.

"Yummy." Lisa scanned Nicolas's backside with a heated gaze, making Jana wonder whether she was talking about Nicolas or the delectable aroma that filled the kitchen. "He is such a great cook."

She folded her arm into the crook of Jana's and led her to the old butcher block table that sat before a bay window looking out over the immaculately groomed backyard. Three place settings and three glasses of orange juice were arranged before them. "Do you remember that his family owns an Italian restaurant?" Before Jana could speak, Lisa continued, "He plans on taking us there tonight." Lisa pushed Jana down into a chair and then took one of her own.

"Tonight?" Jana's gaze flickered to Nicolas's firm ass and then back to Lisa. She leaned into her friend and whispered, "Um... He doesn't have anything on under that apron."

A delightful smile raised the corner of Lisa's mouth. Her gaze slowly caressed up and down his exposed backside. "I know. Isn't it great?"

Yeah, it is fucking fantastic.

Jana felt a frown tug her brows inward. "I really think I should leave." As she began to rise, Lisa's hand caught hers, stopping her midway.

"Come on, Jana. Where's your sense of adventure? We're all adults. The three of us could have some fun."

Three of us? What the hell was Lisa talking about?

Lisa's eyes sparkled with mischief. "You're not chicken, are you? Scared you might see something you like—want?"

Jana harrumphed. "Chicken? Me?" She wasn't afraid of a naked man.

"Prove it. Sit down." Lisa patted Jana's hand.

Lisa was goading her and damn if Jana didn't rise to the occasion, easing back into her chair.

An expression of triumph fell across Lisa's face. "Trust me, Jana. This will be one breakfast you'll never forget."

As usual, Lisa was vibrant and bubbly as she updated Jana on the news of the neighborhood. There was something about her friend that usually had a calming effect on Jana. But today Lisa made her feel dumpy. Here Jana was dressed in a pair of faded jeans, a spaghetti strap shirt and tennis shoes, while Lisa had on a skimpy green sundress that clung to every curve, and matching sandals to top the ensemble off.

And, of course, there was that arrogant man wearing only an apron strutting around the kitchen.

Lisa glanced over her shoulder, taking another peek at him. When she turned back she gave Jana a wink, then leaned in close. "Isn't he gorgeous? Can you imagine having a taste of him every morning and every night?"

Sitting with her hands clenched tightly in her lap, all Jana could say was, "Mmmm..." The sound came out on the sarcastic side, but she couldn't help it. The green-eyed monster had taken that moment to rise and send the heat of envy flooding through Jana's warm body as she wondered just how good Nicolas really was. A sour dose of guilt made her bring her thoughts back in line.

What kind of woman lusted over her friend's man? Because lust could be the only explanation why her breasts felt heavy and her nipples strained against the cotton of her shirt. With her every movement the material stroked her nubs, adding to the discomfort building between her thighs. And it didn't help that Lisa had given her the seat facing the stove. She saw every seductive move Nicolas made. When he turned around she read the writing on his apron.

I'm the chef and you will do it my way.

Well, how appropriate. Jana couldn't help scanning his length and noticing the huge bulge beneath his apron. *Damn! Damn! Damn!* She should get out of here.

At the far end of the counter, he flipped on a compact disc player and the music of the Pussycat Dolls began to play. The beat of "Don't Cha" seemed to raise Jana's pulse—or was it the man looking at her with such heat in his sapphire eyes it made her insides melt?

The CD player had to be a new addition to the kitchen, because Lisa's mother's philosophy was that when you sat down for a meal it was family time. She allowed no interference and even demanded that each person around the table contribute. It was the only time Jana had felt a part of a family unit.

A plate in each hand, Nicolas moved toward the table. Even though he was almost naked, he walked with confidence and authority, like he owned the kitchen and possibly everything in it. Before Jana he set one omelet surrounded by an arrangement of peaches, watermelon, and strawberries lightly bathed in thick cream. Then he went back and retrieved the other plate with the sterling silver dome on it. This one he set in front of Lisa.

Jana fumbled with the fork next to her plate. Everything looked delicious. Her stomach growled, reminding her that she hadn't eaten since breakfast yesterday.

Lisa reached for the dome and then looked up at him.

He slowly shook his head.

"We're playing outside the bedroom?" Lisa asked with hesitancy in her tone.

Nicolas grasped her chin between his thumb and forefinger tilting her chin toward him. He leaned forward and kissed her so lightly Jana wondered whether their lips actually touched.

"I'm changing the rules." His deep, sexy voice sent a tremor up Jana's spine and Lisa must have felt it too because Jana saw her friend's body shiver. "Do you accept these changes?" he asked.

Lisa eyes grew dark. Her tongue slowly circled her lips, as her chest rose lifting her breasts. "If it pleases you, Milord." Her voice dropped in pitch, grew sexy and warm like honey.

Milord? What game did these two have going? Jana sat rigid in her chair.

Nicolas's nostrils flared. "Oh, baby, it would please me beyond your imagination." With his words the heat in the room spiraled upward. Add the sexy beat of the music playing in the background and Jana could see exactly where this was going.

That did it. She was out of here.

Well, she would be leaving just as soon as her legs responded. She had her thighs squeezed tightly together to control the ache throbbing between them. Her fork fell out of her hand, making a clinking noise that neither of the other two people in the room seemed to be aware of.

Lisa dropped one shoulder and the strap of her sundress slipped down her arm. "What may I do to pleasure you, Milord?"

He lightly rubbed his thumb across the bare skin of her shoulder. "Strip for me," he breathed and Jana felt his words as if they caressed her nipples, teasing them to even harder buds.

Jana jolted from her chair, the back legs scraping across the tile floor before wobbling and settling down. "That's my cue to leave." Her heart was fluttering madly.

A brief look of concern filled Lisa's eyes and then vanished. "Jana, do you trust me?"

"With my life, but this is a whole different ballgame. I shouldn't be here. Especially, if you guys are going to—" Heat flared across Jana's face.

"Fuck?" A Cheshire cat grin curved Lisa's perfect lips.

Jana swallowed hard, her face growing warmer as her gaze went from Lisa's to Nicolas's. His expression was sultry.

"Well...yeah," Jana said, before she pivoted, moving away from the table when she heard, "Brrrock..." Lisa held on to the last note, before saying, "Chicken."

Jana spun around to face Lisa as her friend starting clucking and laughing. "I'm not chicken," Jana insisted.

"Face it. You're scared shitless. Brrrock..." Lisa mocked her.

"She looks scared to me," Nicolas added with a slight smile.

"Oh. Fuck you both," Jana fumed with embarrassment.

Nicolas raised one brow. "Now that's an idea."

"Jana." Lisa's voice softly dropped as she became serious. "Have I ever led you astray?"

Jana shook her head. It was true. Lisa had been the only one in her life who had tried to protect her against her foster father. She had been there through every step of Jana's recovery in the hospital and even afterward following her to California to make sure that Jana was settled. When Jana needed Lisa she was there. "But—"

"No buts." Lisa narrowed her sights on Jana. "All I want to do is break down some of those walls you've erected. What I'm asking of you may sound unconventional, but just trust me." She pulled Jana's chair back to the table. "Now come back here and sit down."

Jana took a step toward the table. "I don't see how any of this—"

Lisa pressed her index finger to her lips. "Shhh... Come sit down. Trust me."

Why Jana conceded she'd never know, other than she did trust Lisa more than she trusted herself. There was something about Lisa—something about their friendship she never wanted to lose. Besides, it wasn't like she hadn't seen Lisa naked. Last night she'd seen both Lisa and Nicolas in an intimate position. If she was being honest with herself, it had been damn arousing.

Quietly, Jana took a seat.

When Lisa and Nicolas locked gazes Jana ceased to exist, she had no presence in the room. She could slip through the door and never be missed. The pair had mentally erased her from the kitchen. Hell, by the looks they gave each other they had erased her from the planet. The knowledge didn't do much for a girl's confidence.

Or had she just become the invisible woman? She raised her hand before her eyes. Nope. Not invisible.

Nicolas extended his hand to Lisa and assisted her to her feet. Their bodies came together, as they wrapped their arms around each other. His long fingers curled in the back of her dress, wadding the material so it rose and revealed the swell of her ass and a hint of a lacy thong beneath.

Again he captured her mouth, but this time it was a real kiss, deep and demanding, one that took Jana's breath away and left her wanting. Her mouth began to water. Her lips quivered with need. The beat of the music echoed in her head.

With a slow caress he moved his hand up Lisa's back, raising her dress higher, revealing more perfect skin, before his fingers curled at the nape of her neck, winding through her hair as he pulled, forcing her head back. Then he pressed his mouth to the arch of her neck.

Lisa's lips parted on a gasp.

Jana's heart slammed against her ribcage.

She'd give anything to be kissed like that.

When Lisa and Nicolas finally parted Jana felt her chest rise and fall with excitement. Damn, she hadn't known watching lovers interact would be so heady, so arousing. Thank God Lisa had persuaded her to stay.

Without a word Lisa floated across the room until she stood in the middle of the kitchen, then her body began to sway to the music. With the toe of one foot she slipped one sandal off and then the other. She kicked them out of the way and they made a swishing noise as they slid across the polished tile. The entire time her brown eyes were glued to Nicolas's.

Silently he moved around the table and took a seat beside Jana. "Eat," he said, continuing to stare at Lisa as he picked up his fork.

It was a demand, not a suggestion.

But who could eat?

Lisa was seductively moving her palms over her shoulders, then dragging them across her breasts, circling them and weighing them in her hands, before she stroked down her abdomen and thighs to the hem of the dress.

Jana was mesmerized by her friend's sexuality and further astounded by how Lisa was affecting her. A naughty smile slid across her friend's lips. Every so often she slid her tongue over them, invitingly.

Eyes focused on Nicolas, Lisa began to sing along with the song. "Don't cha wish your girlfriend was *hot* like me?"

She slipped the dress up to her waist, displaying a thong that rode on her swaying hips. Repeatedly her body undulated to the music as the dress rose higher and higher.

Just as the swell of her breasts was revealed Nicolas said firmly, "Eat."

Jana startled. Her gaze darted from Lisa to Nicolas.

There was a "Don't make me repeat myself" tone in his voice that held all the warning Jana needed. She clutched her fork in one hand, stabbed a peach and crammed it into her mouth and chewed. Her action won her one of his beautiful smiles. Then he turned his attention back to Lisa's performance.

When Jana looked at Lisa again she was naked with the exception of her thong. The song had ended, another one began. As she dipped her fingertips into the waistband of her panties, Nicolas said, "Stop."

Immediately, Lisa's hands stilled.

"I want to reveal you myself. Take your stance." With his command Lisa parted her legs shoulder-width; she thrust her chest out, placed her hands behind her, and then bowed her head.

The bite of omelet that Jana had begun to swallow stuck midway down her throat. She choked, fighting for air. But neither Nicolas nor Lisa paid her attention. He pushed back his chair and rose as Jana reached for her orange juice and took a swallow, washing down the lodged food.

Nicolas was trapped in a world of sensations. Lisa was a temptress, her sexuality raw and inviting, while Jana's struggle with what was happening before her was exciting him beyond control. Blood filled his balls and rushed down his cock as the temperature in his body soared.

He could feel Jana's arousal, smell Lisa's heat above the omelet he had yet to sample. Hell, this was much better than food. If he thought Jana was ready he'd take them both right here, right now.

Instead he continued on his path, seducing Jana through Lisa.

Moving to stand behind Lisa, he removed his apron and tossed it aside so he was naked, but hidden from Jana's view. He watched as Jana's breathing increased and her eyes widened. Her full breasts rose against her shirt, tempting him as he pressed his body to Lisa's backside. Lisa's skin was chilled from the morning air, but he knew she burned hotter than a roaring fire inside, and if he wasn't off his mark, her friend sitting at the table was just as hot.

Lisa had been one of his most receptive playmates. He couldn't help but think what it would be like to dip between Jana's thighs and taste her woman's juices.

With a thrust of his hips he slid his cock between Lisa's legs. He knew that Jana could see his erection, as her gaze dropped to the apex of Lisa's thighs and her grip tightened on the fork she had picked back up.

He set his hands in motion circling Lisa's neck, smoothing them across her shoulder blades and cupping her breasts. As he stroked and caressed he moved his hips back and forth, his cock skimming against Lisa's wet panties.

She wanted to be fucked. He could smell her desire, heard it in her soft whimpers.

When he dragged his palms across Lisa's taut stomach, his fingers closing in on her thong, Jana shifted in her chair. He almost thought she would rise and join them. Instead, she pinned her warm blue gaze on him. Hunger blazed in her eyes. He pushed her further, letting his fingers disappear beyond the scant material of Lisa's thong. A gasp filled the room. He could have sworn both women moaned in unison as he sank a finger deep into Lisa's heat.

It was pure torture. Blue balls were in his future if he didn't find relief soon. But he wasn't finished with Lisa, and he sure as hell wasn't finished with Jana.

Pushing Lisa's thong down her slender legs, Nicolas fought to breathe, fought to regain the control he felt slowly slipping away. He had never devised a plan like this to seduce a woman through another. Yet he had to admit it was one hell of an exciting game. No one would be a loser in this adventure.

As he stripped Lisa of her panties he dropped to his knees, knowing that he revealed himself to Jana through the vee of Lisa's legs. He carefully supported Lisa's waist as she stepped from the thong and then kicked it aside. He knew Jana could see his hands stroking Lisa as he pushed them between Lisa's parted thighs. Gently, his fingertips touched her abdomen. With a long, smooth caress he pulled his palms back through her legs to skim her moist folds.

"Face me." His voice almost failed him, coming out hoarse and ragged.

Lisa turned, her blonde hair spilling across her face as she looked down upon him. He wedged her legs further, and then cupped her ass in the palms of his hands as he leaned in to taste her. He felt her quiver beneath his touch. Her body spasmed sending ripples of sensation across his tongue.

"Milord, may I come?" she murmured, her hips thrusting, burying into his face.

"Yes, baby."

His consent was all she needed. Her body jerked. She grabbed handfuls of his hair and pressed herself firmly to him, riding his face hard until the last of her climax subsided. Then she collapsed to her knees, wrapped her arms around him and captured his mouth with hers.

She was sweet on his tongue. But he needed to be in her, needed to seek his own release. He broke the kiss. "Hungry?" She scanned his length and whispered, "Yes," as her gaze settled on his engorged erection.

He rose and assisted her to stand. In unison they turned toward the table. Jana was breathing hard, her face flushed with desire. Her hands gripped the table tightly until her fingers bit into the wood.

Palm pressed to the small of Lisa's back, Nicolas guided her forward. "Kneel," he said as he took his seat beside Jana, turning so he sat somewhat sideways on the chair. "It would please me to have your beautiful lips sucking my cock while I eat."

The stunned look on Jana's face was priceless as Lisa crawled between his legs and took him into her mouth. As she sucked, swirling her tongue around his cock, he clenched his fork, sliced into his omelet and placed a bite in his mouth. With as much strength as he could muster he tried to chew slowly, tried to give the façade of control, while his body was becoming a living furnace.

"How do you like the omelet?" he asked Jana.

"What?" She jerked her gaze from where Lisa's head bobbed between his thighs and looked toward his face.

He almost groaned when Lisa took his sac into her small hand and began to massage it. "The omelet." He held his breath for a moment. "Do you like it?"

"The omelet?" She was like a mocking bird repeating his words.

Fuck, this was difficult, but he continued all the same. "Yes. Do you like it?"

"Like it?"

Clearly Jana was bewildered and he had held on as long as he could. "Excuse me." He weaved his fingers through Lisa's hair. With several thrust of his hips fire licked his cock. He released a throaty groan and let his climax wash over him. Lisa gagged and he loosened his hold, giving her the room and air she needed as she swallowed, milking his cock. After a final pump into Lisa's mouth he slipped from between her lips and drew her from the floor into his lap.

"Thank you," he murmured close to her ear. "I put a dome over your breakfast to keep it warm, but if it isn't warm enough I'll reheat it."

"It'll be fine, Nicolas." Lisa snuggled close to him. "Would it please you to be fed?"

"You are such a treasure, but I think it's time for you to take your seat." He gave her a light push off his lap. When she rose, he slapped her firmly on the ass. She squealed and lurched forward laughing, while his brand flashed a light pink on one cheek of her butt. "Why don't we all just relax and eat our breakfast?"

They both turned their attention to Jana. She was anything but relaxed. The wild look in her eyes, her rapid breathing, said it all. She was prime for the taking.

Chapter Five

And some would call *her* crazy!

Game of chicken or not, Jana shouldn't have stayed. Yet there was no use in trying to hide the fact that their performance had turned her on. It had been *hot*.

As Jana watched Nicolas and Lisa finish their breakfast and chat about the recent rise in gas prices, she wondered if it was possible to have dreamt what just happened. The fact that she was the only one at the table with clothes on confirmed that she hadn't completely lost her mind.

Lisa and Nicolas *had* casually had sex right in front of her. If you could call giving head casual sex.

They were relaxed and enjoying each other's companionship. Jana couldn't claim the same. Even on the lonely nights when she had switched over to an adult movie it had never been as arousing as what she had just experienced. Desire dampened her panties. Her breasts ached and her nipples stung causing her to take shallower breaths so they wouldn't rub against her shirt.

She was hot, horny and wound to the point she felt like a child's jack-in-the-box, ready to spring from her skin at any moment.

She'd never seen Lisa so uninhibited or so sexy. Sensuality rolled off Lisa's skin. Her lithe body moving to the music, the look of ecstasy on her face and especially how she had affected Nicolas was a total turn on. Jana would be lying if she didn't admit the desire to dance naked with Lisa. But the ultimate was how Nicolas touched Lisa, caressed and teased her body. It had been outright torture sitting there watching him and wishing to join them.

Jana had never met a man who made every nerve ending scream as Nicolas did. Even the macho dominance game he played she had to admit was exciting. She wanted to be touched by him, wanted to feel him between her thighs. The tingle in her nipples returned with a sudden surge. A fresh flood of desire drenched her panties.

Dammit! What she needed was a man. Lisa's was off-limits.

"Jana? Jana?" Lisa gave her a nudge with the palm of her hand.

A rush of heat filled Jana's cheeks. "I'm sorry. What did you say?"

"I said that after we clean up, perhaps we could go shopping." Lisa leaned forward and whispered, "Are you okay?"

Clean up? Oh no.

As fucking hot as Jana's body was the last thing she wanted was to watch two naked people bound across the kitchen bumping into each other, laughing and playing, until they got down and dirty on the floor.

And hell no, she wasn't okay.

Furthermore, the only store she really cared to go to was the Rent-a-Stud Escort Service. Briefly she wondered if they had a set of twins available, because it was going to take more than one man to work the tension from her body.

"Jana?" Lisa looked at her with concern in her eyes.

"No. Yes." Jana couldn't believe that rational thought had completely escaped her. She took a breath and began to speak slowly. "Why don't I do the dishes and straighten up the kitchen, while you two get ready. I'm already dressed." She was sure three shades of pink rose in her cheeks.

Lisa's soft, warm laughter filled the room. "You are, aren't you? Well if you don't mind. It won't take us but a minute or two." She rose, whipped around the table and gave Jana a big hug. "I'm glad you're here."

The look of expectation in her friend's eyes made Jana say, "Me too."

As Nicolas and Lisa left the kitchen, Jana knew in her heart that she had to move out before something got out of hand. Nicolas was attracted to her. Hell, he was probably attracted to any woman who wore a skirt. But the worst part was that she was drawn to him, always had been since she was a teenager. He felt like a drug sliding through her veins, trying to take control.

The fire he stirred inside felt alive—made her feel alive.

She wanted him.

Jana would never, ever, hurt her friend; to ensure it wouldn't happen, leaving was the only answer.

By the time Jana cleared the table, loaded the dishwasher, and picked up her friend's clothing and the shoes she'd left behind, Lisa entered looking as fresh as the morning dew wearing a pink sundress and sandals the same color. She was beautiful, but Jana had noticed that her friend had lost a good ten pounds since the last time she visited her. She was almost too thin. And her hair—it used to be long and flowing. It was still beautiful but short, not even brushing her shoulders. Lisa tried to visit at least once a year, always making the trip to California and never asking Jana to return to Arizona.

That was why it had surprised Jana when Lisa admitted to sending Jana's résumé to Medical Devices. Their hiring manager was at USC interviewing fresh-outs—engineering students right out of college. Lisa had called with the time and place, saying, "The rest is up to you."

Actually the rest was history. The job sounded fantastic and offered a great career path. The money was more than Jana had expected to receive. When she'd discussed the job possibility with Dr. Tate, she'd said, *It would be a good opportunity to vanquish the demons in your life. What do you have to lose?*

Her sanity?

Okay, the doctor promised that wasn't possible, that Jana was ready to begin anew.

So here she was back in Chandler and wrestling with more than past demons—there was a whole crop of new ones to add.

"Are you ready to go?" Lisa asked.

Jana dried her hands on the dishtowel and folded it neatly before setting it on the counter. "Yeah, just let me grab my purse."

As she headed out of the kitchen and down the hall she met Nicolas. He gifted her with one of his sexy grins. The close quarters of the hallway made it difficult to avoid him as they came within touching distance.

His hungry gaze scanned her from head to toe. "Has anyone ever told you how beautiful you are, Jana?"

Unease slithered across her skin. "Shouldn't you be saying things like that to Lisa and not me, or any other woman for that matter?"

With a brush of his knuckles he smoothed his hand across her cheek. "So soft."

Jana swatted at his hand. "Stop that. I don't know what game you're playing, but I won't be a pawn in it. I won't hurt Lisa."

He ran his fingers across her lips, sending tremors through her body. The smell of soap and aftershave sent her hormones into overdrive. She tried to move, but her damn legs failed her once again.

His laugh held a hint of male satisfaction greeting her frustration.

"It looks like you two will be on your own. There's a problem at the restaurant. I need to check in." Before she could dodge him, Nicolas planted a kiss on her cheek. "I'll see you tonight, doll." There was a sensual promise in his voice that made Jana more than uncomfortable.

As he moved on, she ducked into her bedroom and retrieved her purse, thankful that when she returned to the kitchen Nicolas was gone.

Lisa was frantically digging through her purse. She pulled out a tablet box and took out a small white pill.

She looked up at Jana and said, "Headache." Quickly she moved to the cabinet, opened it and grabbed a glass. After using the water dispenser from the refrigerator to fill her glass, she threw back her head, downing the pill and chasing it with a swig of water.

"You okay?" Jana asked.

A tight smile spread across Lisa's face. "I'm wonderful. Especially now that you're here." She went to the table to gather her belongings, put them into her purse and then said, "Let's go."

Chandler Mall had been built shortly after Jana left Arizona. It was amazing to see the progress all the surrounding cities had made. Where she remembered fields and more fields of farmland, subdivisions had sprung up in their place. They passed by one and then another new development in Lisa's yellow Corvette. The rapid growth made it hard to believe she once knew this area.

Big, expensive homes were everywhere, making Jana wonder who could afford such luxury. Every sign they passed advertised homes beginning in the high five- to six-hundred-thousand-dollar range.

Of course, that was nothing compared to the cost of living in California. Dorm life for four years hadn't been too bad. The last year she shared an apartment with two other women.

However, the job in Tempe that awaited her was a new beginning and the end to a past she wanted to forget. Medical Devices offered a promise of a new life and the means to make it happen. Not to mention she didn't have to start until late October. That gave her just about two months. She was officially on vacation, a vacation that had started out on really wobbly legs.

With the thought of California, those nagging words from her doctor once again appeared. *Don't put off the ugliness in your life. Face it head on. And most importantly, deal with it immediately.*

Jana really hated to bring it up, but for her own sanity she had to ask. "Lisa, you're not in an abusive relationship with Nicolas are you?"

Lisa reached across the console and squeezed Jana's hand with hers. Her face grew solemn. "Honey, no. Nicolas would never hurt me." Then her mouth twisted into a wicked grin. "Unless I asked him to."

Jana's mind went blank. "What do you mean?"

Lisa steered her car into the parking lot in front of Robinson Mays. It was already ninety-five degrees and climbing. The temperature in the car was twenty degrees cooler than the outside air.

"Surely you can see that we dabble in bondage and domination." She released a blissful sigh. "I love to be spanked by him." Just their luck, there was a parking spot up near the front. As Lisa came to a stop she continued, "It's a lifestyle neither of us live twenty-four-seven, but we do like to play once in a while. In fact, our relationship is built on the physical. We don't want anything else."

Was her friend freakin' nuts? She had one of the most handsome men Jana had ever seen. He was successful and educated, even if he hid it well beneath a cover of arrogance and authority.

Jana was still trying to process what Lisa had said as they climbed out of the car. Lisa used her automatic lock and the car made a clicking sound as the doors were secured.

"I'm not looking for anyone to tie me down." Lisa laughed before adding, "Emotionally." They began to walk toward the entrance of the department store. "Nicolas and I met at a party. He was in between subs and I was in between boyfriends. One thing led to another and we simply hooked up."

"You can't possibly go for this bondage, domination thing." Jana couldn't help letting her doubt slip into her voice.

A grin spread across Lisa's face. "Actually, I do. Nicolas is a skillful lover. He isn't into humiliation or extreme pain, but he can put you on the daring edge." The sound of their shoes slapping the asphalt rang in Jana's ears as she listened to her friend. "Yes, there is some spanking," she grinned, not looking at Jana, "some constraints, and other delicious things, but there isn't anything wrong with it."

The expression Jana held must have given away her surprise, because in the next moment Lisa said, "Hey, don't knock what you haven't tried. Maybe someday you can see what I mean. I know Nicolas would be happy for you to join us. Me, too."

Unbelievable! Jana did *not* hear her friend just invite her into a threesome. Or did she? She shook her head. Nothing rattled inside, maybe she misunderstood.

Lisa grunted, opening the large glass door and allowing Jana to pass through it before she continued. "I wish I could explain exactly what joy I experience, especially at this time in my life. It's like releasing all my problems, all my cares, for at least the time I spend with Nicolas. He's in charge and I'm dependent upon him to see to my needs. My only job is to pleasure him and feel." She turned her head. "*Ohhh*, look at that dress." With that, Lisa's attention was pulled to a slinky evening gown of black silk.

It was a lot to comprehend. Jana's mind struggled with the idea of allowing herself to become dependent on another, even letting him tie her up. That would require a hell of a lot of trust, trust she only felt for Lisa. Yet Jana had dreamed of having a man do just that—take care of her. The right man. A good man.

But would that be taking a risk? Sure as hell it would. To allow herself to feel that kind of trust...could she do it?

Trust.

Too many times in her young life she had been rendered helpless and there wasn't anything pleasurable about the pain or the humiliation. Like always, when she thought of her foster father, her body tensed and she touched the scar at her neck. The thought of trusting any man went straight out the window.

Dammit! If it was the last thing she did, she'd get over her insecurity. Yeah, trust didn't come easily for her, but she was working on it.

A gentle hand on her biceps brought her out of her wanderings. "Are you okay, Jana?" Lisa had the black gown draped over one arm. "I'm worried about you."

Jana laid her hand atop Lisa's. Nodded. "I'm fine. Just never know when the past will raise its ugly head."

"He can't hurt you anymore."

"I know, Lisa." Jana attempted a smile that fell short. "I'm doing much better. I'm here aren't I?" She didn't mention that she'd closed her eyes tightly when they'd passed by her old house. Or that it had taken several miles between her and that house before she could breathe normally again.

Lisa took Jana into her arms. "Yes, you are doing better. Huge step. Major." She hugged Jana tightly, and then released her. "Now let's spend some money."

And spend money Lisa did. If Jana didn't know better, she would have thought her friend won the lottery or someone had died, leaving her a fortune. By the time they left the mall, both of their arms were filled with merchandise and Lisa had purchased that black evening gown they'd seen earlier for Jana.

"How about a light lunch?" Lisa asked as she pulled into Applebee's and parked. "Nicolas is taking us to his restaurant tonight."

Now was Jana's opportunity to step aside, avoid any uncomfortable situations. She opened the car door, responding as she got out. "You know, Lisa, perhaps I'll just stay home tonight. I have some reading—"

"No! You can't," Lisa replied quickly. "I mean, he's doing this especially for you. We both want you there."

"All of this makes me somewhat uncomfortable," Jana admitted.

Lisa cut the engine. "Then I'll stay home too."

"No. You go and have a good time," Jana insisted.

Lisa shook her head. "We can call for take-out. Then you, Nicolas and I can watch a movie."

Crap. Okay, it didn't look like Jana was going to get out of this get together. Which was better, an intimate setting in Lisa's living room or a restaurant full of people? She would just make sure that Nicolas and she were never in a room alone. Ever!

Chapter Six

"What? You're a connoisseur of fine wine and women?" Jana knew she sounded condescending, but she couldn't help it. The damn man stroked every woman walking by with his hungry gaze.

He brought his attention back to Jana, sliding his eyes over her light green silk blouse. "No. It's just that I appreciate each one." The short, emerald green skirt Lisa insisted she wear was creeping up her thighs. She resisted the urge to tug it further down her legs.

She snorted. "Appreciate. Yeah. Right." Just her luck. The call Lisa received from the medical center had taken her away before she could even order dinner. Now Jana was stuck in this circular booth with the one man she swore she never wanted to be alone with.

It wasn't safe to be alone with him. He did something to her libido the minute he came into the room. Now he was only an arm's length away, causing her heart to pummel her chest. His white polo shirt stretched tight over his chest. His tanned skin begged to be touched.

Among the tinkling of silverware, forks and knives striking plates as people ate the delicious offerings of Marchetti's. Marchetti's was a large restaurant with booths aligning the wall, tables in the center. Grape vines bordered the ceilings. Exquisite art donned the walls.

"Take for instance the brunette at the table in the corner, by herself," Nicolas continued. Jana's vision followed the path of his gaze. "Some would call her homely."

Yes. Jana could see that. The woman was thin. Her short hair was dull and lacking luster. Her facial features were uninteresting and non-descriptive. The poor woman was boring.

He inhaled deeply. Jana didn't know if it was the Chicken Parmesan the waiter just passed by with or if Nicolas was trying to breathe in the woman's perfume from a short distance away.

His expression softened. "Look at her hands. Delicate. Soft." He pinned her with a look as if he were staring at a runway model with appreciation and lust. "See the way she holds her wine glass, strokes the shaft slowly, gently. That is how she would touch a man." His voice lowered, dropping deeper and quieter. "She would touch to please. Find the secret spots that would release the animal in her man." A fire burned in his eyes as if he believed his own words. Then he sighed and leaned back in his seat. "But sadly, many men would pass her by, her love lost on a passing affair, because he couldn't see what I see in her." He paused and took a sip of his wine. "She would also make a good mother. Her children would be cherished."

Jana couldn't help staring at him in disbelief. *Was this man for real?* Good looking, sexy and passionate, and a hopeless romantic, too.

"She went from sex goddess to mother in one leap. What makes you think she would be a good mother?"

He smiled as if he knew a secret. "See the family in the corner booth?"

How could Jana miss them? The noise was enough to make someone think they were at the playground instead of the posh restaurant Nicolas owned.

Beneath a beautiful chandelier that sparkled with elegance, a flustered mother and father had their hands full with three rambunctious boys. Corralled between the adults it was one fight after another, until they separated the hellions by placing one at each of their sides, which now allowed the children on the ends freedom to roam, sticky fingers touching the marble statues and fresh flower arrangements adorning the room. It was like herding cats to keep the boys contained within the booth. Their parents' expressions were haggard and tired.

"When the three-year-old passed by her a moment ago she struck up a conversation with him. Then she wiped his running nose. Most people would have ignored him, found him annoying, even disgusting. She didn't." He shook his head. "Wouldn't."

As he spoke it was as if the woman morphed into this beautiful creature. Features Jana had never recognized were now apparent like her hands, her slender neck, and the unusual violet of her eyes.

Jana glanced back at Nicolas. He was staring at her. "What?"

"Do you want me to tell you what I see in you?" From the hungry look on his face she would rather not.

"No."

Again, he leaned back in the booth. That mischievous grin she remembered back when she used to watch him with his friends slipped across his face. "Scared?"

Hell *yes* she was scared. She had always wanted this man. The years hadn't changed anything. "Not interested." She played indifferent, reaching for her wine and taking a sip. Then she released a heavy sigh to drive the point home.

A light danced across his features as his grin grew. "Liar."

"Whatever." She brushed him off with a tilt of her head. But if she thought that her impassive behavior was going to stop him, she should have thought again as she took another drink of her wine.

"You are scared—scared of the attraction between us."

When his foot slid up her leg, Jana choked on the alcohol that chose that moment to go down the wrong way. Air. She needed air as her windpipe closed.

Within a heartbeat, Nicolas was by her side. "Gentle breaths." He patted her back. "One and then another."

I'm dying. She wheezed in a breath that went nowhere. She inhaled again, making a rather unbecoming sound like a cross between a snore and an asthmatic attack. The whole time Nicolas was there, talking, touching her softly.

It took a moment, but finally Jana could breathe again. Her eyes were misty and nose running as she excused herself and hurried toward the bathroom.

What the fuck! She leaned against the counter and stared at herself in the mirror. It was no mistake that Nicolas was coming on to her. And there was no mistake that Lisa didn't mind. How Jana wished she could deny that he made her body burn. She had fantasized about being with him since she was just a teenager. What would it be like to make love to Nicolas Marchetti?

She couldn't—could she?

Nah... She shook her head. It would be weird. He was Lisa's boyfriend. But the fact was, she needed to feel the touch of a man. She wanted to find someone to love.

Nicolas just wasn't the man for her.

Jana grabbed a tissue, dabbed her eyes, then blew her nose with a loud snort.

She needed a plan to get through dinner and then go home alone.

Concerned, Nicolas watched the bathroom door, and was relieved once Jana exited. He stood as she approached. Her eyes were swollen, her adorable nose red. "Are you okay?"

"Fine." Sitting at one end of the crescent-shaped booth, she refused to scoot over, forcing him to sit at the other side. "The wine just went down the wrong pipe." Picking up her glass, she hesitated then set it back down.

He slid clear around on the semi-circular seat until he was within touching distance from her. Her mouth went dry. She glanced at him, feeling her palms start to sweat.

The salad had arrived in her absence, and he busied himself tossing it, mixing the dressing and cheese, before placing a generous helping on her plate.

When he attempted eye contact she glanced away. She had grown distant, not that she had previously been warm by a long shot. He was back at ground zero.

Serving himself a heap of salad, he picked up his fork. "Where were we? Ah... Yes. I was just about to tell you what I see in you."

"I wish you wouldn't," she said, looking down into her plate as she stabbed at a piece of lettuce.

"Strength," he offered the single word.

Her head shot up. "*Strength?*" Their eyes met and he felt her surprise. Obviously she'd expected something superficial. Like how her eyes sparkled beneath the light like two crystals, or perhaps how silky her hair looked draped across her shoulders like a red curtain.

The salad was good, fresh and crisp, the dressing not too tart he noticed as he took a bite. He would have to remember to compliment Antonio later tonight.

Nicolas let her think about what he said before he continued. "Look at what you have achieved in such a short period of time." He picked up the basket the waiter had set before them and offered her a breadstick, but she shook her head. "You've been alone since you were eighteen. Moved to a different state. Started a new life where you had no friends or family to rely on. You have a college degree and have a brilliant career ahead of you. How many people can say that?"

A warm sensation filled him when she smiled. "A lot of people have degrees."

"True. But not all of them have put themselves through school," he countered taking a sip of his wine.

She stabbed another piece of lettuce with her fork, but didn't put it in her mouth. Instead she shrugged. "I was given a scholarship."

"You earned that scholarship. Even so you did this by yourself—alone." He placed his hand over hers. "Jana, Lisa says you are a strong, beautiful person. I know she's right."

A soft expression fell across her once-tight features as she extracted her hand. "Thank you." She grinned, dropping her gaze once again to her salad plate.

"What?"

Continuing to smile, she met his eyes. "You're not exactly what I thought you were."

He pulled his brows together. "What did you think I was?"

"Well, arrogant for one."

Nicolas feigned surprise as he flinched at her words.

She giggled, the sound like bells swaying in the breeze. "Superficial and a whoremonger."

He pressed his palms to his heart. "I'm hurt."

"As if," she said. Her eyes danced with laughter for the first time that night.

"Well perhaps whoremonger is accurate, because I sure want to taste your lips right now." An ache began between his thighs, tightening and pressing against his black slacks. His sight was riveted on her full lips. How soft would they be against his? Would she whimper softly beneath his attack?

"Nicolas. I'm sorry, but I'm simply not attracted to you." She swallowed hard, giving away the fact she lied. "If I've done anything to mislead you, I apologize." Her hands left the table.

It was a challenge he couldn't ignore.

"The thought of me pressing my lips to yours, of my tongue delving between them doesn't make your nipples hard?" He waited only briefly before saying, "Tell me your breasts aren't heavy. That a slight tingle hasn't begun slowly filtering through them, aching for me to stroke them? Place my hot...wet...mouth on them?"

He trapped her gaze with his and paused. "Tell me you're not moist just thinking of how my hands would feel caressing your body, stroking the flame that burns in your belly, building it into a raging wildfire. Because that's exactly what I would do to you."

With his last words her eyelashes lowered halfway, the thick fringe hiding how her eyes had grown steamy. The increased rise and fall of her chest was a dead giveaway that he had aroused her.

He continued.

"I would touch every inch of your body with my hands and mouth. I'd make you scream for me to take you. Then when every nerve ending grew so raw that your skin was alive, I would enter your pussy slowly until you tossed back your head and screamed my name.

"Nicolas," he said his name in a whisper. "Your orgasm would explode as I filled you."

"Stop." She breathed the word.

What the hell had he done? His cock was rock hard. His palms itched to touch her. His mouth watered to taste her. This was torture and he had driven himself to this unbearable point. He couldn't find the strength to release her from the hold he knew he had on her.

"Stop? Or do you really want me to lay you on this table in front of all these people? Grab your ankles, slowly parting your legs, before I bury my face between your thighs, licking and sucking your clit?"

Jana gulped down a gush of air. "Fuck." She squirmed in her chair.

"Oh, doll, I will do more than fuck you," he promised, the idea sending his hormones into a frenzy of desire.

"No. I didn't mean— Oh shit! Just stop, Nicolas, stop." She pressed her palm to her mouth. She mumbled through her fingers, "This isn't right. You're sleeping with Lisa."

Nicolas's hand slipped beneath the table. He cupped his hard erection as his eyelids grew heavy. *God, I wish this was your hand, doll.* "Lisa and I have an agreement." He ran his fingers across his engorged cock. "There is no commitment between us." He reached for her hand, removing it from her full lips, and she didn't fight him. Instead her hand trembled. What would she do if he placed her hand between his legs, showed her how she affected him? He scooted closer to her.

Jana was almost his. He could feel her surrender in the softness of her skin, the way her fingers intertwined with his.

The server arrived with their main course and the moment was lost.

She jerked away from his touch. A light blush crossed her cheeks as her spaghetti was placed before her.

Damn!

But the evening was still young and Lisa had promised to stay away the entire night.

Chapter Seven

Two weeks had passed and Jana was strung tighter than barbwire on a fence post. She entered Lisa's home office and sat in front of the computer. The small room was neatly organized, with shelves containing several medical books, romance novels, and knickknacks on one wall. Family portraits were hung on another and a third wall was swallowed up by a picture window. A candle on the desk gave off a light scent of vanilla.

Nicolas was relentless in his pursuit of her. The night Lisa had been called away on a medical emergency, leaving Jana alone to dine with Nicolas, had been the worst.

Damn. It made her horny just remembering the seductive words he spoke.

Jana stared at the black screen before her. She would be lying if she said Nicolas's words that night hadn't affected her. She'd been so aroused by the time they arrived home that it took everything she had not to accept his invitation for a night of pleasure. Just remembering the evening sent a wave of heat across her body. She was thankful when the air conditioning kicked on and a cool breeze caressed her skin.

It had been extremely difficult knowing he lay naked down the hall from her that night. Lisa hadn't returned home until late the following morning. Jana had even had to deal with Nicolas's attempts at seduction the next day.

Oh my. What a hardship that had been.

Jana placed her fingers on the keyboard, but they didn't move.

In fact, Lisa's emergencies and the occasional headache always seemed to bring Nicolas and Jana together.

And the weirdest thing about the whole situation was that Lisa had encouraged her to sleep with Nicolas. Well, maybe she didn't come right out and say it, but the insinuation was there. A suggestion that barely ever left Jana's mind.

With a few keystrokes she typed in Medical Devices' internet address and pressed the enter key of her computer. Lisa had insisted that Jana utilize the now-converted office. It was a small room that Lisa's mother had used for sewing and crafts.

As Jana's new place of employment's site popped up on the computer screen, she noticed a picture of Nicolas on Lisa's desk. He was bare-chested in a pair of faded blue jeans. The cocky smile on his face was so endearing that Jana picked up the picture, bringing it closer.

There was definitely more to Nicolas than what she'd first thought. Three nights ago Jana had one of those dreams that woke her in a scream. Apparently, he had heard and rushed to her side. He had held her cradled in his arms, stoking her gently. He spoke of Italy to distract her. In great detail he described the city he had lived in. Luscious green hills covered with grape vines and dotted with olive trees. He shared a story about a scrawny kitten he and his brother had kept hidden from his parents for over two weeks. When his father discovered the animal, Nicolas immediately had to find a new owner. The elderly lady down the street had taken the homeless cat in with a promise that he and his brother could visit anytime.

For two hours he had talked to her, helping her to relax and laugh. When her eyes grew heavy, he kissed her forehead and said goodnight. She had slept late that day, her dreams filled with just one man.

Jana set the picture down and drew her attention toward the computer screen. Medical Device's website hadn't changed since the last time she'd visited it. She knew it was nervous energy and a need to do something that had brought her to the computer.

Again her gaze swayed toward Nicolas's picture.

She was becoming used to having him around the house, used to his sporadic appearances while she was taking a shower. No one in the house seemed to be worried about the bathroom door's broken lock, except for her. And each day Jana was entertained with some sexual foray between Nicolas and Lisa. Breakfast took on a whole new meaning.

Just the thought of their slick bodies in motion made her breasts grow heavy. She squeezed her thighs together, fighting the ache that slowly developed.

Hell, she was beginning to think they were doing it on purpose just to see her reaction. Or maybe they just got off on having an audience. Her fingers tightened around the wireless mouse as she moved it to select another page within Medical Devices' site. Of course, she could have complained, but didn't. It was better than cable television and her nights were filled with the rhythm of her vibrator.

She read once again the history of the company, but her thoughts were tugged back to Lisa and Nicolas. Jana had mentioned several times about moving out, each time faced with a flood of Lisa's tears.

On more than one occasion, Jana had walked in on Lisa and Nicolas, Lisa restrained by either her wrists or both wrists and ankles. Kitchen, office, living room, they didn't seem too particular where or when they played. Sometimes Lisa was blindfolded and sometimes Jana could hear the snap of a whip and the blissful moans of her friend. There were no tears, no screams of pain and suffering, only those of ecstasy.

Clearly the game they were playing was not abusive. Even if she didn't understand the dynamics, who was she to pass judgment on the rights and wrongs of what others did behind closed doors? Only, with Nicolas and Lisa, closed doors was never the case.

She chuckled, selecting another page. Clicked on several more links, but her mind continued to drift back to the strange situation she found herself in.

Both Nicolas and Lisa talked openly about multiple partners, not to mention the heightened awareness brought on by pleasure-pain in their bondage play, making it sound interesting and exciting.

But Jana still had her doubts on the benefits of this lifestyle. Once she found a man she could trust, she wouldn't want to share him with anyone.

She plugged the word bondage into the browser and pressed Enter. Selecting one of the multiple listings, she waited for the picture to appear. Perhaps being tied up wouldn't be too bad. But she would have to really trust him—right now Lisa was the only one she would relinquish that kind of power to.

What an odd thought. She shook her head.

On her screen was a picture of a woman with her hands bound behind her, a collar around her neck. Hooked to the collar was a chain fastened to the ceiling. Cuffs circled her ankles forcing her legs apart. Beside her stood a man with a leather paddle in his hand. The title said, "You May Already Be into SM".

The following questions appeared:

Can you get off by having your nipples bitten?

Jana's eyes sprung wide. She loved having her nipples pinched and bitten.

Do you enjoy being fucked hard and wild?

Yikes! Did she have to admit to that one too? She squirmed in her chair and leaned forward.

What about lovers who tie each other up with silk scarves?

Jana relaxed, her shoulders dropping as she inhaled and said, "Never done that one."

Do you like to be spanked?

No! Emphatically no. Then she paused. Tommy, her last boyfriend, had occasionally swatted her playfully on the ass in passing. She had found that arousing, even looked forward to his next whimsical mood. And yes it stung, not to mention she hadn't been turned off by it.

What did that mean?

She scrolled down and froze when she read: *Congratulations! You may already be a pervert.*

Uneasy laughter spilled from her lips as she read on to discover that there were many forms of BDSM. One of the most common mistakes was linking BDSM with nonconsensual violence, rape and brutal acts—like abuse. "The failure to distinguish between nonconsensual fantasy and the reality of consensual play is all too familiar," she read aloud, before she heard a door slam.

Frantically, she pushed one button and then another, the screen going blank just before Nicolas entered the room.

"Hey," he said, and then frowned. "Is everything okay?"

Jana's heart was running a mile a minute. It pounded so hard it throbbed in her ears. Then a sense of relief rushed over her—that was close. She fought back the giggle that teased her throat.

"Fine. I'm fine." She released the mouse and lowered the cover on Lisa's Powerbook, before pushing to her feet.

He reached out and placed his hand on her shoulder. "Are you sure?"

Nicolas was too observant.

He continued to search her face. "I have some time off and—"

"Lisa isn't here." She took a step away from him.

What looked like frustration wrinkled his brows. "I know that. I just thought perhaps you'd like some ice cream."

"Ice cream?" The surprise in her voice was obvious even to her. Crap. She hated it when he threw her off guard, which was becoming more and more frequent. Today ice cream, yesterday he had asked her to go to the zoo, but an emergency call from the restaurant had interfered with the trip.

Damn Nicolas.

"A little milk, sugar and vanilla, perhaps a strawberry or two... Ice cream. Harmless ice cream."

She had to laugh at his teasing. For once the rogue looked harmless. His hands tucked in faded blue jeans. The Arizona State University T-shirt he wore looked like it had seen better days. He looked casual, relaxed. Even his hair looked like it had been finger-combed.

"I'd like that," she said. For the first time, she wasn't scared things might get out of control with Nicolas. He was an enigma to her and she couldn't help but want to know more about the person behind the charismatic persona he wore.

He extended her his hand. She hesitated, staring down at it before lifting her gaze to meet his.

Sapphire eyes twinkled as he said, "Take it. I promise not to bite." His warmth folded around her hand. He raised her wrist to his mouth and set a gentle kiss upon it. Through half-shuttered eyes, he whispered, "Well, maybe a nibble or two."

She tried to wedge her hand out of his, but he held tightly. "I-I really shouldn't go," she stuttered. What was she thinking?

"Come on. It's too late to chicken out now." He winked and she felt her heart melt.

This was wrong. She shouldn't consider going anyplace with this man, but she wanted to.

With a deep, calming breath she gathered her courage. "Okay." It was just ice cream. As he escorted her out of the house, his hand slipped away from hers, sliding across her hip to settle in the small of her back. Without protest, she allowed him to guide her to his truck, loving the feel of his hand on her body.

Man oh man. So this was what playing with fire felt like.

Maybe this wasn't a good idea, Nicolas thought. He tried to look away, but the way Jana's tongue swirled around her ice cream cone had an innocent sensuality that drove him crazy. Thankfully, the table hid his rise of excitement each time he thought about her licking and wrapping her tongue around his cock.

Her light floral perfume rose above the sugary sweet smell of ice cream and confectioneries.

He needed a diversion. "Are you looking forward to starting your new job?"

Jana glanced up at him and frowned. "Yes and no."

When he leaned over and wiped the ice cream off her upper lip, she startled. What he had wanted to do was lick the chocolate off her lips and then sample her kiss, but the noisy Girl Scout troop at the counter gave him pause.

"Uh...thanks." She took another swipe at her cone. "I'm anxious to get deep into the trenches of this company, but scared shitless to see what it involves."

Honesty? Was this the first time she had truly been honest with him sharing her real feelings—her fears? It must have surprised her as well, because she immediately grew quiet.

Two young girls were giggling and whispering into each other's ears as they looked at him.

What? he thought of asking just before he felt cold wetness upon his hand. Ice cream dripped down the side of the cone, making a mess as it ran down his hand and onto the table. Quickly he licked the sides of his cone, then using several napkins wiped up the remainder. He'd been so entranced watching Jana's tongue glide around her ice cream cone that he hadn't been enjoying his own.

"I've never experienced the unknown growing up in a family business." He shifted in his chair, trying to ease the discomfort growing between his thighs. "I just focus on keeping the business successful so that my younger brother can continue to go to college. With both my parents gone he's all I have—he depends on me."

Jana cocked her head and her expression softened. "Joey was several years younger than I was, but I remember him following you around from time to time."

Nicolas laughed reminiscing how his brother trailed him like a shadow. Then something clicked inside. "You remember my brother?"

"Uh... Well, it's just that—Lisa and I, we used to see you guys around the neighborhood." She shrugged and then took another lick of her ice cream.

"But he was younger than you."

"And you were older than me by four years. Does it matter?" she asked.

Just how much about him did she already know? And where did she get all this information? He couldn't remember ever speaking to Lisa about his brother. She didn't really seem interested in his family. Not really disinterested, but aloof.

But Jana was interested.

She picked up a napkin and dabbed at the corner of her mouth. "What's his major?"

Damn. He had wanted to lick that spot of ice cream off her lips. "Joey's a history buff. Don't know what he'll do with the knowledge, but he's happy and that's all that matters."

She smiled again. "You love him."

"Yes." His response came quickly. His love for Joey was probably similar to that between Lisa and Jana. His brother meant everything to him. He watched as her tongue made a long swipe around her ice cream cone.

"Your mom and dad?"

He didn't really want to talk about his father. But his mother had been the light of his life. "My father passed right after you left Arizona. Mom died last year."

"I'm sorry." And she was. He could see it in her eyes. For a moment they just stared at each other, then he dropped his gaze to his watch.

"Damn. I need to get back to the restaurant. You guys are coming over to my house for dinner tonight aren't you?" What he wouldn't give to spend the rest of the day with her.

She picked up her purse and tucked it beneath her arm. The ease in which she asked, "Was that the plan?" showed how comfortable she was getting around him.

He gave a slow nod as they moved toward the door. Oh, yeah. He'd wanted to get her to his home on more than one occasion.

"Then I guess we'll be there." She passed by him and out the door he held open.

After they climbed into his four-door truck and he started the engine, the oily scent of diesel filled the cab. A comfortable silence lingered between them as he shifted the vehicle into gear and pulled into the traffic. Jana was easy to be with. Even the light fragrance of her perfume was unobtrusive. She was the type of woman a man could simply enjoy while holding her hand and walking along the ocean or mountainside.

That was until she was mad or edgy. Even then he relished the fight in her. He especially enjoyed their banter and the chase. She always appeared trapped in the "flee or fuck" mode. While he guessed her mind told her to run far and fast from him, her body was giving the opposite signals.

He had no doubt she wanted him as much as he wanted her.

Nicolas glanced at Jana and she smiled, a smile that sent warmth radiating through his body. This was a side he hadn't seen in her, or at least she hadn't shared with him before. She usually wore her hard-as-nails exterior or the fragile girl persona. The multiple facets to her personality made him feel like he could be with her a lifetime and never completely know her. But something inside of him knew he wanted to try.

As they pulled up to Lisa's house he turned off the truck, got out, went around to her side and opened the door for her to exit. For a moment he thought of taking her into his arms, but then thought better. The time would come when she didn't run from him. And when that time came, it would be all the sweeter.

There was a slight awkwardness in the moment as Nicolas stood before Jana. Almost as if he debated on kissing her. The strangest part of the situation was that she wanted him to. Wanted to feel his lips pressed to hers.

Dammit! Was it wrong to want to taste passion? To desire what Lisa and Nicolas had together? Or was that just a dream? They kept saying nothing existed between them.

"Tonight." His whisper almost sounded like a promise.

"Yes. Of course. Tonight." She stumbled from her wandering thoughts and took a step backward, before pivoting and leaving.

When she got into the house, she collapsed on the closest chair with a huff.

What would happen if she gave in, let Nicolas kiss her, let him touch her? Well, it didn't matter because it was never going to happen.

She pushed to her feet and headed for her bedroom to choose what she would wear tonight. After ten minutes she said, "Girl, you're taking an awful long time to pick out an outfit for a man that doesn't matter."

"But he does."

When she heard Lisa's voice, Jana turned quickly, almost losing her balance. A flush of embarrassment heated her face. "Lisa."

Her friend held up her hand. "Nicolas is everything you've ever wanted. Why not for once in your life be greedy? Take what you want."

"But, Lisa—"

"Jana, there isn't anything I have I wouldn't share with you, including Nicolas. I love you. All I want is for you to be happy."

Jana stood speechless.

"Think about it." Then Lisa floated out of the room, leaving Jana with a lot to consider.

Could she simply slip into a relationship with Nicolas when he was having one with her best friend? And what about this bondage stuff? Did she dare give him the trust needed to even experiment with BDSM?

The thoughts made her breasts grow heavy and that familiar tingle began in her nipples.

Was it possible?

Chapter Eight

Olive oil, butter and garlic simmered in a large frying pan. The oil popped and sizzled as Nicolas tossed in moist broccoli and stirred for preparation of the rigatoni he planned to serve with their main dish, Chicken Marsala. The rich scent of garlic, herbs and spices filled the air.

Before his mother had passed away she used to tease, "Garlic to an Italian is like apple pie to an American." Feelings of his recent loss surfaced, but didn't stay long. He grinned, remembering her many antics. His mother had been a hoot. He loved to listen to her soft laughter. She smelled of almonds, a scent that always warmed his heart. With her gone he felt something was missing in his life.

She would have liked Jana.

Adding chicken broth to the pan, he covered the dish and strolled away from the stove. With a dishrag he wiped down the large island in the center of his kitchen. His mother loved cooking while her family gathered around her, everyone participating in some small way.

With her in mind he had designed his custom home located just south of the restaurant. Upon entering, his guests walked into a great room consisting of a living room, dining room and kitchen. The openness lent itself to entertaining and gave him a sense of home as he cooked.

He placed a chicken breast between two pieces of wax paper, then gave it a whack with a wooden kitchen mallet. Lisa and Jana had arrived only minutes ago and were touring his home. He would have liked to have shown Jana around himself, but earlier a broken waterline at the restaurant had flooded the northeast side of the restaurant, causing him to start dinner late.

Now he found himself in a rather odd mood—antsy—with no idea whether it was the problems at the restaurant or Jana who had captured his attention from the start. The idea of seducing her had become an obsession. Usually a patient man, he was finding it extremely difficult to keep his mind off her.

Man, she looked great tonight. She wore a black evening dress, while Lisa had on a flesh-colored gown that almost made her appear as if she had nothing on at all. A sizzle behind his back drew him to the rigatoni on the stove. He raised the lid and used a fork to check the tenderness of the broccoli.

Done. After adding a hint of basil, he pulled the pan off the fire and set it aside.

What he wouldn't give to strip Jana of her clothing and pour rich red wine over her body. A wicked smile surfaced. Side by side, he and Lisa would lap the sweet alcohol from Jana's soft skin, one lick at a time.

The thought hardened his cock. He shifted his hips. Fuck, he was horny tonight. Hell, when was he not horny when Jana was around?

Feminine laughter caressed his ears. Like an invisible rope it tugged, begging him to follow as he heard their footsteps descend the stairs to his basement. He turned to the island counter, retrieved the mallet and gave the chicken another whack, hard. All he wanted at the moment was to be caressing a certain redhead with kissing and fucking on the menu.

His erection jerked against his pants as if fighting its constraints. Heat rushed through his body and it wasn't from the gas stove behind him.

Would Lisa show Jana the dungeon? It was a special place he kept locked, but Lisa knew where he hid the key. She'd prepared the room for one of their bondage scenes when he had once again been delayed.

The restaurant business could be demanding.

As he finished preparing the chicken, he switched off the burner and wondered what had captured Jana's and Lisa's interest downstairs. They'd been there for a while. Instead of completing the final touches to the dinner and putting it into the oven, he decided to check on the women.

When he reached the downstairs, he was surprised at the laughter coming out of the dungeon. He'd never found anything in the room funny, but evidently they had. As he grew closer he heard Jana say, "I can't believe this swing."

He peeked around the corner into the room. Jana's legs were spread wide, laced through the swing supports hanging from the ceiling, while Lisa gave her a push now and again. They were like two young girls at the playground.

His playground.

Both had kicked off their shoes and appeared to be relaxed and enjoying themselves. From his position, as she swung higher, he could look straight up Jana's dress, but a pair of black panties hid what he wanted so badly to see.

Lisa stopped the swing. "I want to show you his toys." She assisted Jana out of the contraption while they both giggled. "If the swing and hobby horse surprised you, wait until you see his toys. They're going to blow your mind."

Nicolas couldn't believe he was eavesdropping on their conversation, but he couldn't help enjoying their girlish mannerisms. They were like two high school girls down on their knees as Lisa pulled out the suitcase that contained all his special equipment. She flipped open the lid and Jana gasped.

Lisa's face sparked as she dug through his case.

"Oh my God, what *is* this?" Jana held one of his glass butt plugs by her thumb and index finger as if it contained some type of disease.

"Six inches of anal bliss," Lisa said as she continued to rummage through the case.

The confused look on Jana's face was priceless. "Anal?"

Lisa stopped what she was doing and looked up. "A butt plug, silly. Don't tell me you haven't ever seen one before." Jana didn't respond and Lisa chuckled. "I can't believe it."

"Hey, don't laugh at me. I've been busy." Jana's tone sounded playful and young as she placed the plug back into the suitcase. "While you were learning the ins and outs of sex, I was reading and going to school, remember?"

Lisa shook her head and went back to digging through the suitcase.

Nicolas loved the carefree way Jana teased with Lisa, and it was hard to believe she'd been through so much shit in her past. For the first time, he saw her at ease, even happy. She reminded him of how she looked earlier today at the ice cream parlor when she had smiled at him.

"Here. I found it." Lisa extracted a seven inch vibrator with clit stimulator. "This is a woman's best friend. BOB."

Jana's brows dipped.

"Oh, Jana." Lisa shook her head again. "Battery Operated Boyfriend. BOB. I really have a lot to teach you."

"I know what a vibrator is." Jana's voice rose with indignation.

"Strip off your panties."

Nicolas's heart skipped a beat.

"What?" Jana squealed. Her eyes shot wide.

Lisa grabbed a tube of lubrication and covered the vibrator. "Take off your panties."

"Here? What if—" She looked toward the open door, but Nicolas was watching from the crack between the door and frame, and he knew it was doubtful she could see him.

"He's busy. He'll never know what we're doing and even if he did he wouldn't care. Now get those panties off, girl."

Jana moved slowly, hesitant, but Nicolas could see the excitement in her eyes. Lisa had said Jana was a scientist and naturally inquisitive.

Blood rushed into his balls and cock as she drew her dress up, hooked her thumbs in her panties and brought them down so quickly her dress fell, robbing him of a peek.

"Okay go lay on that soft mattress in the corner." As Lisa spoke she drew out a small butt plug and lubed it too.

"I'm not sure about this, Lisa." Still, Jana moved toward the mattress.

There were mirrors on the ceiling and wall that would give her a good look at what she was doing. Not to mention he'd be getting a great view, too. His breathing had elevated and he wished he could join them, but it would probably halt their fun. *Shit.* He had no choice but to resort to voyeurism, at least for now.

"Lie down," Lisa said as she dropped to her knees.

Jana bit her lower lip before saying. "Lisa?"

"You do trust me, don't you?" Lisa asked as she patted the mattress.

Jana's eyes met Lisa's. "You're the *only* person I trust."

Nicolas heard the truth in Jana's soft words and for some reason a pang struck him in the chest. He wanted that trust, and not because he wanted to fuck her. He wanted her to feel the same way about him as she did Lisa.

"Come on then. You'll have the orgasm of a lifetime."

"What about Nicolas?" There was edginess to Jana's tone, as if she expected him to pop out around the corner, which just might be a possibility if he got any more aroused.

Lisa brushed her hand through the air. "He's lost in his cooking. C'mon, lay down." Nicolas couldn't see Lisa, but he knew her well enough to know there was a twinkle in her eyes. "Wait. Take off your dress. Bra, too."

Jana's expression was tentative as she grasped the hem of the dress and drew it slowly up, giving him a good look at the patch of auburn curls at the apex of her thighs. As Jana revealed more flesh, he followed the flow of her hips to the curve of her small waist. After she slipped the dress over her head she stood for a moment and clutched it to her chest. With a slight tilt of her chin she threw it aside. She was wearing only her strapless bra. A visible shiver raked her body as she reached behind her and unfastened the bra, letting it fall to the floor.

She was beautiful. Her breasts were full and round, her nipples a rosy pink. Previously, when he had seen her naked in the bathroom, she had been flushed from the warm water. But as she stood before her friend, her skin was tinted a light shade of innocent pink that he found simply adorable.

Nicolas was swollen to a bursting point. He reached down and unzipped his pants, setting his engorged erection free. Damn if he wasn't as stiff as a board. The throb he felt clear down the shaft was begging him to join the ladies.

As Jana knelt, her long red hair brushed her nipples and he swore they tightened more. Nicolas would have liked to see

Lisa's face because he was sure she was as aroused and excited as he was.

With hesitancy in her movements, Jana slid upon her back.

"Relax, Jana." Lisa's voice was soft and warm. "Since it's just the two of us, let me tie you up."

"I-I don't know."

"Puleeese..." That little shrew. Lisa had the sweetest way of getting what she wanted—when she wanted it. "Okay?" Lisa asked again.

Nicolas didn't hear Jana respond. But when Lisa reached for the pair of thigh cuffs, he knew she had won. He was glad she had chosen this type of restraint instead of the ones that would stretch Jana's arms above her head. The two soft straps of material connected by a short chain with cuffs on the ends were less intimidating. They would restrain her wrists close to her legs. The last thing he wanted to see was Jana distressed. He preferred seeing her as he had only moments ago—happy and full of life.

As Lisa pulled the larger strap apart, the ripping sound of Velcro sent a tremor through him that shot down his cock. It was easy to imagine it was his hand circling Jana's thighs with the larger strap. God, what he would give to watch her eyes grow dreamy with excitement as he secured the smaller constraint around her wrists that would keep her arms by her sides.

Well shit! He was so aroused he didn't think he'd make it through the next part of the show. But it would take a natural disaster to move him from this place.

Not in her wildest dreams had Jana ever expected to be lying naked before her best friend, her wrists tied to her own thighs, in Nicolas's home, while he unsuspectingly prepared dinner. Her belly clenched. Damn, what if he wandered down and caught them?

Just how much more bizarre could this picture get?

Plenty. Lisa pulled her dress over her head, revealing she wore nothing beneath it.

"Now I'm comfortable," Lisa murmured. Then she gave Jana what was probably supposed to be a reassuring smile, but only moved her up the tension scale. "Relax. We're going to have fun."

Fun for whom? Jana thought as her nipples drew tighter. God, she couldn't believe she was doing this. And she couldn't believe how excited she was becoming.

Lisa's hands were soft as she placed them on Jana's calves and began a deep massage. "I've never asked you how you feel when Nicolas and I enjoy sex in front of you." She looked up through heavy lashes. "Does it arouse you?" Her fingers danced on the inside of Jana's legs moving toward her thighs.

It was automatic—Jana's legs squeezed together.

"We might just have to do something about that." Lisa moved away blocking Jana's view, but it wasn't long before Lisa's fingers gently circled Jana's ankle and wedged her legs apart. Before Jana understood what was happening, her legs were spread wide and secured with another set of straps that Lisa connected to D-rings at each side of the mattress. Actually, there were four—one on each corner.

"I don't know about this." Jana's voice cracked.

"Sweetie." Lisa leaned over Jana then pressed her warm body against hers. She whispered, "I would never let anything happen to you. I love you. Please believe that."

Okay, this was just freakin' weird. Yes, she and Lisa had fooled around, but they were teenagers at the time, experimenting, finding their sexuality. This was different. The softness of Lisa's body, the press of her hard nipples against Jana's flesh was arousing. A flush of heat surged across her skin.

Shit. Was she supposed to think like that—feel that way about her closest friend?

"Lisa?"

"Shhh... Just let me show you the joys of toys." Lisa eased back resting on her knees. Her eyes were dark with desire and Jana couldn't help but think her own reflected the same.

There was something heady about doing something daring, risky, against the rules of society. And truthfully, Lisa looked happy. Fulfilled. Although she had said that her relationship with Nicolas was only physical, Jana couldn't help but wonder if he put the smile on Lisa's face. The thought no sooner left her mind when the most delicious throb began between her legs, slowly inching its way between her slit.

"Lisa?"

"Shhh... Relax... This is a woman's best friend." Lisa purred. "I don't know how I ever lived without a vibrator." As she pushed the toy deeper, she whispered, "Feel the wide girth. Nicolas is thicker—longer, he fills you like no other man can."

Jana's eyelids felt heavy as they slid closed. Hell, she was no stranger to a vibrator. But she was to a woman's touch that was softer than a man's.

"Do you enjoy watching Nicolas and me fuck, Jana? Does it make you hot for him?" Lisa asked as she picked up the rhythm of the vibrator, thrusting deeper, harder, faster.

The protruding ears of the clit stimulator began a slow vibe surrounding Jana's clit, sending the most delicious waves throughout her.

What was Jana supposed to say? Her breasts felt swollen, aching to be touched. Nicolas's face flashed in her head. "Yes," Jana answered before she realized what she just admitted. But it was true. She had been hot and bothered from their many episodes. And yes, she had wanted to join them, but most of all she had wanted to feel Nicolas inside her body. As Jana climbed the peak of sensation she had no defenses.

"Does this feel good?" Soft and sexy, Lisa's voice caressed Jana's skin as if she stroked her with her free hand.

"Oooooh yes." Jana's response was breathy. She was so close it wouldn't take long before she was engulfed in her orgasm.

Lisa extracted the vibrator, leaving Jana feeling empty as her womb throbbed and her clit pulsated. "Lisa?"

"I know. You want me to continue fucking you with Johnny boy here, but you can't come yet. There are still many wonderful things to experience. Do you remember that butt plug?"

Jana's eyelids flew open. "You wouldn't." Oh crap. Oh crap. Oh crap. She pulled against her restraints and found she wasn't going anywhere.

"No." Lisa smiled sweetly. Then she held up a smaller version of the previous plug. "You never start with something that big, unless it's your man's erection. I haven't told you how good it feels to have Nicolas's cock lubed, hard and sleek, thrusting in and out of that special place."

Oh God. If she continues on with the dirty talk I'm liable to do anything she wants. "Lisa. Please."

"Please what? Would you like me to insert this, or should we call Nicolas? You know he's attracted to you."

Fuck. What was she supposed to say?

"He wants you," Lisa whispered.

Hearing the words sent flames licking across her skin, as Lisa's words raced to Jana's logical brain. It was exciting to know that a man she had lusted for wanted her, but how did that really make Lisa feel? Another flood of moisture dampened Jana's folds.

Lisa leaned forward and placed her palm on Jana's cheek. "It's perfectly fine. I want him to want you."

"What?" Okay, now Jana was totally confused. Lying there with her wrists strapped to her thighs, her legs parted and tied to the ends of the mattress, she felt helpless. But before she could say anything else Lisa inserted the vibrator and set it to softly flutter. Then the most exquisite throb teased Jana's clit.

"It's a clit stimulator. Isn't it wonderful?" Lisa asked.

Wonderful? No, this was a slice of heaven. Jana had never felt anything like it as it stimulated her nerve endings, sending tingles throughout. Her own vibrator must be centuries old, because she had never seen or felt anything like the one buried deep inside her.

Every part of her body responded. She could feel the air against her skin like light fingertips, heightening her awareness. Again, she closed her eyes. The vibration was like an echo reaching deep inside her. Nothing existed beyond the pleasure she felt between her thighs. When something cold nudged against her anus, she didn't even have the will to argue.

Slowly, she felt her backdoor open, stretching wider. Bittersweet pain met the plug as it slipped past the rings of muscle to bury deep inside her. She gasped at the unusual sensation of fullness in one orifice, while the other shook with delight.

Then the vibrator stopped and Lisa extracted it once more, leaving the butt plug in place.

"Lisa. I need—"

"You need to come, sweetie, don't you?"

"God, yes. Please." How had Jana stooped to begging her best friend to fuck her with a toy? She needed to climax. The tightening in her body made her writhe. Her mind was a mass of confusion knowing one thing and one thing only. "Fuck me, Lisa."

"Keep your eyes closed. Don't open them until I tell you."

"Okay. Anything. I'm burning up inside."

"Anything?" Lisa asked.

If she didn't, she was going to explode. "Just let me come."

There was a moment of silence. She felt Lisa's touch on her face, and her fingertips lightly pressing against her eyelids.

Strong hands, rougher and larger hands than Lisa's, gripped Jana's hips. She startled and tried to open her eyes, but Lisa's fingertips held them closed. A whimper left Jana's trembling lips as she pulled against her constraints.

"Relax, Jana. Let Nicolas bring you to the most amazing climax you'll ever have." There was a hint of desperation in Lisa's voice, as if she needed it as much as Jana did.

Jana's body was on fire. It didn't matter whether it was a seven-inch vibrator or one gorgeous hunk of a man.

"Can I fuck you, Jana?" Nicolas's whiskey-deep voice washed over her, stealing whatever resistance she had left. Truth was she wanted him to fuck her. She'd wanted it for several weeks now. Hell, it had been years—going back to her high school crush.

Jana couldn't speak; she just nodded several times. The feel of his palms on her ankles as he freed her legs sent shivers up her spine. She still couldn't open her eyes because Lisa held them shut and her wrists were still bound to her thighs. Nicolas lifted her hips.

"Raise your head," Lisa said as she slipped beneath Jana, pillowing Jana's head in her lap.

Nicolas penetrated her with one thrust, driving deep inside her and forcing a cry from her lips. He was long and thick and all male.

Seconds passed and Jana's breath still hadn't returned. Slow and steady, he moved in and out of her slick pussy. He touched a particularly sensitive spot and she gasped.

It felt good to have a man inside her, buried so deep that he felt part of her.

"Open your eyes, doll. I want to see them as I fuck you." He spoke softly, sensual words that sent tremors up her pussy. Heat rays surged through her body as he slid in and out between her legs. She couldn't breathe. When Lisa removed her fingers, Jana opened her eyes and released a breath in one gush.

Jana's and Nicolas's gazes locked.

It was beyond anything she could imagine. His thrusts were slow, seductive, driving her wild. There were no words to describe how drop-dead gorgeous Nicolas was. He looked like a warrior, naked and strong, ready to conquer and she was his conquest. The thought curled her toes. She couldn't count how many nights she had dreamt of Nicolas, of making love to him.

A hint of satisfaction raised the corners of his mouth, but it was the darkness in his eyes that sent goose bumps across her flesh. He left no doubt in her mind he wanted her.

She was thrown into a feeling of chaos as soft palms cupped her breasts. Lisa's fingers pinched Jana's nipples easily at first, growing firmer with each of Nicolas's powerful thrusts. The sound of flesh slapping flesh, the butt plug lodged in her ass, his large cock invading her pussy, and a woman's touch on her breasts threw her completely over the edge.

Jana's back rose off the mattress, a scream burst from her parted lips, as the most earth-shattering climax ripped through her body. Lisa pinched her nipples, hard, then harder. Jana convulsed, legs trembling, as waves of sensation filtered to every extremity. It was like receiving electroshock without the pain, the penetrating burn shooting through her veins. It felt like it lasted forever as she jerked with each ripple of orgasm.

Then Nicolas gave a throaty moan and she knew he had followed her over the edge of ecstasy. He moved several more times within the cradle of her thighs before he released her legs and crumpled atop her. His weight didn't feel crushing but comfortable. It was as if more than sex had just created a bond between them.

He smelled good, a spicy male scent that mingled with sex and another overpowering scent. Garlic. It was on his hands that cupped her face as he rose and then he took her breath away with a kiss.

No, it couldn't be called just a kiss. It felt more like a victory celebration after her surrender. Jana had no strength and no desire to resist him. Her tongue was hungry. His was hungrier. He took her mouth with such force there wasn't much to do but accept him. When his hands swept across her body building the fire inside her, she melted in his arms.

Nothing could have prepared Jana for what she felt, but Lisa was right. This man had given her the most amazing climax she had ever had in her life. And he just kept on giving...

When he finally pulled away, he left her wanting more. If her hands hadn't been fastened to her thighs she would have pulled him back to her mouth. Her tongue slid across her lips, capturing more of his taste.

He grinned. "Don't do that, doll, unless you want me to take you again." There was a sexy promise to his voice.

"Hey, what about me?" Lisa playfully pouted.

Complete and total embarrassment raced across Jana's face. She had forgotten about her friend. For a moment only she and Nicolas had existed.

"I would never forget you. Come here," he said.

Now, wasn't this awkward? Lisa's full breasts hung just above Jana's mouth as Lisa and Nicolas kissed. His cock was still buried deep within her body, the butt plug in her ass. She could feel him harden as he made love to another woman's mouth. His hips began to move, stoking Jana's fire once again.

Chapter Nine

This was every man's dream. Nicolas couldn't believe that he had two women in his dungeon and they were all his.

Yeah, he'd shared women with his friend Trent. But he'd never had two women all to himself.

Jana had been amazingly responsive. Not to mention that when he'd climaxed it had actually felt like the ground shook. Something different had happened and he wasn't sure what it was or if he felt comfortable with it.

Of course, it didn't help that he had spent fifteen minutes or more watching Lisa tease Jana into a sexual frenzy. And the witch had even known he stood just beyond the door, because when Jana had reached her peak of arousal, Lisa had motioned him in, mouthed that he should take off his clothes and put on a condom.

Lisa had orchestrated the entire show.

Talk about being friggin' hot.

When his body had touched Jana's his skin went up in flames, but when he had entered her warmth, the unbelievable tightness of her pussy almost undid him. Her cry as he filled her was beyond exciting. It was as if she had never been touched, not by a real man. She was everything he thought she would be and more.

And then there was Lisa. Her breathing was labored, her eyes dilated. She needed to come, but she saw to her friend's pleasure first. The intense expression on Lisa's face and the way she responded to his kiss said she wanted to be fucked, now.

Not exactly how Nicolas had thought to see his sub perform. In fact, Lisa actions had been that of a Dom. The expert way she coaxed Jana into each situation and directed him on every move to ensure her friend would accept him was skillful. He was beginning to see Lisa through different eyes. She wasn't exactly what she had pretended to be this last month and a half.

Had he been duped? Or was she so intent on bringing her friend into the mix that she took the initiative?

As a Dom he should be angry. Yet, Lisa had been right. Jana felt so good as her hips rose unconsciously to meet each of his thrusts. He knew it was unconscious because her worried expression said her thoughts were someplace else. Was she already regretting what just happened? He couldn't allow that.

He wanted her. Wanted to brand her his. Where this strong obsession came from he didn't know. The odd sensation was uncomfortable, but he felt helpless against its pull, as if talons held him fast.

Instead of focusing on his failure to control his swirling emotions, he scowled. "You acted without my consent." Lisa's brows furrowed, her back went rigid as her lips parted. For a moment he thought she would argue with him.

Lisa deserved to be punished. It was necessary for each of the women to remember he was in charge. He was their Master.

Then her face softened and she fell into her role. Setting back on her hunches, Lisa bowed her head. "Yes, Milord."

He ignored Jana's look of surprise as she lay beneath him, his cock still deep within her warmth. As he spoke, "I'm displeased with you, baby," he dislodged Jana's butt plug and set it aside. Her pussy convulsed around his cock. She groaned, a raspy sound as her body squeezed and tightened, causing him to grow even firmer. The look of arousal that slid across her face set him afire. He pushed deeper into the vee of her thighs.

"How should I punish you?" It took the strength of his inner-demon to focus his attention back on Lisa instead of Jana. As he glared at Lisa, his hands smoothed across Jana's taut abdomen, feeling her ribcage before he closed in on her breasts. They were heavy in his palms. Knowing Lisa liked the sting of a flogger across her body made him grind his hips into Jana.

Through feathered lashes Lisa glimpsed up at him. "However would please you, Milord."

Yes. Nicolas wanted to mark Lisa's skin with his touch. Perhaps spank her like the naughty girl she was, or drag his flogger across her delicate skin and watch goose bumps rise as she became more aroused, her chest expanding with her heated breaths. He tweaked Jana's nipples hard, causing her to whimper. He glanced down, relishing the look of pleasure on her face. She liked the feel of pressure. Would she like his nipple clamps?

Damn. This was making him hot as he thrust between Jana's delicious thighs. Her eyelids had fallen to half-mast and her full breasts rose invitingly into his palms. If he didn't have Lisa to attend to, he would fuck Jana every which way possible. Then he'd take her in his arms, caressing her as she slipped into a dream state, dreams he knew would include him.

Struggling with his desire, he fixed his hot gaze back on Lisa. Although she needed a good whipping, he didn't want to ruin the progress made with Jana. She had felt too many *real* beatings to watch another receive them, even if what he and

Lisa would do was only in play. The times they had played at Lisa's house had been so light that Jana would know it was all for pleasure.

Again, Jana's sex convulsed around him, pulling him deeper. She was getting close to reaching another climax as she writhed beneath him. He prayed that the used condom he still wore held out, because he would not be denied his pleasure. He wanted her and at the moment that's all that mattered.

Nicolas ground his teeth together as fire licked his shaft. He skimmed his hands down the softness of Jana's flesh and gripped her hips. "Look at her, Lisa. Place your palm over her heart, feel her excitement." Lisa leaned forward, her mouth close enough for him to capture her lips as she did his bidding. Instead of a kiss, he let his hot breath flow across her face. "For your punishment you'll watch and feel Jana's orgasm. There will be no release for you, until I say you have earned it."

Red flames of anger sparked in Lisa's eyes, so hot he felt the burn. He had never witnessed this much defiance in her. Hell, she had never disobeyed him. Something was different about Lisa and had been for the last couple weeks.

But what?

The thought disappeared as Jana writhed beneath him. Closer. He needed to be deeper inside her. "Wrap your legs around my waist."

The second Jana locked her ankles around him, she arched and her back came off the mattress. The most exquisite cry pushed through her parted lips, robbing him of his breath. Wave after wave of pleasure caused her to buck beneath him. As her pussy squeezed him tightly, he lost it. His balls drew up against his body and he exploded. It was like shooting electricity through his cock. The force—the burn—was so powerful it felt as if he were being ripped in two from the inside out.

Lisa's body shook, pushing her to the edge as their gazes locked. His hold on Jana's hips grew firmer. To see Lisa fighting her release while Jana bathed in hers drew out his orgasm longer than it had ever lasted.

He managed to say, "Hold!" to Lisa. His fucking heart thrashed against his ribcage hard enough he thought it would jump from his chest. As the pressure continued to release, he sucked in a breath, and then another.

There was something omnipotent about giving and taking pleasure from two women at once.

"Hold," he repeated firmly. His erection gave a final jerk and then lay quietly in Jana's cradle.

Damn. That was wonderful. His body felt relaxed, sated. Jana's expression said she felt the same.

But not Lisa.

The anger was gone from her eyes and only deep dark passion remained. "I don't know if I can," Lisa whimpered. "Please, Milord. May I come?" Her hand slowly pushed between her legs. The scent of sex permeated the room. She withdrew her hand and slipped her finger into his mouth. He sucked, gently tasting her sweetness. "Please?"

"Nicolas." Jana's sweet voice rose. He cast a glance toward her as Lisa slid her finger from his mouth. "Let her climax."

How he wanted to make her happy, to see her smile once again, but he couldn't. Instead he became impassive, shading his real feelings beneath a cold indifferent mask. "She defied me. Like Lisa, you need to learn to obey or face the consequences." His last words made Jana's brows shoot upward. "Perhaps she'll remain naked for the rest of the night and wear a clit stimulator."

Lisa groaned. Her mouth opened and then she snapped it shut.

Man, he hated to leave the warmth of Jana's body, but it was time to take control. He pulled his hips back, losing part of the condom within her. As he reached to retrieve the slippery rubber, he smoothed his fingers across her folds, creating a tremor against his hand. She was beautiful, spread wide for his view. It made him hot just seeing her restrained in the thigh cuffs. The black straps circling her delicate skin were a real turn on.

"Lisa, put on the harness," Nicolas demanded.

Without a word she rose, swaying slightly as she caught her balance and moved toward the suitcase from which she had taken the vibrator and butt plug. She reached in and extracted a red heart connected to elastic straps. Wide-eyed, Jana watched her friend crawl into the harness one foot at a time, then ease it around her hips, ensuring the heart rode low and pressed against her clit. She held the controller in her right hand.

"Come here." Nicolas's cock sprang to life as she approached with her hips swaying seductively. As he rose, moving from between Jana's thighs, she drew them together. With a scowl, he said, "Keep your legs spread open. I didn't give you permission to hide yourself from me." She hesitated. His voice dipped low. "Don't make me tell you again."

Jana's limbs sprung wide as if spring-loaded. He almost choked while suffocating a laugh...

Shit! Jana froze. Did she just comply with the arrogant man's demand?

A flicker of male satisfaction brightened his eyes. Well, hell. The smugness on his face was as if he thought she had just

Mackenzie McKade

handed him the reins of control. She glanced down her length realizing that in her current predicament he actually did have control. She knew it was only perception as she tried to test her bindings. They were Velcro. How hard would it be to wriggle her way free? As she pondered the possibilities of escape, Nicolas motioned to Lisa to follow him.

There were two chains extending from the ceiling. On each end of the imposing chains was a Velcro strap similar to the ones she wore on her thighs and wrists. Without being told, Lisa handed him the controller and raised her hands above her head. Holding the black box between his fingers, Nicolas proceeded to capture and bind Lisa's wrists with the straps until she was perched slightly on tiptoes. Then he smiled and pressed a button on the controller.

Lisa's response was immediate as her body shook and swayed. "*Ahhh,*" tore from her throat. "Please," she gasped.

Jana tensed. Please what? She waited for Lisa to continue, but her friend's head lulled back, her hips shooting forward.

Please continue?

Please turn the fucking remote off?

What?

When Nicolas pushed another button, Lisa's body melted, as if every bone turned to jelly. Muscles and tendons bulged at her shoulders and arms holding her dead weight.

Jana wanted to scream, ask if her friend was all right, but when Lisa drew her head up her eyes were dreamy with desire. She wet her lips in a flirtatious attempt to get Nicolas to give her what she needed.

An orgasm.

Instead he turned and pinned Jana with a dark gaze that sent shivers racing up her spine. Without a word he

102

approached, bent and helped her to sit up because she still wore the thigh cuffs restraining her wrists. The connection between her thighs and wrists was long enough that she could stand upright. Why she kept her mouth shut, Jana had no idea. All she knew was that his hands felt wonderful on her. She'd never had a climax like the two he had given her. Lisa was right about Nicolas. He was wonderful.

And if she were honest, she was even turned on not being able to move her hands, which rolled into fists with her anxiety as he positioned her standing behind something that looked like an arm sling hanging from a chain connected to the ceiling.

"Doll, will you trust me? I want to secure your head."

Her heart lunged against her breastbone. Excitement and fear pulled her in different directions.

"Trust him," Lisa whispered with an air of confidence in her voice. "I do."

Jana swallowed hard. Could she, too? God, she wanted that feeling of believing in someone so much that she could give over control—like she had with Lisa. Somehow, even though she wanted to deny it...to truly trust Nicolas... Maybe?

No. Yes. Maybe.

Before she realized it, she murmured, "Yes." *Shit.* She was going to let him put her head in that contraption and keep her from moving it.

Holding the control to Lisa's clit stimulator, he guided Jana to take one step forward, then another, until she stood in front of the sling. He brushed back her hair, releasing a deep, angry growl.

Damn. He must have seen the scar left by a broken beer bottle her stepfather had cut her with the night before her high school graduation.

Gently, he traced the scar with his fingertip, and then guided her chin, resting it in the cradle of the sling, before he disappeared from her sight. The sling wrapped snugly around her cheeks and ears. Within seconds the strap raised, lifting her chin and securing her until she couldn't move her head. Before she could catch a breath, Nicolas was back kneeling before her.

Through heavy eyes filled with lust he gazed up at her. "Now, I'm going to shackle your ankles." He placed the controller on the ground and began to softly caress each of her legs with his strong hands. "Will you trust me?"

A whimper slipped out between her trembling lips.

"It isn't necessary." He gave her a tender smile. "But I can't stand not being able to see your pussy." His gaze slid over her body to rest on the apex of her thighs, and his dark eyes ignited a spark inside her. "You are so hot when your legs are parted and you're waiting for me to fuck you."

Jana knew he was seducing and manipulating her. Still she said, "Yes."

Without another word, he secured her ankle with a cuff connected to a chain that was attached to the floor. His touch wasn't in the least bit threatening as he dragged her free ankle to the other side, parting her legs and baring her once again for his pleasure as he secured her.

He knelt before her, his powerful hands smoothing up her calves, past her knees, applying pressure across her thighs until his thumbs rested in the bend where her thighs and pussy met. When he buried his nose in her slit, Jana's nipples tightened into painful nubs. A rush of moisture released to meet his touch and sent the heat of embarrassment across her face.

"That's it, doll. Get good and wet for me." His voice was like sandpaper, rough and coarse against her sensitive skin. The first wave of excitement radiated up her pussy. "Beautiful." He blew lightly on her folds, making her clit ache. Then he scooted back on his knees before he picked up the controller and rose.

Something like pride brightened his eyes before he pivoted and walked toward what Lisa had said was a love sack. It looked like a large overstuffed beanbag big enough for three or four people. His taut ass and the impressive span of his back immediately captured her attention. Nicolas was gorgeous. He grabbed handfuls of the material and dragged the bag across the room, situating it until he was center stage. Then he sank down in its folds, his long, hard cock jutting out in front of him.

"Beautiful. Both of you." His fingers folded around his erection, while he held the controller in his other hand. "Did you know I have dreamt of this?" He stroked Lisa with his gaze, and then Jana, starting at her feet and stopping only when their eyes met.

Shocked at his open admission, Jana didn't know what to say. Her gaze darted to the side, trying to see how it had affected her friend. But Lisa's sight was pinned on his hand and the slow caress he performed as he moved his fingers up and down the length of his erection.

"Do you want my cock in your pussy, baby?"

Lisa answered Nicolas's question with a breathless murmur. "Yes. Please, Milord." He turned his attention back to Jana. "And what about you, doll?" He grew even longer as Jana watched his hand slip over his flesh. "Would you like me to fuck your gorgeous mouth?"

The dampness that formed between her thighs screamed *yes*. Jana couldn't believe this man aroused her like no other had. Her love life had never been the greatest. It wasn't that she didn't like the act, but her fantasies had always seemed so much better. And it was hard to get close to a man.

Hard to trust.

Jana hadn't trusted anyone but Lisa, yet she let this man tie her up. Although fear rode the boundaries of her mind, what she really felt was excitement. Jana's eyes were riveted on Nicolas. From the corner of her eye, she saw that Lisa's hips had begun to thrust with each movement of Nicolas's hand. Jana had never seen a man masturbate. And Lord, was it turning her on.

Nicolas growled his displeasure. "Doll, when I speak to you I expect an answer. Do you want me to fuck your mouth?"

Jana's gaze darted to Lisa. She still watched Nicolas. The images of Lisa going down on him—several times since Jana had arrived from California—sent Jana's pulse into overdrive. Blood rushed through her veins and pounded in her ears. She did want to wrap her lips around his cock. Feel him shiver at her touch, his fingers threading through her hair, holding her head as he thrust in and out of her mouth. She wanted to taste him.

Breathlessly she whispered, "Yes."

The rhythm of his hand increased. "Yes, what?"

"Yes, Milord. I want you to fuck my mouth." *Oh shit! Did I say that?* Jana's gaze again darted to Lisa, but her friend appeared to be unmoved by her words.

In fact, Lisa smiled.

Milord? The title had come easily.

Nicolas removed his hand from his cock and rose to his feet. "Honesty? You've earned your release."

Within seconds, Jana found herself free of her bonds, including her thigh cuffs and the head constraint. God, she loved the feel of his strong hands on her body. When he clasped his hand in hers and began to lead her back to the love sack, Jana wondered what would happen next. Already she had experienced a lifetime of emotions.

Who would have thought that the geeky gal behind the row of test tubes would actually like being restrained and fucked by her best friend's man? And since she was being honest with herself, she had been more than aroused at Lisa's touch and what she did to her before Nicolas had arrived and once he had entered her.

As she sank deep into the softness of the love sack, she wondered what her life would be like a year from now. It was an astonishing thought, because Jana had never dreamed about her future, never considered she really had a future. She just lived one day at a time. Even going to college was a strategy to give her direction, take any real decisions from her. Then she graduated, tossing all the decisions back into her lap.

Like an itch left unscratched, a hint of insecurity rose. It gnawed in the back of her mind.

When Nicolas drew her into the curve of his warm, hard body she couldn't help the sigh that slipped from her lips. The small action caught his attention and he captured her mouth in a hungry kiss. Then he stretched his large frame and lay on his back.

"Doll, take me into your hand. Stroke me, but don't make me come—not yet. If I do you'll be punished." There was something in the way he spoke, the dark shadow that crept into his eyes, that made Jana feel he meant every word.

She was confused. Baffled. How did you jack a man off and not expect him to shoot come into the air? Guess she'd find out. Wrapping her fingers around his large girth, she marveled at how soft yet hard he was. Tentatively, her hand began to slide up his length as she inhaled the heady scent of masculinity that rose from his heated skin.

God, he smelled good enough to eat.

Lisa moaned, drawing her attention. Her friend writhed against her bindings. From her anguished expression, Jana knew Lisa wanted to join them. Briefly, Jana wondered if she had looked that way this morning when she wanted desperately to join Lisa and Nicolas during one of their forays.

Through shuttered lashes Nicolas studied her. His bare, sexy form sprawled out beside her was something she had dreamt of and it had all come true, because of Lisa. She glanced again at her friend.

"Do you want Lisa released?" The warmth of his voice flowed over Jana's body like a second skin.

"Yes," she murmured.

A devilish smile creased his mouth. "Bad enough that you would pleasure her?"

"Yes." Jana frowned, then her eyes shot wide. "What?" *Me pleasure Lisa?*

"What?" he repeated.

"What, Milord?" she corrected trying to grasp Nicolas's meaning.

"That's better." He ran his fingers through her hair. "Do you want me to release Lisa and see her come bad enough that you would go down on her?"

Oh, my God, did he really ask if she would perform oral sex on Lisa? *Shit! Shit! Shit!*

The expression of relief on Lisa's face was not what Jana wanted to see. Perhaps she could just hang from the ceiling a little longer. *No.* That wouldn't do. But what he was asking was something she had never done. Even when she and Lisa had fooled around as teens they had never gone *there.*

Chapter Ten

Once again Nicolas had shocked Jana. The love sack was cool beneath him as he relaxed on his back, her fingers wrapped around his firm erection. He watched her, looking for any signs of retreat. Would Jana actually pleasure Lisa?

She removed her palm from his cock to clutch her hands together, and bit her lower lip. The anxiety and innocence in Jana's expression was endearing against the backdrop of his dungeon. His own personal playground.

The obvious excitement that had begun to overtake Lisa was heady as she pulled gently against her bindings. She was beautiful, wrists cuffed, restrained above her head, so she stood perched on her tiptoes. The red heart vibrator nestled in her blonde pubic hair, black elastic strips high on her hips. He couldn't wait to activate the small black controller he still held in his hands that would send vibrations through her clit.

He glanced from one beautiful woman to the other. What would be more exciting than to have them making love to each other? The emotion was there between them. He had sensed it immediately. This wouldn't be just an act, but would touch each of their hearts.

It would be special to them—to him.

Plus it would be fuckin' hot.

"Her orgasm is up to you, doll." He reached and fondled Jana's nipple. She drew back sharply, giving him an angry look. "Careful, doll. My patience is fading."

Jana sucked in the corner of her bottom lip and bit down so hard that when she released it he could see the imprint of her teeth. "Yes," she said.

Light and heady, he realized that he held his breath. "Yes?" he asked when what he wanted to say was, *Hot damn!*

Jana's gaze whipped from Lisa to him. "Yes, Milord." She said it with such sarcasm that he fully expected her to follow it up with a list of obscenities meant just for him. Instead she glared at him. "Will you release her now?"

He nodded as he rose. *With pleasure,* he thought as he approached Lisa. "Let's get you ready," he said, switching the controller on as he approached her.

"Shit." The single word squeezed from Lisa's thin lips as the clit stimulator hummed. When he released her wrists she fell into his arms.

"Thank you, Milord." Something in Lisa's tone made him feel like she thanked him for more than just releasing her from her bonds. She was so sexy looking at him that he couldn't help but dip his head and taste her lips. Her arms snaked around him, holding him tightly as he feasted on her. Not wanting her to come before he had the opportunity to watch the show between them, he flipped the controller off, and then broke the kiss.

When they turned as one to face Jana, she was standing. A light pink colored her entire body. She attempted a smile that fell short. Nicolas couldn't help the laughter that burst from his lips.

God, she was adorable.

With a brush of attitude, she pressed her fists into her hips and shot him a look that could kill.

If he was going to pull this off he had to remain in control. Had to make sure she knew he was in control. White-hot excitement built inside him. He loved this game of bondage and domination. Lisa had accommodated him when he'd adjusted their contract without her consent. He slid his hand down her back and grasped her ass.

He owed Lisa big time.

Unexpectedly, Lisa broke away from him and walked slowly, seductively toward Jana. She stood before her friend and leaned forward, whispering, "He wants a show. Let's give it to him."

Nicolas couldn't help but know that Lisa wanted him to hear. She even moved aside so he could see the devilish twinkle that stole the anxiety from Jana's eyes, seemingly putting her more at ease with what was about to happen.

There truly was more to Lisa than he imagined.

He watched with heated interest as Lisa smoothed her knuckles over Jana's cheek. Jana caught Lisa's hand in hers and brought it to her lips, letting a finger slip into her mouth.

Lisa was good.

The sexy blonde slid her finger in and out of Jana's mouth as she arched her back and released a soft moan. Which did two things; it encouraged Jana to carry on with what she thought was just a show as she drew her body closer to Lisa's, and it literally lit a fuse in him. Nicolas could feel his blood simmer as if set to a slow burn. The women certainly did a job on his balls, which pulsated like a son of a bitch, sending the throbbing straight down his shaft.

When Lisa withdrew her finger, she cupped Jana's cheeks and planted a kiss on her lips that had Jana stumbling back in surprise. Her back went rigid and she stood motionless. Lisa moved with Jana, continuing the kiss, then she ran her tongue up Jana's face toward her ear.

Nicolas couldn't help but be drawn to them. As he neared, he caught the last of Lisa's words. "...make it believable, or we're both in for a good spanking." Jana was hesitant at first as she placed a small kiss on Lisa's neck. Then Lisa returned her lips to Jana's and the kissing started for real. As their lips parted, Nicolas could see Lisa's tongue dart within Jana's mouth, tasting her. Jana slipped her own tongue through Lisa's parted lips.

Fuck! Nicolas would give his left nut to be in the middle of those two wildcats, because now they were really giving him a show.

Delicate hands began to trail over each other's bodies. Beautiful female forms moved gracefully together, almost as if they were slow dancing, rubbing each other into a sexual frenzy. Lisa found one of Jana's nipples and pinched, eliciting a deep, throaty moan from Jana. Both women's breathing had elevated to small pants of excitement.

Nicolas's cock jerked painfully. They were killing him.

It didn't take long before both women were enjoying the fullness of one another's breasts, their hands cupping, fingers pinching, pulling and rolling. As the scene grew hotter and hotter, so did Nicolas. When Lisa dipped to capture Jana's nipple in her mouth, her friend gasped at the sudden movement, but she didn't resist. No, in fact she threw back her head and jutted out her chest.

That was the ball breaker.

Nicolas had held out as long as he could. In a couple of strides he was standing next to them. Lisa's lips curved into a smile around the taut nipple in her mouth.

The action shook him to the core. The controller he held slipped from his hands, making a clicking sound as it hit the floor.

Lisa released Jana's breast and began kissing her again. Their breasts pressed against one another and their nipples grew harder as they touched.

Man, he was a lucky son of a bitch.

He knelt, retrieving the small controller, before placing his palms in the small of their backs to keep their hips pressed firmly together. With one push he set the clit stimulator to buzzing, servicing both the women at once. It had an amazing effect as they ground their hips together. Soft moans of pleasure seeped from their locked mouths.

But there was so much more that could be done with these two. He flipped off the vibrator and laced his fingers through their silky hair, ran his hands down the napes of their necks to their spines and back down to the swell of their asses.

Beautiful.

Lisa broke the kiss, releasing Jana and turning to accept his waiting mouth and arms. She was hungry as her tongue darted in to taste him and their teeth made contact. He bent slightly, his hard cock slipping between her legs. She was so wet and ready. In a surprising move, Jana moved behind him and snuggled up close to his backside.

If anyone had ever told him that he would be sandwiched between these two women he would have called them a damned liar, but here he was. And it was heaven.

"Milord, fuck me." Jana's warm breath teased the nape of his neck, sending a tingle up his spine.

Lisa withdrew from his kiss. "No, Milord. Fuck me." Her sexy voice slid across him like silk.

Nicolas was speechless and so friggin' hard. Who would have figured that two gorgeous women would be begging him to fuck them and at the same time? This was great for a man's ego. But he hadn't gotten the thrill he had wanted seeing these two women bend to his demand and do something they had never done before. He couldn't wait to see Lisa hot and moaning as Jana licked and sucked her pussy.

Wait! He had a better idea.

With a quick move he maneuvered his way free. He reached out and took Jana's chin between his thumb and forefinger drawing her gaze up to meet his. "I believe that doll still needs to pay off her debt to me for releasing you, baby." Jana tried to jerk away, but he held her firmly. "Don't refuse me. You might not like what I have in mind for punishment." He could see she was nervous about going down on her friend, but perhaps she was excited, too. Just in case he was wrong he said, "Do you agree to provide both Lisa and me the pleasure we desire?"

Jana swallowed hard. Then her tongue whipped out and nervously wet her lips. "Yes."

"Yes?" he asked, loving the way she had said his title before. It was a power thing. He knew. They knew. What the hell, he was the Master in this game for as long as they wished to play.

Jana's teeth snapped together as she snarled, "Yes, Milord."

Beneath her quiet exterior Nicolas knew she had the heart of a wildcat. She was still uncomfortable with him, but what would she be like once he broke her to his touch? He wanted her eager beneath him. And he wanted to know the real woman who had been beaten so badly she had climbed into a shell and fought her way back into the world.

"Then let me gather a few things to make our game more interesting." As he turned to retrieve what he had in mind he overheard Jana say, "Shit, Lisa. What am I going to do?"

"Just play along, sweetie. He wants to have fun with us. That's what this is about—fun. Relax and enjoy yourself. I plan to." Nicolas wasn't sure if Lisa's words were comforting to Jana, but he didn't hear her say another word.

When he turned, Lisa was stroking Jana's hair lightly. Jana's eyes were bright as she looked at the things in his hands. Again he had the thigh cuffs, but to his ensemble he had added two sets of velvet-lined handcuffs and a three-foot spreader bar with ankle cuffs.

Lisa surprised him once more. With her other hand she gently caressed Jana's body, fingertips drawing light circles, then long flowing waves that made Jana's nipples pucker. Each stroke was used to calm and excite and break Jana to Lisa's touch.

A quiver of unease slid across Nicolas. He could easily become the third wheel with the unique relationship these two women embraced. Then Lisa silently blew him a kiss and winked.

Damn. This gal could win an Oscar. She was special, as was the angel beside her.

"You ready to begin?" Nicolas asked as he strode forward with his tools.

Lisa pulled Jana closer to her own body and in a sensuous breath that teased the hairs around Jana's ear, she said, "As you wish, Milord. We only exist to pleasure you."

Nicolas's cock jerked with excitement, drawing both their gazes. His balls suddenly throbbed under Jana's scrutiny.

What the hell was wrong with him? He had taken Jana twice already. Why did he have the uncontrollable need to hold

115

her and rain soft kisses along that scar at her neck? Lisa moved Jana's hair aside and ran her fingertips along it as if she knew what he was thinking. Or maybe Lisa used her actions as a warning, a caution for what he was about to do.

"Follow me," he said, leading the way out of the dungeon and down the hall, stopping when he came to the bottom of the stairs. "Baby, move up the stairs about a third of the way." Lisa had told him once that she loved his pet name for her. She gifted him with a tender smile and then began to climb. That probably wasn't a correct description of what she did as her gorgeous ass swayed, taking each step with an air of sensuality that even had Jana captivated as she stood beside him. Her blue eyes were smoky, radiating heat. Hot. Hot. Desire.

Oh. My. God. Jana had never seen Lisa like this. The only way it could be described was pure and unadulterated sex appeal, as the black straps to her clit stimulator rested on her hips, and then disappeared between the cheeks of her ass. Fuck. Even she was turned on by Lisa's behavior. She moved like a sensual cat in heat. She slinked, the sexy look she tossed over her shoulder when she reached the point Nicolas requested made Jana's heart jump.

Yes, she and Lisa had kissed, touched each other, and even masturbated together, but they'd been inquisitive teenagers, hormones raging, caught up in the moment of discovery.

Tonight was different.

They were mature adults. Jana had never really thought about the differences between a man and woman.

It was hard to ignore now as she watched Nicolas climb the stairs after Lisa, giving Jana an amazing view of his magnificent physique. She loved the tight muscles in his ass, the veins that ran along his arms, and especially the large sac that hung between his thighs. Her hands ached to caress it, perhaps to suck it into her mouth.

It was the subtle differences between a man and a woman Jana had noticed when Lisa touched her. Like how soft her friend's hands and lips were. How light her kiss was compared to Nicolas's hot pursuit. Even their scents were different, from Lisa's soft musk to her light, minty breath. Men had an earthy, raw smell that surrounded them. In fact, everything about a man was hard, demanding, and even a little rough around the edges. Lisa was satiny, a piece of clay begging to be molded.

Jana's heart picked up a beat when Nicolas slipped the clit stimulator off Lisa and then secured her wrists using the velvet handcuffs, one to each handrail of the stairs.

Breathing didn't come easily to Jana at that moment. She really had to work to draw oxygen into her lungs.

At first it had been scary touching and being stroked by a woman. God. Did she have to admit to being excited about feeling her friend's breasts in her hands? Or how arousing it was to stand with another woman doing the things she loved having done to her?

Lisa's breasts were larger, firmer because of her breast implants, whereas Jana's were squishy. She silently laughed at her choice of words. But there was nothing wrong with her breasts. Even their nipples were different. Jana's were larger, rounder, longer, darker in color than Lisa's smaller, pinker, perkier versions. But what had been a complete rush was feeling Lisa's breasts pressed against her body. It had made Jana immediately wet with desire. For a woman!

Bottom line, shouldn't she be upset, even repulsed—a woman touching another woman—and then going down on her? Even if it was only to give Nicolas a good show?

But how could Jana feel disgusted? This was Lisa, the only person Jana had ever truly loved.

Confusion slipped into Jana's mind when Nicolas secured the thigh cuffs around Lisa's thighs, allowing the wrist bands to dangle at her side. Her friend's hands were already bound, which meant only one thing. Nicolas was going to bind her to Lisa using the smaller restraints, her face aligned with Lisa's pussy.

Again, Jana's heart jumped, skipping a beat this time when he placed a bar-looking thing between Lisa's ankles and then strapped the bindings in place. When finished he stood and turned to face Jana. She could see pride shine in his eyes.

He crooked a finger, calling her to his side.

As Jana placed her foot on the first step, she had to admit that Lisa made a hot image, bound as she was on the stairs, wild as her short, mussed hair framed her sexy features. The man beside her looked like the devil himself.

A shiver shook Jana.

When he touched Jana's arm, sizzling hot flames licked her sensitive skin. She grew hot. And damn if her nipples didn't betray her by drawing tight. Not to mention the cream that developed between her thighs. With just a simple caress Nicolas made her weak and she slipped upon her knees.

With deft fingers, he bound her using the wrist restraints connected to Lisa's thigh cuffs and then moved behind her. She tried to look over her shoulder, tried to ensure he made his way down the stairs, but she wasn't that lucky.

"I'm not going anywhere, doll. While you pleasure Lisa, I'll pleasure you."

Jana found her voice, which had been unnaturally absent tonight. "It's not necessary." Nervous energy flowed through her veins. What had she gotten herself into?

A brush of air touched her shoulder as he murmured in a deep, sexy tone, "I'm going to have some fun, too."

Okay, she couldn't fight that logic. Lisa was right. Nicolas was insatiable.

Nicolas positioned himself behind her, as his hands slid between her thighs. Her gaze darted downward and she couldn't help the tight squeal that left her mouth.

"Easy, doll. All I'm doing is making you easier to accommodate me." He parted her thighs, exposing her further. "Beautiful," he whispered and she again felt his warm breath on her moist folds.

When he slipped a finger into her wetness, the abrupt invasion made her fall forward, grasping Lisa's thighs. Jana's gaze met Lisa's. Her brown eyes were soft with tenderness. *You can do this*, she mouthed adding, *I love you.*

Yes, she could do this. Jana mimed, *I love you, too.*

Lisa smiled, then puckered her mouth as if blowing Jana a kiss before sliding her tongue across her full lips. Jana focused on her friend's face, trying to ignore the thick fingers moving inside her. Slowly, she moved her bound hands so she could grasp Lisa's ass cheeks and stabilize her stance.

Lisa thrust her hips forward. Jana took a deep breath of courage and buried her face into Lisa's pussy.

Relief filtered across her with a hint of shame at being afraid. It wasn't at all what Jana expected as she smoothed her tongue over Lisa's swollen folds, felt the tiny bumps of hair follicles that lined her friend's labia. Lisa released a deep groan, her thighs parting further as she bent her knees. Jana flicked her tongue across the velvety surface, once more eliciting another moan from Lisa that curled around Jana's body like silk. Then she pressed her tongue deep into Lisa's slit. The feel was wild against her tongue, soft, like taffy folding around her, drawing her further into Lisa's cove.

The scent was different, hard to describe, but not unpleasant. The taste, however, surprised Jana. She hadn't known what to expect; still, the light, sweet taste was not it. Maybe the fact that Lisa ate tons of fruit contributed to her unique flavor.

Who knew? Who cared?

Jana hadn't expected to like what she was doing, but once again she had to admit to being aroused and it wasn't just because of what Nicolas was preparing to do to her. He had taken the opportunity to crawl between her thighs to taste her. With each lick of his tongue across her slit, desire burned.

Was Lisa feeling the same exquisite sensation?

When Nicolas ran his tongue over Jana's clit, Jana mimicked the action against Lisa's. The sensation was strange and stimulating. Lisa's hidden nub swelled against Jana's tongue, hardened and then pulsated like it had its own heartbeat. And darn wet. The flood Jana released on Nicolas's tongue would rival the wave of desire Lisa freed.

Lisa's legs began to quiver. She bent her knees, opening herself even wider as the shaking intensified.

"God, Jana."

Jana didn't recognize her friend's ragged voice as she wrapped her tongue around Lisa's clit and sucked.

Lisa exploded, her pussy contracting in small jerky motions, discharging a thinner, sweeter fluid than that of the lubricating moisture. When Jana tasted Lisa's climax she moaned deep into Lisa's pussy. Her friend thrashed against her bindings, making it difficult to continue. Then Nicolas touched a sweet spot inside Jana and all thoughts of Lisa disappeared.

Nothing existed except Nicolas between her thighs.

Chapter Eleven

An omnipotent rush of power and dominance surged through Nicolas's veins as he brought Jana to orgasm. She writhed above him, desperately clutching onto her friend's thighs for support. Breathless, she trembled beneath his touch, whimpering softly.

As he rose from beneath her, he'd never felt so invincible as he did at that moment. Strong energy built, growing inside him with full vital strength. Forceful and powerful, he could taste its red-hot potency upon his tongue.

They performed as he commanded. He held them in the palm of his hands. The godlike power invigorated him.

The illusion that he could do anything surfaced, which included opening the condom packet that slipped through his moist fingers.

When he finally had the damn thing on his cock, he remained quiet, admiring the bound women on different levels of his staircase. Lisa strapped to the banister, Jana shackled to Lisa. He reached for Jana, his palms gripping her hips. With one thrust he entered her from behind. She made a sound between a cry of surprise and a groan. She was wet, drenched, and so tight that he lost control the second he thrust deep between her swollen folds.

"Fuck." The cry tore from his throat. It was like expelling fire as his orgasm ripped through his shaft, but different because there was such a forceful pulse of pleasure. He couldn't help collapsing against Jana's back, driving her forward. He couldn't breathe. His balls spasmed. Nicolas tensed from the intense pleasure/pain. Seconds passed as he lay there, feeling the last of the rippling spasms die out, leaving him relaxed and sated.

The haze around him began to clear as he heard his name spoken.

"Nicolas." Lisa's voice didn't sound right. High-pitched and shaky, she cried, "Oh God, Nicolas, release me."

"Lisa, are you okay?" Jana asked as concern tightened her features.

Blood drained from Lisa's face leaving her as white as a sheet. The area around her lips turned blue.

As Nicolas struggled to get to her his movements were sluggish, awkward. Jana was in his way. He had to free her first in order to get to Lisa. With haste, he undid her wrists from Lisa's thighs and then literally pushed her down the stairs. He heard her body thump as she rolled, heard her deep groan.

Fuck. What had he done?

When he finally got to Lisa her eyes rolled back. Her skin was cold. Without delay he worked on the spreader bar to release her ankles. She groaned softly and then collapsed on the stairs, pushing them both down a couple steps making him land atop her. He struggled to rise, hearing Jana's frantic cries. "What's wrong with her? What have we done to her?"

Nicolas hurried to release Lisa's wrists and worked to lift her into his arms. When he had her securely in his embrace he took two steps at once, heading up the stairs toward his bedroom.

As he laid her limp body down on his bed she opened her eyes. "My purse. Get my purse." Her request was almost inaudible.

He turned and saw Jana disappear through the open door.

With a brush of his hands he moved Lisa's hair from her face. "Baby, are you okay?"

"Fine," she managed to say. But he knew she was anything but fine. Light, shallow breaths barely moved her chest. Her face had twisted into a mass of pain. "Water."

Nicolas sprang from the bed, heading for the kitchen, passing Jana on his way. The worry in her eyes reflected his own concern. Nothing mattered but taking care of Lisa.

The kitchen smelled of garlic and a handful of other seasonings and herbs from his half-cooked dinner. From the cabinet he retrieved a glass, filled it with water from the refrigerator, and then moved hastily back to the bedroom. When he arrived, Lisa was sitting up against his pillows. Some color had flowed back into her face, still dark rings around her eyes remained. Jana was offering her a tiny white pill that she took and placed on her tongue. Nicolas handed her the glass of water and she took a small drink.

"Thank you," she said, laying her head back against the headboard.

"I'm calling the doctor." Jana sprang to her feet, moving toward the telephone on the other side of the bed.

"No. Please, Jana." Life seemed to spring back into Lisa. She forced a laugh that simply did not sound like she was having fun. "I'll be okay. I just get headaches from time to time. The doctor said there's nothing they can do for them."

"Bullshit!" Jana barked.

"Really, Jana. Watch, in five to ten minutes I'll be just fine." She reached for her friend's hand, but Jana was already in motion.

Jana turned about sharply to face Nicolas. "What happened?"

Nicolas was speechless at the accusation in her eyes. Nothing he had asked them to do would have caused Lisa's reaction.

Jana pressed her fingertips to her forehead. Her eyes closed briefly. "This is my fault."

"That's ridiculous. We did nothing Nicolas and I haven't done millions of times." A huff left Lisa's thin lips. Then she cringed like pain overtook her. She took several deep breaths releasing them slowly. "Well maybe not millions of times. Jana, calm down. I enjoyed what we did together." She waved her hand. "Come here."

Jana's movements were stiff as she approached the bed and then sat beside her friend. Lisa took her into her arms, laying her head on Jana's shoulder. "I loved what we shared. Please don't think poorly of yourself or Nicolas." She held her free hand out to him and he went to her. "Beside me. I want both of you beside me."

Lisa's eyes were red, tired, as he pulled back the comforter and sheets, letting both women climb beneath them before he took his place next to Lisa. When he wrapped his arm around her he accidentally touched Jana and she pulled back like he'd burned her.

"Children, play nice together." Lisa chastised them, sounding like she was almost too tired to speak. "I'm sleepy. Can we just sleep for a while..." No sooner did Lisa speak, before she fell into a deep slumber. The same couldn't be said for him or the other woman in the bed.

Nicolas didn't know how long he had lain there when exhaustion overtook him.

Nicolas woke curled around Jana. Lisa was nowhere in sight. His concern for Lisa remained, but it felt so good, so right holding Jana against him in his bed. Many women had shared this space, but he had never gotten the sense that they actually belonged there, as he did with Jana.

The thought gave him pause. What the hell was he thinking? Jana didn't even like him much after last night. And he wasn't feeling all that great about himself either. He still couldn't figure out what went wrong.

As he tightened his hold on Jana, the sweet scent of her musk was overridden by a delicious smell wafting through the open bedroom door. His stomach growled, reminding him that he hadn't eaten since mid-afternoon yesterday.

Who was in his kitchen?

What time was it?

As he rose slightly to look at the clock on the nightstand next to his bed, Jana moaned and shifted onto her back. She was beautiful. He couldn't resist tasting her as he pressed his lips to hers. Within seconds she was kissing him back, her arms snaking around his neck.

Then she froze, which could also be said of how her icy blue eyes looked when she opened them and saw who held her. With a jerk of her head their mouths parted.

Her palms struck his chest and then pushed. "Get off me."

He made no attempt to move, instead he adjusted himself further so that he pinned her to the bed with his body, his rigid cock pressed against her hip. "Jana, you have to believe that what happened last—"

"I should have never participated. It was wrong." The whole time she stared at his mouth. He could see that she wanted him to kiss her again. "Lisa—where's Lisa?"

He cupped Jana's chin. "No! It wasn't wrong. I won't let you belittle what happened last night. It was beautiful. Special. Even Lisa recognized how good we all are together."

She shook her head in denial.

"Dammit! Doll, you know you enjoyed what happened between us. You're just having next morning regrets." This happened all the time to people. They allowed their desires and their frame of mind to butt heads in the morning. In Jana's case, it was compounded by Lisa's sudden illness. He should have anticipated Jana's response.

"Now. Now. Children, I thought I told you two to play nicely." Lisa waltzed into the bedroom holding a tray covered in food that set Nicolas's stomach to growling again. She wore one of the transparent nightgowns she kept at his house. The kind that made him feel like he had infrared vision, able to look through shadows and see everything. In this case it was the dips and curves of her lithe body.

"Lisa—" Jana's face flushed as she tried to rise, but was held immobile by Nicolas's body atop her. "Nicolas, let me go. Lisa, what do you think you're doing?"

Nicolas started to shift when Lisa said, "Keep her right there." She moved closer to the bed and he could see that although her eyes appeared weary, she seemed like she was back to her same old self.

Jana squirmed, trying to get out of Nicolas's embrace. "Lisa!"

Lisa ignored Jana's cry as she set the tray at the foot of the bed, then shimmied out of her gown. Like a panther, she slowly climbed upon the bed, making sure not to disturb the tray. She looked up through feathered lashes as she crawled across the bed in a sensual sway. "Now we are going to have breakfast in bed, *together.*" She ran a fingernail down Nicolas's leg, sending a shiver up his spine which hardened his cock even more and pressed it firmly against Jana's belly.

She gave him an agitated look that said, "Barbarian."

Hell. He *felt* barbaric trapping one woman beneath him against her will as another slinked her way toward him with a hungry expression like he was on the menu this morning.

Lisa continued, "Then we are going shopping, *together.* Nicolas tells me he has something special for us." She bent, tracing her tongue along his bare thigh. "Mmmm... You taste good. After that we are coming home and fucking, *together.*"

When Jana opened her mouth, Lisa leaned over Nicolas and pressed a finger to her friend's lips. "No argument. As you can see I'm perfectly fine. It's Saturday. We have the whole weekend to *really* get to know each other."

Screw breakfast. He was ready to fuck now.

What was Lisa up to? Jana wondered.

Nicolas released Jana and she scrambled from beneath him as he twisted to lie on his back. She sat upright, glared down at him and shivered. There was no doubt in her mind he knew she had enjoyed last night's experience. More surprisingly was that she had trusted him. It may have only been during the throes of passion, but she had trusted someone other than Lisa, which was something she hadn't done in a long time.

But to accept that she liked being bound, that she liked a man dominating her, went against her grain. She should be stronger—more in control.

Damn him! For beginning to break down the defenses she had built throughout the years.

Yet she couldn't deny the feelings she'd had all along of having a man be in control, and how much BDSM had turned her on when she researched it on the internet.

Lisa crawled to one side, placing Nicolas in between them, then reached for the tray and handed it to him. Jana looked at her friend over the muscled chest of the man who sat between them in bed. The tray covered his cock and probably wasn't very comfortable.

Good!

Jana's indelicate snort drew Lisa and Nicolas's attention. She simply raised a brow. From the looks of his earlier erection, the one that had jabbed her in the stomach, she would guess the rise in his knees was to put distance between his family jewels and that of the warm tray.

Jana glanced at Lisa. She really did look like her old self. Yeah. Her eyes were drawn, but whose weren't this morning?

Their evening of discovery had swallowed up the night. Then whatever had happened to Lisa had stolen several more hours of sleep. Jana had stayed awake listening to Lisa's soft breathing, while Nicolas lightly snored. It was only when Lisa turned on her side and snuggled into Jana's back, like she used to when they were younger, that Jana fell asleep. For a moment she'd been sixteen again, safe, at least for the night.

Jana hated the feeling of insecurity that consistently raised its ugly head. She looked down at the knife lying on the tray and wondered if there was any way to cut the head off the demon. When she looked up, Nicolas had a rather sheepish expression. His knees fell flat on the bed as he placed the tray firmly on his lap like a shield.

Surely Nicolas didn't think the object of her frustration hid beneath the tray? She really wasn't mad at Nicolas, more herself.

Jana couldn't help the laughter that spilled from her mouth. Color flooded up Nicolas's neck, surging across his cheeks, peaking at his ears.

"What?" Lisa asked.

"Nothing," Nicolas responded sharply. His expression was priceless. Then his face softened and one of those devilish handsome grins crossed his strong features.

Lisa leaned forward. "What did I miss?" She glanced back and forth between Jana and Nicolas.

Damn Nicolas. Damn him for being so irresistibly sexy.

She couldn't help thinking about their night together. Moisture gathered at the apex of her thighs with the thought. She crossed her arms over her chest to hide the tightening of her breasts. She had enjoyed his domination. Enjoyed the fact she was forced to experience something new and special with Lisa that, on her own accord, she would have never done.

"Nothing," Jana insisted. "I think breakfast is over." She tossed her legs over the side of the bed and rose.

"But you haven't eaten. Where do you think you're going?" Lisa asked, getting off the bed with haste. The way she moved around the bed to intercept Jana wasn't like that of a sick woman.

"I'm going downstairs to get the outfit you bought me. Then I'm getting dressed. And either you can drive or I'll call for a taxi. I'm going home." Jana headed for the door, stopping as Lisa caught her by the arm with her fingers. Jana gave her friend a warning look.

Home? This was the first time in a long time that Jana had referred to any place as home. But it was true. Lisa's house did feel like home to her.

Lisa planted one hand on her hip. Her head and shoulders wagged side to side exactly the way her mother's used to when she was mad at Lisa. "No you don't, young lady."

"Cathy, is that you?" Jana asked and then broke into laughter. "You sounded just like your mother."

Lisa giggled. "I did, didn't I?" She drew Jana into her embrace. "I guess it's true."

"What?" Jana asked hugging her back. Funny, but it seemed natural to be hugging her friend, even if both of them were naked.

"The apple doesn't fall far from the tree."

Engrossed in each other, Jana hadn't noticed that Nicolas had risen until he moved beside them. He again wore a pair of faded jeans, the top button undone.

He took Jana's breath away as she stepped from Lisa's arms. She'd never seen a sexier man.

"Maybe she's right, Lisa." He placed a palm on her arm.

"No!" Lisa's fists flew to her waist, knocking away his hand. "I—we have planned the weekend for fun, and I intend to enjoy myself." Jana could see tears well in Lisa's eyes. Perhaps it was because her friend was tired. Again, with an outburst of emotion that Jana had never seen, Lisa said to Jana, "I can't do it without you." Then she glanced at Nicolas. "Or you. Please, let's put what happened last night out of our minds." Then a smile slid across her lips. She wrinkled her nose in her cutesy way. "Well, not all of it. I believe some parts should be repeated—tonight. In fact, I insist. Now let's eat and then get dressed."

"I don't have any clothes other than the dress I wore last night," Jana said, thankful for a reason to put distance between her and Nicolas as she stepped away.

"Oh yes you do." Lisa winked at Nicolas. "Courtesy of our host. We'll dress for his pleasure. As a sub, your Master's pleasure is all that matters. Now let's eat. Everyone—back on the bed."

Master? Nah... This lifestyle wasn't for her. Or was it? Jana wondered as she crawled upon the bed. She watched Nicolas slowly slip his jeans off and move to the bed. With ease, he situated himself between them. His warmth touched her and for a moment her breath stilled. A tight release of air slipped between her lips.

Lisa was the only one who talked as they ate. "Jana, thanks for last night. I knew the three of us would be great together."

Okay, this was where Jana needed to express her concerns. She set her plate containing her half-eaten breakfast back on the tray, eased off the bed and then stood. "Lisa, I fully understand your desire to play this game, but it's not for me." There. She'd said it. This lifestyle wasn't for her.

Then she thought about the BDSM website she had visited and its revealing questions. The only question she answered with an absolute *no* had been being tied up. Last night threw that one out the window. Maybe, just maybe, she should go along with Nicolas and Lisa and see what this lifestyle offered. She had already taken the first steps.

Jana shivered at the heated glare she received from Nicolas as he rose from the bed and walked around Lisa to invade Jana's personal space. She fought the urge to step backward. His presence overwhelmed her.

Before she was aware of what was happening he had her in his arms, devouring her mouth. She thought to fight, but her body thought differently. All her defenses melted like ice on a summer's day. It was senseless to resist. The only way she would succeed was to put distance between them and it didn't seem like that was happening any time soon.

When he allowed her to catch her breath he placed his mouth next to her ear. "Do you want to play this game with us, doll? It's your choice." He nibbled on her earlobe. "I'll never force you to do anything you don't want to do." His voice was low, sensually twisting and drawing her closer into his sexual spell. When he kissed her neck chills raced up her body. "But if you concede," his warm breath blew across the area he had just kissed, "you must obey me without question." He waited for a moment and then said, "Do you agree?"

Jana was confused. Her head told her no, but her body screamed yes. She wanted to know more about this world. Wanted to share in what Lisa and Nicolas had.

"Yes," she whispered as her eyelashes brushed her cheeks.

He ran his tongue along her neck and her knees slightly buckled. "Choose a safe word."

Safe word? "A what?" she asked.

"A word to use that will tell me that you want to stop this game. And then I'll never touch you again."

Now that wasn't what she wanted to hear. Since she had a taste of him, doing without was simply out of the question. "How about, stop."

He tried to stifle his amusement, but she heard the laughter in his voice. "Choose another word. That one won't do."

"Red."

"That'll do. Now, on the chair across the room is a box with your name on it." Deep and sexy, his voice wrapped around her like rope, each word binding her closer to him. "Take it with you to the guest bathroom. After you shower, get dressed." He moved his palm to rest on the small of her back. Then his hand slipped down to grip her ass. She startled but didn't say anything. "Leave your hair down and free. You will be rewarded for your obedience. Now go." The firmness in his tone made her shiver.

She took a step backward. Her eyes locked with Nicolas's. Her nipples beaded, revealing how his words had affected her.

Jana glanced at Lisa and saw only reassurance in her friend's nod. Could Jana do this? Excitement raced across her skin.

"Trust me, Jana. You're mine." The determined look in his eyes said he believed it to be true.

She was his.

Chapter Twelve

It was noon by the time Nicolas pulled his truck out of his driveway. The sun was bright as he flipped his visor down, shading his eyes. He was looking forward to their trip to the mall.

Lisa was her cheerful self. "Isn't it beautiful today?" Her vibrant personality made him smile. She chatted on about how each day should be cherished as if it were the last.

Several times, Lisa attempted to pull Jana into the conversation, but Jana acted preoccupied and only gave clipped answers as she gazed out the window.

Something had told Nicolas that Jana would be uncomfortable when he took hold of the reins. But he could do no less.

He wanted her.

No, that was an understatement.

She was his.

If Jana didn't realize it now, he would make sure she understood and accepted that fact soon. She craved his touch as much as he craved hers. If he had to keep her abed until she finally surrendered, he would. His cock sprang alive, pushing against the zipper of his jeans with the thought of her submission. The two small controllers hidden in one of his pockets just made him grow firmer and uncomfortable.

Damn the obstinate woman. Her scent flowed from the backseat to tease him. She did things to his body no other woman had, not even Lisa. From the corner of his eye he glanced at Lisa dressed in the short tiger print sundress he had chosen for her. Jana wore a leopard print sundress. Yes, Lisa was sexy and a wonderful sub, but Jana woke something in him that no one had ever touched. Even when she was dressed in a T-shirt, jeans and tennis shoes, which she favored, he found Jana sexy and sensuous.

He wanted her.

What the phenomena was he didn't know. What he did know was that every moment spent with her was special. The times she smiled brightened the room.

Perhaps it was the life he knew she'd lived. Did he just feel sorry for her? No, he felt pride in what she had been able to overcome. Was it her insecure side he saw every once in a while? No. He had been with plenty of women who needed a man to survive. Jana didn't need a man. She had proven that by establishing herself professionally. She was a chemical engineer. You didn't get to a position like that without determination and strength.

Whatever it was about her that intrigued him better be quenched, and soon. The triangle between the three of them could never be more than just fun. He had no plans for anyone to get hurt in this arrangement.

Especially Jana.

A car darted in front of him as he steered his truck toward the off-ramp at Chandler Boulevard. He jerked back on the steering wheel and received the first sign of life in the backseat when Jana squealed with surprise. The tight sound made him want to take her in his arms. Instead he ignored her and continued to exit the highway.

As he pulled into the parking lot in front of Nordstrom's, he wondered whether he should use the valet service or just find a parking space. His answer came in an open spot just two spaces down from the last handicap vacancy. Close enough.

Nicolas opened the truck door and climbed out. He tucked his red cotton polo shirt into his jeans, and then bent and tied the undone shoelaces of one of his tennis shoes. Before he could reach Jana's door she was out and around the car. In fact, she opened Lisa's door and her friend climbed out.

"Well, thank you. Are you the valet today?" Lisa teased as she placed her purse beneath her arm.

"Funny." Jana's response was dry.

Lisa waited for Nicolas to catch up and then she gave him a beautiful, sparkling smile. "What are your wishes, Milord?"

With a pinch of his thumb and forefinger he raised her chin for a kiss. "Only to have fun, baby. Where would you like to go?"

She shuttered her eyelashes. "Where else? Victoria's Secret to find something you'll like." Her voice was low and sexy and he loved what it did to him.

He was already getting hard just thinking about the skimpy lingerie and what it would look like on his girls. "I was hoping you'd say that. Shall we go through Nordstrom's on our way?"

Placing his palms in the small of each woman's back, he led them to the glass doors and held them open to allow them to pass through. The minute he stepped inside the store a flood of perfume hit him in the face, overpowered his senses and immediately clogged his nostrils.

How did anyone work in that type of environment and breathe?

To the left were women's purses. To the right were children's clothing—young girls. For a minute Lisa paused, looking at the ocean of pink. Her smile faded and then as quickly as it was gone it reappeared as she spun around in the other direction. "Come on, I need a new purse." And then she was off, heading quickly in the other direction.

Jana frowned. "Lisa, you bought two new purses yesterday." She followed, keeping her distance from Nicolas. He noted that she walked awkwardly due to a certain surprise he'd hidden in her clothing.

That's what had Jana out of sorts. He silently snickered. She wasn't pleased with the small electronic device in her panties. She'd balked at putting the underwear on, but had finally given in, Lisa had told him, before they left the house.

Lisa stopped abruptly. "I did? I bought two yesterday?" Then she brushed her forgetfulness off with a hand through the air. "Then you need one."

"I don't need a new purse. I don't need anything," Jana insisted.

Yesterday, before he arrived at the restaurant, Nicolas had stopped at an adult store to find something special for Lisa and Jana. The salesclerk, who had more piercings than he had ever seen on one person, suggested a remote control clit stimulator that came with its own special pair of panties with a built-in shield to hold it firmly against the wearer. The young woman said it would feel a little unusual walking around. Yet she assured him the benefits would be worth the temporary discomfort.

The best thing about the remote control devices was that he could activate them from twenty-five feet away. The darn things even worked through walls.

Damn if it wasn't making him hot just thinking about teasing the women. The anticipation must be killing Jana, not knowing when he would zap her. She probably thought he would activate the box as soon as they entered the store, but there was more fun in the anticipation.

Call it foreplay.

He adjusted his hips to accommodate the swelling between his thighs. Quickly, he scanned the nearby merchandise, knowing he needed to buy something soon to use as a shield to hide his obvious excitement of what he had planned.

Amazingly, they were able to get out of Nordstrom's with a handful of items that Lisa had to have. Jana had yet to purchase anything. She seemed more concerned about Lisa's spending habits. Although Nicolas had offered each time to pay for her purchases, Lisa insisted on spending her own money, which would be unacceptable when they got to Victoria's Secret.

Nicolas knew exactly what he was looking for. He had seen the sexy ensemble on a mannequin in the display case several days prior.

He slipped his hand deep in his pocket and touched the controllers. *No. Not yet.*

As they moved down the aisle, Lisa peered into every store window. She loved to shop.

Nicolas couldn't say the same about Jana.

Every once in a while he could see her eyes brighten at a particular shirt or piece of jewelry, yet she kept a tight hold of her purse. She wasn't a frivolous spender. He could almost imagine the wheels in her head turning as she prioritized each item between wants and needs.

That was the kind of woman he needed beside him to run his restaurant.

The thought brought him to a dead halt. What in the hell was wrong with him? The answer was only six feet away entering a novelty store.

Jana.

No woman had ever consumed his thoughts like she did. He had only known her for two weeks, and yet he had grown unusually attached to her. When he woke in Lisa's arms each morning it was to wonder how Jana had slept. Did she dream of him? Did she have another nightmare?

He followed the women into the novelty store and laughed when Jana put on a Halloween mask, raised her curled fingers, and roared at Lisa. Finally it looked like she was getting into the shopping excursion. As she pulled the Bride of Frankenstein mask from her head she released a giggle that forced him to take a breath, watching her toss her red mane behind her shoulder. When she was happy, when she felt free—or was it safe?—Jana was an entirely different woman.

He admired her strength, loved the fight in her, as she struggled to overcome her demons.

Just as she reached for another mask, Lisa swayed and almost fell before Jana grasped her arm. "Are you okay?"

"Yeah. I just stepped on something." Lisa bypassed the masks and moved on to look at a cow costume with outlandish udders.

As Nicolas followed he looked down to avoid whatever it was that had tripped Lisa, but she must have kicked it beneath the shelves, because nothing lay on the floor.

The girls had a great time in the novelty shop looking at the new things that had just been put out for Halloween. Rows and rows of costumes were aligned against one side of the wall from the very scariest to the sexiest. In fact, he picked up a French maid and naughty schoolgirl costume before they left.

Jana and Lisa linked arms. Nicolas fished out the two remote controls he kept fondling in his jeans pocket. He set his packages on the floor. Holding a remote in each hand he pushed the on buttons simultaneously.

Immediately, both women's laughter died, their knees buckled, but neither fell. Thank God. They did, however, turn and give him a dirty look—both of them.

They spoke briefly to each other, words he couldn't hear and figured he didn't want to hear. He could only imagine what the topic was about, before they continued to walk. The grace was gone from each of their steps; instead it was more of a dip, thrust and roll, reminding him of the "can't chew gum and walk at the same time" adage.

He burst into laughter, receiving strange looks from a couple that passed him as he reached for his packages.

When Lisa and Jana headed toward a bench not more than ten feet in front of them, he turned off the stimulators. Both women threw another aggravated look over their shoulders in his direction. He could have sworn they smiled as they turned their backs to him and once again began to converse.

He flicked both controllers on-off-on-off-on-off. He couldn't help it. It thrilled him to have such power over their bodies, giving and taking away their pleasure with the push of a single button. Their expressions were priceless as they grasped each other for support, making him feel like a real bad boy.

And tonight he'd show them what a real good man he could be.

That. Damn. Man.

Jana was contemplating murder. That was if the black box wedged between her legs didn't feel so good.

Yes. She had been worried about this entire trip, especially when she pulled on the panties and saw what Nicolas had in mind.

Lisa had said, "It'll be fun. Just think about never knowing when he might activate the clit stimulator. Never knowing when the tingle between your thighs will force you into his arms, begging him to fuck you." Her face had grown dreamy. "Anywhere—not caring who watched."

Jana adjusted her dress and attempted to gather her wits as the final wave of sensations died a slow death between her legs. Not knowing when her body would go up in flames again was not fun.

Liar. Truthfully, it was exciting and made her hungry to feel Nicolas's touch.

Last night had been a mistake.

Or was it?

Excitement and regret clashed. The conflicting emotions knotted, twisted and churned inside her as if they were trying to be set free. Nicolas played with both her and Lisa's bodies like they were his own personal toys. Did he really feel that way? Was this really just a game?

The excitement she felt when he had said, "Trust me, Jana. You're mine," was beyond anything she had ever felt before. Truth was she did want to belong to someone—someone like Nicolas. But a three-way affair would never work out.

She fought not to look behind her. To not see what Nicolas was up to.

Who knew that he was a god between the sheets and evidently a devilish rogue outside them?

Jana was just like any other woman. She wanted a family of her own. She had leeched off Lisa's for far too long. Her deepest, darkest secret was to have a man to love her, children she could care for and keep safe. She hadn't even revealed this fantasy to Lisa.

Sharing a man wasn't what Jana had in mind, even if it was with her best friend. She couldn't regret what happened between them. It was an experience she would always treasure, and stirred emotions inside she had never experienced.

"Lisa." Jana couldn't help asking one more time. "Are you okay about—you know? What happened last night?"

Lisa's expression softened. "Did you enjoy yourself?"

Heat flushed over Jana. "Well, yes."

Lisa squeezed her arm. "That's all that matters."

"Don't you love him?" Jana prepared herself for Lisa's answer.

A rather unladylike snort left Lisa's perfect lips. "Are you kidding?" Not exactly the response Jana had expected. "Fun. That's what I'm looking for as I told you before. I want to experience everything." Then Lisa stopped and with both hands held Jana at arm's length. "Will you help me?" A shadow crept across Lisa's eyes and then disappeared. "Have fun, I mean?"

Jana tensed. "Are you okay? I mean is everything all right?"

"What?" Lisa released Jana and started walking toward Victoria's Secret, which was only two stores down. "Man, you can be ridiculous at times. There are just a few things, like the club Nicolas is taking us to tonight, that I want to experience. And I can't do it alone." She turned back to face Jana. "I'm not as brave or as strong as you are. Promise me you'll be there for me?"

"Club?"

"When we get home we need to talk about Trent's party. There are things you might feel uncomfortable with." She paused, reaching for Jana again. Her palms were moist. Her grip on Jana's arms tightened. "Promise me you'll go and try to have fun? It would please Nicolas. I can guarantee when he's happy—you'll be happy."

As they stood before the entrance to the store, Jana said, "But it's just a little awkward."

"That will go away once we're all comfortable with each other. Please say you'll play with Nicolas and me?" Lisa's eyes sparkled with tears.

Did this really mean so much to Lisa? How could Jana turn down her friend? Or was it that she really didn't want to?

It didn't take much coercing for Jana to say, "Yes. Okay. I'll give it a go."

"Grrreat! Now let's spend some of Nicolas's money," Lisa said, grabbing Jana's hand and pulling her into the store.

As Lisa directed her to a bin of panties that could only be described as butt floss, Nicolas entered.

Their eyes met. The heat simmering in his dark blue gaze made her feel as if she were standing within his fire. Speechless, she watched as he lifted the remote controller.

He wouldn't dare. Not here. Not now.

The store was swarming with women. Lisa had walked off toward the perfume.

His thumb stroked the black box as he strolled toward her. She trembled with the power he had over her. It actually sucked the air out of the room leaving her breathless. When he was close enough to touch he leaned close to her ear. His warm breath sent goose bumps across her skin.

"Find something to try on." His sexy, low voice was a warning that tightened her nipples, sending a tingle through them. Then with a wink, he pressed the button.

Once again Jana's knees buckled with the sudden vibration between her thighs. She grasped the bin, bracing herself against it as moisture flooded her pussy.

"Stop," she choked out.

"More," he whispered as he turned the vibrator to a throbbing pulse.

Her spine rolled with sensation after sensation. "Nicolas, please."

"I recommend you find something to try on. Because this time I want to see your beautiful body flushed with arousal." As a salesclerk walked by, Nicolas said, "Excuse me." He picked up a lacy thong out of the bin. "She would like to try this on."

The saleswoman smiled as her gaze scanned Nicolas's length. "Excellent choice." She batted full eyelashes.

If Jana hadn't been in the throes of desire, she might have decked her. Instead she had other things on her mind. One of them was simply walking. Her legs felt like jelly. The temperature in the room was rising. Her heart was racing and she had the uncontrollable need to grab Nicolas and rub her body up and down his. Slide her wetness across his leg while she worked on Nicolas's zipper.

By the time they made it to the fitting rooms, Jana was barely holding back the moan that begged to be released. Instead she gulped down a deep breath, tightened her vaginal muscles and prayed she'd make it into the room. When the saleswoman opened the door Jana dashed inside, tried to pull the door closed, but it halted with a sharp jerk.

Nicolas's hand rested on the door. "Don't forget these." He held out the panties. Her mouth opened as if she planned to berate him, but she gasped instead as the beginning of her climax released. "Come for me, Jana," he whispered against her lips, pushing her over the edge. She grabbed the panties and slammed the door, sure that everyone in the store, hell, the entire mall, heard it. Then she melted on the seat, almost sliding off it as her orgasm washed over her. She arched, jerking with each spasm tightening her pussy, contractions that made her shake.

The deep, throaty groan she released elicited an, "Are you okay, miss?" from the salesclerk.

"She's fine. Just excited about our shopping excursion." His lie stroked Jana's ears as if he caressed the sensitive spot between her thighs. The emptiness inside her screamed to be filled, to taste the girth of his cock deep inside. She moaned again because she couldn't help it. Her nipples felt raw, as if they scraped against sandpaper instead of the silky fabric of her sundress. Again Nicolas supplied a lie. "She loves dressing for me. Do you mind if I take a look?" Nicolas asked casually, but Jana could hear the edge of excitement in his tone.

"We're not supposed to allow a man and a woman in the same stall, but...for you..."

Jana couldn't take much more. The clit stimulator was relentless. As she reached to dislodge the vibrator the door opened and her tormentor stepped inside.

"Gorgeous, honey," he said aloud for the salesclerk's benefit. His voice dropped low and quiet as he issued a warning. "Do not remove my toy, doll, or I'll be forced to punish you." He ran a finger down her arm eliciting another tremor. "I'm not finished with you."

Jana swallowed hard, trying to hold back the scream perched on her tongue.

"I don't think I'll ever be finished with you."

If only it was true, Jana thought.

Trembling, she let her legs part, hoping that the damn thing would move away from her crotch. Leaning over her,

Nicolas slipped a hand beneath her dress and pressed the clit stimulator closer, more firmly against her wet pussy. She arched her back, squeezing, "Fuck you," from her tight mouth, as another wave of electricity surged through her body, tossing her about on the seat. She couldn't have held still if her life depended on it.

Nicolas cupped the back of her neck, pulling her to her feet and to his lips. He took her mouth in a brutal kiss. The thump in her chest was her heart as he released her with a start. "Later. I promise."

Jana couldn't stop her arms from folding around him. She pulled him to her, hungry for more. With a powerful thrust she ground her hips to his. As if to show who was in control, he switched off the stimulator, extracted himself from her embrace, and backed out of the fitting room, leaving Jana alone and shaking with need.

What was going on with her? Why was she letting this man have freedom over her body? Truth was that all this was new and exciting to her. For so long she had lived such a boring and lonely life. Lisa and Nicolas made her feel like she belonged and was a part of something special.

Within a heartbeat she would have easily let him take her, even knowing that a salesclerk stood beyond the door. And if she were truthful, watching him fondle the remote control, teasing her, had made her hotter than hell. She wanted him to activate the vibrator. More astonishing, she wanted to come in front of a crowd. And she would have if he hadn't forced her into the dressing room.

"How did they look?" The salesclerk's sexy purr sounded more like an invitation to showcase the next pair of panties herself.

"Gorgeous. Now I want two of the black and rhinestone outfits like the one in the display case."

Jana tried to remember what ensemble he referred to. Then she heard a low moan in the next stall and knew it was Lisa.

The door swung shut as Jana exited the dressing room. "Two?" Jana heard the rise of hope in the salesclerk's voice. Surely the saleswoman didn't think the second set was for her. The smile on her face fell when Nicolas said, "The blonde in this other room belongs to me, too."

Belongs? Did she belong to him?

He opened his arms and Jana went willingly into them, giving the salesclerk a smirk for good measure. Amazingly, she did feel like she belonged to him, or at least wanted to until this game played through. He pressed his lips to her forehead, then he snaked one arm around her shoulder. As the saleswoman turned to retrieve the lingerie he requested, Lisa exited with a sated grin on her face.

"Thank you, Nicolas," Lisa breathed. He held out his free arm and Lisa slipped next to him.

A young man shopping with his girlfriend walked by with a grin plastered on his face. Admiration gleamed in his eyes. "Yeah. Buddy." His gaze scanned both Lisa and Jana with envy. His girlfriend punched his arm but he just laughed and wrapped his arm around her shoulders as they walked away.

When the salesclerk returned she handed Lisa and Jana each a black corset that laced loosely in front with silver rhinestones, so three inches of their skin would be bared. The tiny matching thong had a row of rhinestones that connected the front and back of the panties.

Nicolas's hand slid down Jana's back until it rested on her ass, and then he gave her a subtle push. Lisa moved forward in perfect unison with Jana. "Girls, make sure they fit. I'll wait for you at the register. Oh, and I want those panties Jana tried on."

Jana hadn't tried the thong on. She hadn't had the opportunity since she'd been thrown into an orgasm that took every bit of her attention. But obviously she would be trying it on in the future.

Once she was in the changing room, Jana slipped her arms into the corset as she thought about what just happened. Who would have thought? Certainly not in her wildest dreams would she have believed she was capable of this irrational behavior.

Yet, it was exciting to push the boundaries of propriety.

Perhaps Lisa was right. Jana slipped one leg and then the other into the panties and pulled them up, riding high on her hips. Maybe they both just needed to let go and simply feel. Widen their horizons. Couldn't she just once grasp onto something that felt so right, so good?

She turned to look at herself in the mirror. Her lips were full and slightly pink from Nicolas's kiss. The black against her fair skin and her auburn hair was striking. Jana couldn't remember when she looked sexier. Pressure built in her chest, emotion she had fought down for years. She wanted to be sexy, wanted to be loved. Not one to dream for the impossible, she knew there wasn't any hope with Nicolas, but maybe someday—someone.

"Jana, I love it. What do you think?" Lisa's voice floated over the top of the dressing room.

"Very pretty," Jana replied, starting to undress.

"Pretty? Nicolas has a wonderful eye for clothing and women. Now we need heels to go with it." Lisa laughed.

And apparently that was exactly what Nicolas had on his mind as he ushered them toward the nearest shoe store. They found the perfect silver and rhinestone stilettos that looked like they were made for the lingerie.

Male pride sparked in Nicolas's eyes. He set down the packages he was holding and pulled Jana into his arms. "Doll, tonight I'm going to take you to places you've never been."

Jana felt paralyzed in his embrace, drowning in his eyes and ready to travel the world in his arms.

Chapter Thirteen

The flickering of the light on Nicolas's telephone announced a message awaited him. He set down his packages, hit the hands-free button and dialed in his password. Over the speaker he heard:

"Hey, buddy. This is Trent. Sorry, but I've been called out of town. We'll have to reschedule tonight's party in about two weeks. Looking forward to meeting your new woman." Then the recorder went dead.

Disappointment rose on quick feet, but maybe this wasn't all bad. He disconnected the call and dialed Lisa's telephone. He couldn't wait to hear Jana's voice, but it was Lisa who answered.

"Hello."

"Hey, baby. Change of plans," he said.

"Oh, yeah?"

"Party's been canceled. Trent had to go out of town. Why don't you and Jana come over and I'll fix you that meal I've been promising? Afterward maybe we could go over some of the aspects of Trent's party to ensure Jana is comfortable with our plans." This was going to work out even better. Jana needed more time to become accustomed to their way of life, and to him.

"Sounds good. What time?" He wasn't surprised when Lisa agreed so quickly.

"How about seven? I need to go to the store and get a couple of things." If he was going to try Chicken Marsala again he wanted fresh ingredients, and the time to properly prepare it before Lisa and Jana stole his attention.

"Until seven." Her voice was a breathy release as she hung up.

Damn, Lisa was hot. But it was a certain redhead he couldn't get out of his mind. His gaze went to his packages, remembering the French maid and naughty schoolgirl costumes, and he grinned. Perhaps a little role play was also on the menu tonight.

After putting away the things he bought from the mall, he exited his house and climbed into his truck. He always kept a well-stocked kitchen. There wasn't much to buy, except some fresh chicken breasts and more garlic, perhaps a fresh bouquet of flowers and candles.

Tonight he wanted things to be perfect. Why it mattered he didn't really know. All he did know was that he wanted Jana to feel comfortable with him and his home.

Again Jana dressed to match Lisa's attire. They both wore short evening gowns, Lisa's red and hers emerald green. Funny, but she hadn't been dressed this formally in over three years and never twice in one year. It just wasn't really her style.

But she had to admit that it made her feel sexy. The way the silk slid over her curves was arousing. And she knew that Nicolas would appreciate her appearance.

As she took one last look in the mirror, Lisa sauntered into her old room. "You look beautiful."

"I look overdressed," Jana retorted, pulling the short thing down only for it to pop right back up where it was supposed to be at mid-thigh.

Lisa sat on the bed and then patted the mattress for Jana to join her. "Come here." Jana took the few steps it took and sat. For a moment her friend just looked at her. "You're having fun with Nicolas and me, aren't you?"

Jana felt a warm blush overtake her face. Man, she hoped this wasn't going to be a heart-to-heart discussion.

Lisa placed her palm on Jana's thigh. "Don't you dare be embarrassed."

"Lisa, it's just sort of weird."

"When has weird ever offended you?" Lisa tittered and then it faded as her features grew serious. "If anyone would have told me that you and I were going to be engaged in a ménage a trois, that you and I would make love, I would have laughed in their faces." Moisture misted her eyes. The deep breath she inhaled was ragged, as if she fought for control to continue. "But I want to let you know how much it's meant to me," she choked. "How much it means to me that we are comfortable with each other. That we have this time together, because I do love you, Jana."

This conversation was awkward. Still, Jana said, "I love you, too. But, Lisa, you have to admit this is weird. You... Me... Nicolas. What's supposed to come from this relationship?"

Again Lisa chuckled. "Ever the logical one." She shook her head and a single tear fell as her expression again went serious. "Nothing—something—everything." She squeezed Jana's thigh. "Don't try to analyze it, just go with it. Nicolas and I are wrong for each other. We both know that, but we have found similar ground to meet on. We like to fuck." She swatted Jana's thigh playfully. "Now let's get going. You haven't tasted anything until you've tasted Nicolas's Chicken Marsala."

Within ten minutes they were in Lisa's Corvette and headed for Nicolas's house. As Lisa chatted about the new homes and schools that were popping up all around the valley, Jana watched her. Her friend's mood swings, not to mention the headaches, had Jana worried.

"When was the last time you went to the doctor about your headaches?"

"What?" Lisa's attention jerked toward Jana and then back to the road ahead of her. "I thought we were talking about the development in Arizona."

"No, you were talking about the rise of homes across the valley. I want to talk about your health."

Lisa's hold on the steering wheel tightened. "There's nothing to talk about. I've gone to the doctor. He's given me these pills. End of story."

"But—"

"Jana, there isn't anything more to say. Besides here we are." She steered the car into Nicolas's driveway.

"This isn't over," Jana warned.

"Yes it is." Lisa switched off the car and was out of there in a flash. Her hips swayed as she approached the front door to Nicolas's house. "Coming?" she yelled over her shoulder.

"But— What's the use." Jana shook her head, as Lisa graced her with a bright smile.

Lisa didn't bother knocking; she just turned the doorknob and walked in. The house was alive with smells that made Jana's stomach growl. She hadn't realized how hungry she was or how much she enjoyed seeing Nicolas again until he came around the corner.

Dressed in a black and white tux, he was a vision. A woman's fantasy. Her fantasy.

His wavy ebony hair was a stark contrast to his shirt. When he looked at them a bright smile broke across his face.

Lisa raised her chin to receive his kiss.

Nicolas looked suave and elegant as he left Lisa's side and approached Jana. Her heart leaped and her pulse sped.

"Doll," he murmured before capturing her lips. The kiss was tender and sweet. When they parted he kept an arm around her shoulders. "I hope you girls are hungry."

"I am," Lisa replied.

"Me, too." Jana gazed into his sapphire eyes. Hungry for a lot more than food. The thought gave her pause and she almost laughed aloud. She was becoming a brazen harlot. Whenever she was around Nicolas, all she could think about was sex.

Nicolas found it difficult to think about anything other than sex when Jana looked at him that way. Her innocent sexuality made his cock respond, growing firmer beneath his slacks. If he didn't put distance between himself and this woman they'd never make it through dinner. He released her and strode toward the kitchen.

"It's beautiful," he heard Lisa say as she made her way to his large dining table. "Flowers and candles. How lovely, Nicolas."

"Nothing but the best for my girls," he said, heading for the light switches. All the lights needed to be dimmed in his great room. Lowering one but not the others would ruin the effect. Perfection was what he was seeking. He'd already lit the candles. The wine was on the table, as well as the salad. The main course was in the oven to keep warm until they were ready for it.

As he entered the dining room, shadows flickered across Jana's face. It warmed him to see her smile. She looked content, if not happy.

"Ready to eat?" He first held out Lisa's chair and then Jana's, sitting them on either side of his own chair, before he sat. "I'm sorry that the party was canceled. Trent said he would reschedule it in two weeks."

"Great. That will give us time to prepare you," Lisa said to Jana.

"Prepare me?" Jana's voice rose with concern.

"Salad?" Nicolas asked Jana. She nodded, and then gazed back at Lisa, awaiting an answer.

"Why of course. You don't want to go in there blind." Lisa stabbed a piece of lettuce and placed it into her mouth, chewing and swallowing before she continued. "You know I met Nicolas at Trent's home. It was my first introduction to an EPE club. I found it daring and exciting. A new experience." She looked again at Jana. "You'll love it."

"EPE?" Jana had yet to taste her salad.

"Erotic Power Exchange or what is commonly called BDSM." After a drink of her wine, Lisa said, "I guess the best way to explain it is that sexual partners, of their own free will and choice, actively incorporate the power element in their lovemaking. I find power heady. Don't you?" Lisa's sigh was blissful.

No one answered Lisa. Yet, Jana sat on the edge of her chair, her expression intense, as if she weighed the pros and cons of this unknown world.

Yes, Nicolas agreed silently. Power was erotic. A woman giving away her power was like setting his adrenaline free. He compared it to the same sensation a person got from an intense sport, a runner's high. The endorphin rush was like a drug.

156

"Discovering the boundaries of one's mind is amazing," Lisa said. "The sense of belonging, the trust involved when sharing your darkest dreams and fantasies is life altering. It can be thrilling, relaxing, and," she winked at Jana, "revealing."

This was exactly the reason that Nicolas found it hard to believe that Lisa had known nothing about EPE when they'd first met. Either she hadn't been totally honest or she was a natural, always knowing what to do in each of their scenes. Plus, the expert way she had handled Jana, guiding her into their threesome play had been a surprise.

"I'm not sure that this is for me," Jana said, chasing around a tomato with her fork. She was beginning to falter again. It was as if her mind told her to say one thing, while her body told her to do another.

"Jana, you have to give it a try. Say that you will," Lisa pleaded with her sweetest voice.

Nicolas stood. "Why don't we table this discussion and pick it up in a more appropriate place, like say my dungeon."

"Now?" Jana chirped in surprise as her fork fell from her hand and landed with a clink on her plate.

"No." He let his hungry gaze linger a moment longer on her face, before he promised, "Later. Right now I'm going to get our dinners."

Jana released a sigh of relief. All this talk was making her rather nervous. Yes, it sounded interesting, but scary too. She didn't know whether or not she could go through with it. But there was a voice in the back of her head that urged her on. She'd already gone through more in the last thirty-six hours than she had ever expected to in a lifetime. Hell, in the last two and a half weeks since she'd walked in on Lisa giving Nicolas head.

And what had happened in the dungeon...she had enjoyed herself, enjoyed reaching beyond her comfort zone to experience things that she had only held in the deepest, darkest corner of her mind.

Nicolas was the perfect host as he set a plate before her, filled her wine glass, kissed her tenderly on the cheek, and then took a seat between her and Lisa.

Dinner was delicious as they chatted about matters at the restaurant and Jana's new job. While she put the last bite of succulent chicken into her mouth, she glanced at Nicolas as he asked Lisa about the new wing of the hospital that was planned.

Nicolas was every woman's dream. He cooked, he cleaned, he was interested in the things that mattered to a woman, and he was dynamite in bed, but he had the one hang up that most men did—commitment.

Lisa was crazy not to find someway to snatch this man up. He smiled and Jana felt it straight to her toes. Then the most bizarre thought entered her head. If Lisa wasn't interested in him, maybe, just maybe something could develop between her and Nicolas.

No sooner did the thought rise than she began to chastise herself for the silly notion. Nicolas wasn't looking for a forever after scenario. Same as Lisa, he was only in it for fun.

"Dessert?" Nicolas asked.

Lisa leaned back in her chair. "What do you have?"

"Cheesecake—or me." His voice dropped low and sexy.

Jana's pulse jumped. The heat in his eyes did something to her. Her blood warmed and she felt flushed. And that wasn't the only thing going on. Just the insinuation of sex released a flood of desire between her thighs. She wanted to touch him, be touched by him.

Lisa was the first to respond by rising from her chair and going to him. "I choose you, Milord." She bent and received his kiss.

His strong hands clasped her knees and then began to caress, drawing her dress up and revealing that she once again wore no panties or bra. Within a heartbeat Nicolas had Lisa naked except for her heels.

Moving between his thighs, Lisa began to undo his tie and pushed his jacket from his shoulders. He struggled to help her remove it.

Glancing over Lisa's shoulders, he asked, "What will you have, doll?"

Was there really any choice? *Are you really going to do this?* she asked herself.

Desperately, she needed to feel like she was a part of something bigger than herself. To feel wanted—to belong—to not be alone. "You, Milord," she whispered and pushed away from the table.

"My shoes," he said.

Lisa dropped to the floor and Jana joined her. Each pulled a shoe off and then rolled down his socks as he sat. Then they both rose. Lisa worked at disrobing him of his pants, while Jana worked on the buttons of his shirt.

"You two are hot," he groaned. Jana looked down to discover that Lisa had indeed gotten his pants off and had slipped his hard cock into her mouth. Her head bobbed with a steady rhythm. "Take your dress off, doll."

Jana hesitated only a moment before she rose. Her fingers gripped the hem of her dress and slowly she pushed the soft material up and over her head until she stood in front of him in only her black strapless bra and thong.

"You're so fucking sexy," he said as he pushed his shirt from his chest and threw it to the floor. Her hand opened, releasing her dress. In a silky flow it floated down beside his shirt. As she reached behind her to undo her bra, he growled, "No, I like the look. Keep the bra and panties on, the heels, too." He put his hand on Lisa's head, stilling her. "Lisa, there's a costume on my bed. Put it on and prepare yourself on the bench in the dungeon."

Lisa released the hold she had on Nicolas's cock and moved from between his legs. She flashed him a charming smile, before she stood and walked out of the room. Nicolas pushed to his feet. He didn't touch Jana, except with his gaze, stroking like silk flowing over her skin, raising goose bumps, and sending a shiver racing down her spine.

"Come here," he growled. "I've wanted to fuck you all through dinner. Feel the heat between your thighs, your breasts in my hands, your nipples in my mouth."

Oh my. He was making her hot. Without laying a finger on her he had her wet and horny. She went to him and he took her into his arms, his hands smoothing across her skin, touching and stroking and caressing.

She sighed as her head lolled back, his mouth sucking, licking and biting along her neck.

"Come with me to the dungeon," he said as he began to guide her toward the stairs.

Each step he stopped and caressed or kissed a different part of her body. By the time they were at the bottom of the stairs, Jana was so hot and wet she would have spread her legs for him right there. But he ushered her onward.

Jana wasn't prepared for what she saw. Lisa had dressed in the naughty schoolgirl costume Jana had seen Nicolas purchase at the novelty store. Her short blonde hair was spiked into two ponytails, but it was the position that took Jana's breath away. She was on her belly lying over a bench, her hands above her head holding onto two bars, and she had raised her skirt to expose her naked ass.

When Lisa heard them enter the room she glanced over her shoulder and smiled.

Nicolas took Jana's hand and pulled her further into the room toward Lisa. He smoothed his palm over Lisa's butt and then suddenly struck out, slapping one of Lisa's ass cheeks. Both Jana and Lisa startled.

Nicolas's handprint rose pink against Lisa's pale skin.

"Did you like that, baby?" Again he brushed his hand over Lisa's ass, rubbing the spot where his palm had landed.

"Yes, Teacher Marchetti," Lisa responded, moving her legs further apart until the flesh of her sex was exposed. "It felt good. Spank me more."

Jana couldn't believe what she was hearing and seeing. Lisa had said she liked being spanked, but Jana just assumed her friend was talking about the type of playful teasing that had gone on between Jana and Tommy.

Had Jana's ex-boyfriend left a mark on her ass when he had swatted her? Possibly, but she had never thought to look for one. Lord knew it stung and it had felt good.

Confusion swam in her mind. *This is pretend. They're role playing.* A part of her realized it, but she couldn't help the flashes of memory that came to her.

A picture of her stepfather materialized behind her eyes.

As if Nicolas could read her mind, he reached for her and cradled her in his arms. She tried to pull away, but he held her in his steely embrace. "Not everything is as it seems. Spanking is just one of the facets of exchanging power. There is a point where pain and pleasure blur and the most amazing orgasm is experienced."

"Jana, please. I want this. I need it." Jana could hear the plea in Lisa's voice. "More, teacher."

Hard as it was, Jana tried to control her breathing, in and out—in and out. Nicolas wasn't hurting Lisa. He couldn't be or Lisa would be fighting him. Instead she lay there of her own free will, asking for more.

Nicolas released Jana. Again his palm landed on Lisa's ass. Jana's pulse leaped as she startled. Her strapless bra and panties felt tight around her skin, where earlier they seemed to caress her curves.

Gently he began to stroke his two handprints. "This awakens the nerve endings. It makes Lisa more sensitive to touch and sensations." He swatted Lisa a few more times, alternating it with a tender caress until her butt was a light pink.

It shouldn't be arousing to see Lisa being spanked, but the way Nicolas smoothed his hands over her ass, the softness and firmness of his touch was turning her on.

"Come here, Jana. Feel her heat, her arousal."

Lisa moaned when Jana placed her palm, covered by Nicolas's, on her ass. The area was hot to the touch. Jana couldn't help comparing the size of her hand to the much larger ones marking Lisa's tender skin.

"Now place your fingers between her legs. See how wet she is." Jana jerked her hand back from Lisa, and simply stared at Nicolas. Even though Jana felt a touch of unease, there was excitement as well; the tightening of her nipples, desire seeping between her thighs. "She wants to be touched. She needs to be touched," he encouraged.

Lisa groaned. "Please."

Taking a deep breath, Jana ran her fingertips along Lisa's folds, feeling the shiver that went through her friend's body. Wet didn't accurately describe how Lisa felt. She was drenched. Her hips undulated, rubbing against Jana's hand, and Jana couldn't help but answer their call as she stroked Lisa once, twice, and then again.

"That's right, doll, finger-fuck her. Make her come," Nicolas said as he moved behind Jana. With a snap her bra came undone and was pulled from around her. Strong hands grasped the elastic of her panties and started to peel them away from her hips, sliding down her thighs. When the material circled her ankles, she stepped out of them. Then Nicolas pressed his front to her back. His skin was warm, his body firm, his cock hard, slipping between her thighs, wedging itself along her slit. "Thrust your fingers into her heat, smooth them across her slick folds, and play with her clit. Feel her pleasure grow beneath your touch." His hands gripped Jana's hips before they circled her waist, caressing her ribcage, until he held her breasts. They were heavy, her nipples aching for attention.

"Jana, please." Jana answered Lisa's pleas by leaning over her and then sinking a finger deep inside her. Nicolas's palms skimmed down Jana's stomach until he found her own pool of desire. He cupped her pussy and a fresh wave of arousal anointed his hand.

The experience was unbelievable. With each thrust of Nicolas's finger Jana drove hers deeper and faster into Lisa's pussy. Higher and higher Jana climbed the mountain of ecstasy, while Lisa followed in her path, evident from the spasms within her friend's pussy that clenched Jana's fingers.

When Nicolas gently but firmly began to pat her clit in fast, steady strokes, Jana exploded. Her vision went dark, bright lights splintering, as she fell forward atop Lisa, riding ripple after ripple of sensation.

She only became aware of things around her when a taut, breathy voice said, "I can't breathe." Then Lisa began to giggle, her laughter shaking Jana as she struggled to find her footing. She slipped. He caught and steadied her, before he moved toward Lisa. "That was absolutely wonderful." Nicolas helped her from the spanking bench. Her eyes sparkled as she wrapped her arms around Nicolas and captured his lips. When they drew apart, Lisa said to Jana, "Your turn."

And the most outrageous thing was that Jana was seriously considering it. She couldn't help but wonder what it would feel like to have Nicolas's hands on her ass. The same sensations Lisa felt that made her so wet.

"I don't know," Jana murmured.

"Perhaps not tonight." Nicolas came to stand before her. His penetrating eyes burned into her and she felt as if she would drown in them. "But soon." He gathered her in his embrace. "I need to mark you as mine," he whispered in her ear. The current of his breath, his words made her knees weak.

Mine echoed in Jana's ears. She wanted that, too. So desperately she was willing to work through her fears and take the next step—trusting Nicolas.

"Spank me," Jana whispered, "and make me yours." Then she captured his lips in a heated kiss.

Chapter Fourteen

Stars twinkled through an overcast sky as Nicolas steered his car into the gated community located in the northeast area of Scottsdale. He'd been looking forward to Trent Alexander's party for several weeks now. Both women were wrapped in silver fox fur coats, hiding the black and rhinestone lingerie he'd purchased at Victoria's Secret. He couldn't wait to unveil them, to see the expressions of envy on those around him.

A smile touched his lips. The evening he'd discovered that his friend's party would be delayed hadn't gone to waste, nor had the past weeks. Jana was responding to him and Lisa. They were growing more comfortable as a threesome and Jana was showing her trust in him. She had eagerly participated in several of their bondage scenarios. Nothing too strenuous or outlandish, because he always made sure she felt at ease with the scenes they performed.

As he drove down one street and then another he pondered tonight's arrangements. Again Jana had grown quiet sitting in the backseat, while Lisa chatted up a storm about Trent's parties.

Had it been a month since Jana returned to Arizona?

Through the rearview mirror, Nicolas glimpsed Jana shifting again on the seat. He sucked in a breath as his cock hardened. He wanted her more and more each time they came together.

A gust of air shook his truck as an eighteen-wheeler passed by. Nicolas's body swayed as he slipped back to that moment he knew Jana had become his.

It had been about a week ago. Lisa had been called away to cover a shift at the hospital just as they were preparing for a scene in his basement.

Nicolas steered the vehicle into the middle lane as he recalled the panic in Jana's eyes as she hastily began to pick up her discarded clothes that night. Clearly she didn't want to be left alone with him. She found courage with Lisa by her side. Standing in her lacy underwear, a visible tremor had shaken her as her gaze darted to Lisa as if she expected her friend to rescue her.

A horn blew pulling Nicolas briefly from his mental wanderings. He gave a quick glance in the rearview mirror at Jana sitting alone in the backseat. The trepidation in her eyes drew him back to that night.

Her innocence and insecurity had only whetted his appetite. He couldn't let her leave. It had been what he'd been waiting for—to have Jana all to himself.

Lisa was quick, always saying or doing the right thing to calm Jana. "Nicolas." Lisa had moved into his arms. Her partially naked body was warm against his bare chest as their lips met in a fiery exchange. When the kiss ended she remained a breath from his mouth. Her lips brushed his as she called to her friend, "Jana."

A moment of déjà vu hit him as Lisa spoke Jana's name at the same time he recalled it. They started to chat back and forth, and he was glad Jana was no longer quiet.

He easily slipped back into his daydream. Jana's approach had been hesitant, but Lisa reached out, grasped her friend's hand and pulled her into their embrace. There was a moment where Lisa soothed her friend's fears with a light stroke, gentle, as if she were chasing a child's bad dreams away.

The tender kiss the women shared was a beautiful sight. Just the remembrance of their forms, elegant and curvy, moving seductively beneath the dim lighting in the room made him harden more.

The current throb beneath his zipper caused his foot to slip momentarily from the gas pedal. The truck slowed, and then picked back up as he pressed down on the pedal. He shifted his hips. His pulse sped. *Damn*, what he'd give to be back at his home, Jana in his arms.

His fingers tightened around the steering wheel as he recalled the comfort between Jana and Lisa, their close bond reminding Nicolas he was the outsider in this threesome. It was emphasized further when their kiss turned passionate, breathy.

Then Lisa reached for him, pulling him close and capturing his mouth, her tongue dueling with his in a hot assault as her hardened nipples pressed through the thin material of her bra and rubbed against his chest.

Before he knew what was happening, Jana was in his arms, soft and pliable. He sipped from her mouth like a wine connoisseur, savoring her taste. She was heaven in his embrace as he drew her nearer—lost in the feeling.

When they parted there was a moment of silence where their eyes met and locked. Then she blinked rapidly as if willing away the spell that bewitched them.

"Lisa," Jana's voice quivered as she turned in his arms and gazed around the room.

Lisa was gone.

Jana and Nicolas were finally alone.

Nicolas dodged a small green Lexus that darted in front of him. His meandering refused to let go of him as he struggled to pay attention to the thickening traffic.

The truth? Jana was never far from his thoughts, nor the desire to be buried deep inside her warmth, or to feel the heat rising off her freshly flogged ass. Yes. She had allowed him to flog her in Lisa's presence.

There had been a moment of awkwardness as he held her that night. Her tongue made a nervous swipe across kiss-swollen lips. "I—"

He silenced her objection with another kiss, and then slowly nibbled his way to her earlobe. "Stay with me," he whispered, while his heart hammered. "Let me pleasure you." His agile fingers found the back of her bra and gave a twist. The elastic snapped, releasing her breasts and her softness met his hardness as she leaned into him.

"I-I should go," she stammered, pressing her palms against his chest. He cupped her breast, eliciting a moan from her parted lips as he slid the pad of his thumb across her pebbled nipple.

"No." He groaned low. He was never going to let her go. The thought had shaken him, but quickly vanished. This was right—Jana was right.

Voice light and airy, she murmured, "Yes," even as her hips slid against his stiff erection causing another groan to surface from somewhere deep within his throat.

"I need to fuck you," he growled, his desire rising inside him like a quiet storm sneaking up on him. "*Damn.*" The word was grounded between clenched teeth. He was losing control and quickly. All he could think about was having Jana beneath him. "I want to tie you up and have my way with you." His grasp tightened, as he guided her around until they faced one another. "Surrender to me, Jana. Give me your body—your trust."

Her silence was edgy. Her breathing labored. Her body trembled on each inhale. He could sense her indecision, knew she fought demons of the past.

"Trust me, Jana," he whispered reassuringly. As he palmed her breast, his other hand slipped to the nape of her neck. His fingers closed around her hair, pulling her head back so their eyes met, her slender throat stretched and exposed. "I'll never hurt you." God, he needed her to believe in him. "Give yourself to me. Let me fight the demons for you. Release your fears and worries for tonight."

Moisture gathered in her blue eyes. She'd blinked as if attempting to force them back from the well of emotion they sprung from. "I don't know if I can." The pain in her voice ached with a desperate need to believe.

Her hair was cool silk between his fingers. "You're stronger than you know, doll. Let go. Give me the reins."

Tears spiked her eyelashes, but didn't fall. "Nicolas—"

"Jana." He swallowed hard. Instinctively, he knew she wanted him—wanted to be dominated and release control. "Listen to your heart. You need this—you need me."

"I—"

"Remove your panties." He didn't wait for her to finish her protest.

Her eyes widened. Her throat worked as she choked out, "Nicolas?"

"Remove your panties," he repeated firmly. It was like standing on thin ice waiting to hear the crack, wondering if it would hold or if he would fall into the chilling depths below before she responded. Her need for Lisa was obvious. He couldn't help feel a bit jealous.

When her hands fell from his chest, thumbs hooking in her panties, he fought not to smile. A flood of triumph filled him till he was overflowing with male pride.

Jana was his—with or without Lisa in the picture.

"Nicolas?" Lisa broke into his memories of that night.

"Uh...what?" He glanced in her direction as the vision of Jana's surrender evaporated into a fog.

Lisa frowned, searching his face. Then her gaze dropped to the obvious bulge between his thighs and a grin crept across her face. "Just where has your mind wandered, you naughty boy?"

He fought the heat traveling fast and furious up his throat, singeing his ears. How could he tell Lisa that he'd fallen head over heels for her friend? He couldn't, so he said the next best thing, "Stripping you two naked, paddling your asses until they're red-hot, and then fucking you both senseless."

Lisa reached out and squeezed his biceps, releasing a feminine burst of laughter. "Shall we turn around?"

He gave her a quick grin, then pinned his eyes to the road before catching Jana looking at him in the rearview mirror. He winked. "No, I think we can find something to entertain me at Trent's place."

Color tinted Jana's cheeks, but was followed by a tentative smile. The wary look in her eyes didn't hide that she was uncomfortable with this trip.

A twitch nagged at the corner of his mouth. The first time alone with Jana had been awkward, the second and third time pure bliss. Able to focus his attention directly on Jana and hers on him had brought them closer. In fact, he found himself looking forward to the times that Lisa would leave when she was on call. Guilt was something he was beginning to live with. But Jana was worth it.

More importantly, Jana was beginning to accept him into her arms and body, even without Lisa there to protect her. That was the key to unlocking her heart. He couldn't explain it but just knowing that Jana trusted him made him feel that much more a man.

Her man.

And something about the way that sounded touched him deep inside like no other woman had ever done before.

After Nicolas maneuvered his truck around a sports car and an SUV, he came to a stop down the street from Trent's home. Lisa flipped down the visor and stared into the mirror, running her finger over her lipstick.

He turned, leaning his elbow on the seat. "Would you rather not go?" With another sub he wouldn't have even asked. But this was Jana.

Lisa spun around, her eyes widening as she stared at Jana in disbelief.

Like a blanket, Jana pulled her tough-guy persona over her face. Her shoulders squared. "Are you kidding? I've been looking forward to this." Her hands were folded in her lap and the tightness of her grip revealed her lie.

Strength and courage, just a couple the attributes Nicolas found charming in Jana. She was a fighter and he had no doubts that whatever she put her mind to she would accomplish or get through.

After they exited the truck, several more individuals joined them while they strolled up the sidewalk to the front door. Knowing there was no need to knock, Nicolas opened the door and they walked in. Lisa's and Jana's arms were linked in his.

It was nine o'clock and already the cave was packed. The large basement home of his college buddy morphed into a play party for night crawlers—people who sought their pleasures from the dark side of their dreams and desires. Men and women of every walk of life congregated here.

About eighty percent of attendees were simply curious, as he had been at his first party. Some people were in-between partners or didn't plan to participate and only came for the socializing. Others were energy vampires—people who had no sense of connection to the participants, they were only there for the thrill—the fuck—as if they were watching a porno movie. The remainder of the people would act out their fantasies. They were here to seek a higher plane than vanilla sex could give them.

Some were dressed casually in jeans or slacks, others in full blown leather outfits or naked. Of course, those individuals wore a cape or coat to hide the shocking attire or lack of until they entered the large entryway of Trent's home. The hum of the air conditioning unit kicked on and a gust of cool air caressed Nicolas's face. He could hear the click of ladies' stilettos against the polished marble floor.

There were several men and women formally dressed in tuxedos or gowns, acting as valets, taking guests' coats and wraps as they progressed further down the hall.

Nicolas enjoyed attending Trent's soirees, because his friend ensured that safety and cleanliness was top on his agenda. For every ten to fifteen people at the party his friend posted a man or woman as a dungeon monitor, referred to as a DM. A DM was assigned to each of the rooms, ensuring the proprieties of the rules were followed. Boisterous or rude individuals interfering with the concentration of the participants were eighty-six'd. No alcohol or drugs were allowed, nor were those already under the influence.

Trent took his lifestyle seriously. He was a Master. Yet he usually let his guard down when he entertained Nicolas. They always had fun when they got together.

Nicolas looked around for his buddy. The Master was always first to welcome his guests.

During college, his friend had introduced Nicolas to the fine art of BDSM. Nicolas knew right off that this wasn't a twenty-four-seven lifestyle that he would consider. But it was a great way to spice up a relationship and gave him control of where a relationship went, which was usually down the non-commitment road. His parents' marriage had been a disaster. No way did he want to relive that experience.

A naked man and his Mistress caught Jana's attention. She leaned over to Lisa, said something, and they shared a quiet giggle. He was glad to see Jana had relaxed. Perhaps she would find what many others had, the joys of letting go and just feeling.

The glances of appreciation Lisa and Jana received from men and women alike as they moved through the masses caused his chest to swell with pride. Jana tugged the collar of her coat tightly around her neck as if she were chilled. It was still too warm to wear a coat, but he had known the effect would be priceless.

He was right. The air of elegance as they walked beside him was riveting. The effect was amazing, making him even more thankful that during the two weeks since their shopping spree, he'd had the opportunity to buy the coats and stop by a local jeweler for two other special items.

From beneath his own black leather jacket he extracted two thin, square velour boxes and handed one to each of them. Jana looked suspiciously at the gift. Lisa was thrilled. As they each removed the lids of their boxes, his stomach knotted. He wondered what Jana's reaction would be.

Lisa giggled with excitement as she pulled the silver chain collar dotted with diamonds and a D-ring out of the box. Jana only stared blindly down at the jewelry. Then she murmured, "A dog collar?"

"Oh, Jana," Lisa chastised.

He should have known the jewelry wouldn't impress Jana. The fact she thought it was a dog collar was disturbing. Yes, it was a collar, but there was significance in his gift. He wanted both women to know they belonged to him.

"Fasten it for me, Nicolas," Lisa asked, moving her blonde hair out of the way. His heart raced as he clasped the necklace around her slender neck. "It's beautiful. I'm assuming there's more?"

Darn, Lisa. He hadn't decided whether or not to actually leash the women. Yet, it looked like Lisa was fully expecting it.

"Is this what you want, my pet?" He extracted two silver chains from out of the inside of his jacket pocket. Jana's wide-eyed gaze moved from the box to the leash. Her scowl told him exactly what she thought of it.

No fucking way.

There was no time like the present to take control. He stuffed the leashes away for the time being and approached Jana. From the box she held he retrieved the collar. She made no attempt to lift her hair as Lisa had. Instead, he felt her tense beneath his touch and then a shiver raked her body as his hands slid across her neck and he fastened the collar.

When the beautiful jewelry graced her throat, he slipped out the two silver chains from his pocket. As he snapped the leash to the D-ring, Jana startled, her eyes widening. He turned and did the same to Lisa's collar then released both leashes to dangle down their coats.

A solid pat came across his back. Nicolas turned to face the host of the party. Trent had played halfback for Arizona State University all four years. Blond and tanned, his friend definitely had a way with the women. "Well, well. I see that you still have exquisite taste in women."

Nicolas watched Jana for a reaction to his friend. Women fawned over Trent. Nicolas prayed Jana wasn't one of them. He was pleased when her gaze turned to him instead of Trent's.

Nicolas gave a low nod in respect. "Master Trent." Then he extended his hand.

His friend's hungry gaze was pinned on the women, even as he shook Nicolas's hand. Trent's blatant interest set Nicolas on edge, which surprised him. He had called Trent before the first party was canceled with special plans. Nicolas never reneged. Yet suddenly something crawled beneath his skin. That nagging sensation that his previous agreement with Trent just wasn't right lingered. No matter how Nicolas tried to convince himself it was only for one night, the unease he felt wouldn't go away.

This feeling of jealousy was bullshit. To prove it he said, "Ladies, your coats."

With a drop of her shoulders Lisa's coat rolled from her body and into Nicolas's hands. Jana hesitated only briefly before she wiggled awkwardly from the fur and held it in front of her. She placed it in his outstretched hand, but she didn't release the coat, as if it were stuck to her palms. He gave a slight tug, but she refused to surrender it. For a moment Nicolas thought she might tear the fur out of his hands and go running for the door. Instead her chest rose on an inhale. On the exhale she let the coat go.

Standing beneath the magnificent chandelier above them, the two women stole Nicolas's breath away. Their black corsets, the rhinestones crisscrossing the cleavage between their breasts and ribcage, were sensational, complimenting every curve and mound with ease. The shiny stones lying high on their hips, connecting the glossy material of their panties, glistened beneath the light, having a sparkling effect.

The gasps and sighs of appreciation surrounding them said it all. Lisa and Jana were gorgeous, statuesque beauties. Nicolas handed their furs to a DM whom Trent motioned over.

"Perhaps exquisite was too mild of a description." Trent's arm slipped around Nicolas's shoulders, but his eyes remained pinned on the women. "It will be my pleasure to assist you tonight, my friend."

Well shit! Nicolas wasn't sure about sharing Lisa and Jana with his friend tonight. The thought had been exciting and adventurous at first. Now it just made him wince every time he thought of Trent touching Jana. Lisa too, he added quickly to his thoughts as he let his jacket roll off his shoulders and then his arms. Beneath he was bare-chested, wearing only tight leather pants and boots. He wore a silver chain as a belt, bringing his ensemble together with Jana's and Lisa's. The DM next to his side immediately took his coat.

"Mmmm..." Lisa's purr was soft and low. She scanned Nicolas's length with appreciation.

He waited for Jana to remark, but she remained tightlipped, an action that Nicolas should have known would intrigue Trent. She stood like a statue, as if calculating her alternatives. Whether it was the possibility of escape or hope to wrestle back her coat, Nicolas didn't know.

Either way she was beautiful. Couldn't she see that? Clearly the attention bothered her, but it should have been an awareness that made her stand tall and proud as Lisa was doing. Lisa preened like a flower in the sunlight or a star in the heaven. Every move was meant to entice the crowd. She owned the room.

His friend moved away from him to stand in front of Jana. "May I touch your subs, Lord Nicolas?"

"Permission granted," Nicolas managed through clenched teeth.

With the tip of his index finger beneath her chin, Trent raised Jana's gaze to his. She stared him directly in the eyes. *That's my girl*, thought Nicolas.

"Defiant. I like defiant." Trent leaned forward and flicked her nose with his tongue.

She jerked back, a frown on her thin lips.

Nicolas should have punished her for the disrespect, but Jana was inexperienced. Trent would understand—this time.

Without another word, Trent turned to Lisa. He grasped her hand, turned it over so her wrist faced the ceiling, and licked a slow wet path up the inside of her arm. "Lisa, it's good to see you again. Are you ready for some fun?"

Lisa looked up through feathered lashes. "Of course, Master Trent. That is if it will please, Milord." She turned her attention to Nicolas, as was appropriate.

Lisa was pure sensuality. She attracted men like a magnet. Yet, it was Jana who held his attention. The silver stilettos made her long legs appear even longer. The silver collar and leash identified her as belonging to him. The black, silver and rhinestone ensemble made her fair skin look angelic, but that mass of auburn hair flowing over her shoulders and the fire in her eyes screamed vixen.

A vixen he wanted to release tonight.

He gathered up Lisa's and Jana's leashes. "It would please me for both of my pets to enjoy themselves tonight." The tug he gave on the chains was received differently from each woman. Lisa moved to his side.

Jana stood steadfast, fists clenched at her side. Her breathing had elevated slightly—from nerves or fear, Nicolas wasn't sure. No doubt the leash was the issue.

Lisa opened her mouth to speak, but Nicolas held up his hand to silence her. Even if Trent understood that Jana was inexperienced, Nicolas would lose face if he couldn't control one of his subs. It was his own fault he hadn't realized exactly how Jana might respond. He'd been certain she was ready.

Trent crossed his arms over his broad chest and cocked a brow.

Nicolas slowly curled the chain in his hand, tightening the leash and forcing Jana to his side until they were nose to nose. He pressed his mouth lightly to hers.

Her eyes remained open, challenging.

He kissed her again, but this time there was no tenderness. Teeth meshed, his tongue demanding entrance, and then he sucked in her bottom lip and bit down hard. She squealed, falling back on her heels, but Nicolas held her leash tightly.

"Trust me," he breathed against the corner of her mouth.

"I don't know if I can," she said. "A dog collar? It's humiliating."

Nicolas pivoted and handed Lisa's leash to Trent. Then he turned his full attention back to Jana. This time when he took her into his arms he stroked her gently. Running his hand through her hair, he whispered, "It's a show of my ownership. It pleases me to have you wear it. To let all others know that you're mine." Her features softened with his last word. "Trust me that I won't hurt you or let anyone else hurt you tonight.

178

We're only here to have fun. If you become uncomfortable I promise to take you home." Then a little louder, so his friend could hear, he said, "Submit to me."

In an act of surrender Jana tipped her chin up to receive his kiss. He had won. She was his for the night.

With just a kiss, Jana allowed Nicolas to conquer her fears, at least for the moment. The pride in his eyes showed brightly, filling her with a warmth that rivaled the Arizona summer heat. His wide smile was just for her. She'd never had anyone, other than Lisa, who'd been proud of her and she reveled in the feeling. She needed to please Nicolas, craved to see that smile again.

For once in her life she felt wanted. Held close to his strong body, she needed desperately to believe she could trust Nicolas. He had proven his trustworthiness these past four weeks, but could she trust him around his friend? Would the need to one-up his buddy get out of hand?

"Perhaps you want to show your subs about, Lord Nicolas. I've reserved the Blue Room for you at ten o'clock." Trent's eyes glowed with something Jana would rather not think about as he said, "I'll join you in a while." He handed Lisa's chain to Nicolas.

Side by side, with Nicolas in the middle, the three began to move toward the stairs that led to the basement.

When they reached the basement, Nicolas explained, "There are separate rooms for each play scene. This first room is what Master Trent refers to as the Yellow Room. It consists of a St. Andrews cross similar to what I have in my dungeon, but everything you see here is top of the line." They moved among the crowd, finding a place just inside the door. The scene was just about to begin. "It's important to remember that while a scene is in progress you must remain quiet, respectful to the participants."

Silence was not going to be a problem for Jana. She couldn't believe what she saw. Speechlessly, she watched as a hooded man dressed in just enough leather to hide his cock strapped a woman to the cross spread-eagle. The brunette smiled, her eyes glassy with excitement.

Jana couldn't comprehend how anyone would place themselves on exhibition for the pleasure of others. It was one thing to go through these steps behind closed doors, another to share it with complete strangers. She just didn't know whether she could ever do that.

When the hooded man reached for the halter top the submissive wore and tore it from her body, Jana gasped. The sharp ripping of material filled the room. Jana looked for some reaction from the woman. Her smile had disappeared. Instead of anger, fear or humiliation, excitement reflected in her drawn nipples and the deep rise and fall of her large breasts.

Then the Dom reached for her short-shorts and again the ripping seams caused everyone to inhale sharply as he revealed her shaved pussy. Or perhaps the gasps were from how she looked naked, strapped to the cross—helpless.

Jana closed her eyes. *Just a game. This is ridiculous. It's just a game.* When she felt her composure return, her eyelids rose.

As if Nicolas and Lisa knew what she was feeling they moved to each side of her, enveloping her with their bodies as though guarding her from her own mind. Lisa lightly kissed her on the cheek. Nicolas gave her a supportive hug.

Jana scanned the room for others affected by the scene. But, of course, there were none. Instead their eyes were filled with appreciation and white-hot arousal.

Just a game. She tried to calm the tremor that shook her.

Dammit! She wasn't going to let this bother her. She was going to have fun. Nicolas had promised they could go home if she wanted. But she was hell-bent on not letting Lisa or Nicolas down.

From a table that stood next to the cross the hooded man retrieved several chains linked together. Two chains had small clamps on each end, the longest of the three a larger looking clamp.

When he affixed the first clamp to her nipple, she screamed. Jana nearly jumped out of her skin, sending her leash swaying across her body. Immediately, Nicolas pulled her into the shelter of his embrace. As she leaned her back against his chest, Jana could feel his hard erection, which had evidently been stimulated by the scene. For that matter, Lisa's breathing intensified with each inhale and release.

Shit! Jana's own nipples began the slow tightening that announced her approaching excitement; or was it because Nicolas was quietly grounding his pelvis against her ass?

The brunette on the cross seemed prepared, focused as the next clamp was applied, leaving a single chain with the large clamp dangling at the apex of her thighs. When the hooded man dropped to his knees, Jana sucked in a tight breath of disbelief.

He wouldn't.

Oh. My. God.

He did.

With just a move of his hand he slipped the larger clamp over the poor woman's clit. The most bloodcurdling scream tore from her throat as she threw back her head.

Jana began to shake. She couldn't help it. Nicolas quieted her when he slipped his palms over her silk-covered breasts and began to knead softly. She felt the leather of his pants against her legs, the cheeks of her ass, and his erection pressing into her back.

In a hushed tone, he said, "He's not doing anything she hasn't had done before, or doesn't find pleasurable. Trust me." His deep, sexy voice washed over her like calming water. He stroked her with reassurance. "We should move on. You might not be ready for what's next."

He was right. What she had seen was enough for the first time. "Don't you ever think of putting that thing on my clit," she said, drawing out a quiet chuckle from him as they pushed through the crowd and out the door.

"What about the nipple clamps? Would you let me tease you, make you horny and hot, then slip them on so that the pressure remained while I fuck you?" Nicolas asked as he slipped his hand under the corset and tweaked her nipple.

"I-I don't know," she stuttered, unable to think.

"We'll work on it." He issued the sinful promise, sending a thrill up her spine as they began to move through the crowd. "This next room is the Red Room, or the suspension room." Nicolas ushered both ladies through the door.

Jana's palm flew to her mouth.

What the fuck had she gotten herself into? It was a freak show. Unconsciously her hand drifted to her throat as she felt the collar around her neck and gave it a pull.

Three people were hanging from the ceiling by chains and leather straps. One woman dangled, a foot off the ground, bound by her hands. Muscles and tendons stretched to their limits, pressed against her delicate skin. A man hung by his feet, his hands trussed behind him at the small of his back. Another woman was gagged by a scarf, her arms and legs hogtied behind her as she swung by her waist. Beside each

.

suspended person stood another individual and in their hands a whip or a flogger.

"Dear God," Jana whispered. "They're going to beat them."

"No." Nicolas grasped her biceps, pulling her around to face him. "Not beat them. Pleasure them. Remember, there's a fine line between pleasure and pain, like the spankings and the floggings that I've performed on you and Lisa. Pain can be pleasurable when it's introduced while you're aroused. Think about the scenarios we have acted out." With a thumb and forefinger he raised her chin. His eyes were warm with concern. "Choice is what makes the difference to anything you've experienced. These people choose to be here. They choose to have these things done to them, because they experience an ecstasy that can only be found in this world."

Lisa leaned in close and whispered, "Open your mind, Jana. Let's experience something new tonight."

Jana couldn't believe what she was seeing—hearing. "I-I can't do that."

Lisa's giggle held a hint of unease. "Perhaps this is *too* much for both Jana and me. Let's go, Nicolas."

Nicolas grasped Jana's and Lisa's hands, leaving the leashes to dangle, as they moved on.

They passed a refreshment table with a variety of hors d'oeuvres, fruits and vegetables. To the right was a bar. "They only serve non-alcoholic drinks here," Lisa explained. "No one is allowed to be under any type of influence."

"That's comforting," Jana said.

She couldn't believe how many people mingled, some of them basically naked, wearing only collars, nipple clamps and a variety of other body jewelry. It was obvious who the Masters and subs were, not only by how they were dressed, but how they interacted between each other. Subs took a formal stance when not serving their Masters, while others were cherished as if they were pets or a prized possession. Masters and subs appeared to be comfortable, even happy with their stations.

Even Lisa knew the protocol, which made Jana feel somewhat inadequate. As Nicolas stopped to converse with another Master, Lisa as well as the Dom's sub stood with their feet shoulders' widths apart, placed their hands behind their backs, and bowed their heads. Lisa's actions received a soft look from Nicolas. He reached out and stroked her hair and gave a tug of appreciation on her leash.

The desire to please Nicolas, to see pride warm his eyes, was growing inside Jana, pushing past the fear and anxiety that twisted inside her. She wanted to please him, too. She didn't exactly know how yet, but she could learn. All she had to remember is that this was make-believe. No one was actually being forced to submit. No one would be hurt. Pleasure was their only goal.

"Impressive." The Master speaking with Nicolas boldly scrutinized both Lisa and Jana. "The redhead is new?" He pinned an interested gaze on Jana.

Dammit. What was it about her that screamed newbie? Was the word tattooed across her forehead? Or was there a sign plastered to her back?

"Yes, but coming along nicely." Nicolas winked at her.

His sexy endearment made her nipples tighten. God, what she'd give to be kissing him, feeling his strong hands take control of her body. Given half the chance she'd opt for going back to his place and screwing his brains out.

"Well, if you're interested in sharing or auctioning her let me know," the Master said.

Jana's brows shot up, as she murmured, "Over my dead body." Lisa gave Jana an elbow to the midsection. "Shhh..."

The Dom turned to his sub. "Come, slave, the spanking bench awaits us."

Soft laughter left Nicolas at Jana's expression. "Don't worry. I'm not taking you to the Green Room." Then he pulled Jana against him, his erection pressing into her belly. "But I do have to tell you how much I would like to see your skin pink from my hand, brighter than it was the first time I paddled that beautiful ass." He added to Lisa, "Yours too, baby. Come, ladies, I believe it's time to see to our own pleasures."

Much to Jana's relief the Blue Room was empty. She hadn't known what to expect, but she'd prayed for no audience. She was ready to try a few new things, but being an exhibitionist wasn't one of them.

"This is Trent's playground. Every sex toy you can imagine is here." Lisa pointed to the variety of whips, floggers, clamps and clips hanging from the wall. Many more items lay atop the table pressed tight against the wall. The items clearly outnumbered Nicolas's three times over.

Additionally, there was a spanking bench and an ominous table set off to the side which strangely looked like one you might find at the doctor's office. She couldn't help the sliver of panic that made her pulse race. One wall contained D-rings for restraints, several chains hung from the ceiling and floor, a large fireplace adorned one wall, and an oversized bed which four people could fit to sleep—or play.

Now that was more like it, she sighed inwardly as her stiletto heels clicked against the marble floor, stepping deeper into the room.

An archway introduced a breathtaking bathroom. Visible from where she stood in the playroom was a Jacuzzi that bubbled invitingly, and a walk-in shower not far away. Only the commode appeared to be set off and hidden from all eyes.

Yes, a lot of fun could be had in this room.

A flood of excitement released from between Jana's thighs. By the heated look in Lisa's eyes could she be thinking the same thing, getting Nicolas between the sheets of that great big bed? In unison, they pinned their gazes on him, and then both began to laugh.

"What?" he asked, moving toward them. Muscles rippled beneath his tanned skin.

"We only wish to please you, Milord," Lisa purred, running her fingers through the dark hair on his chest. "What can we do to turn your world inside out?"

And that was exactly what Jana wanted—to show him as much pleasure as he had given her the last couple of weeks.

That was until the door opened and Master Trent entered.

"Let the play begin," he said and removed his robe, displaying an impressive chest and a bulge between his thighs molded by black leather pants.

Oh. My. God. No one had told her it was going to be a foursome.

Chapter Fifteen

Several weeks ago a foursome sounded fun and exciting, but now Nicolas wasn't sure as he stood in the middle of Trent's playground. This particular room was the talk of all his friends' parties. Referred to as the *land and sea ecstasy*, participants could easily ride the waves submersed in the Jacuzzi or shower, or lose themselves in the bed with as many partners as was desired.

Man, I hope I don't end up regretting this decision. Anxiety slid across his skin as he glanced at Jana. Bottom line, Nicolas didn't want to share her, not now—not ever.

Nicolas had enjoyed the playground's amenities before, usually with Trent and several experienced subs. He gazed about the bedroom at the whips, floggers and other toys hanging from another wall. The floor was marble with throw rugs of several different textures, each designed to heighten the senses.

By the look of disbelief on Jana's face as she stared at Trent, Nicolas had shocked her once again. She didn't run screaming from the room.

A good sign. Yes?

He had made these plans to include Trent before he had really known Jana. It was just something he thought would be fun at that moment.

While Nicolas's experience as a Lord was not extensive, Trent was an expert. His friend knew Jana was inexperienced. Not to mention that Lisa was fairly new. Nicolas trusted him not to go beyond the limits they had discussed.

A strong and determined wave of confidence rose in Nicolas, making him square his shoulders. These were his women. It was his responsibility to ensure their comfort zones were not breached and the pace taken was acceptable, not Trent.

"Master Trent, my pets will see to our pleasure this evening." Nicolas motioned to one of the two lounges off to the right, a table between them. "Please take a seat." His friend sat and then eased his long form across the lounge to lie down. Nicolas did the same.

As the two men relaxed, a DM opened the door to the playground and slipped through it, pushing a cart weighted with food, slices of meats and cheeses, fruits, and a variety of other items, including a can of whipped cream. Among the rich smell of chocolate there was sparkling cider and bottled water, even a couple of non-alcoholic beers.

Moments passed and no one spoke while the small table between the lounges was arranged. Afterward, the DM left the room.

"I didn't know whether you had dined." Trent winked as he bent one of his leather-clad knees. His chest was smooth, free of all hair.

"Excellent suggestion," Nicolas said. Food was a great way to break the ice and ease into sexual play. The idea helped to relax Nicolas as he started to toe off a boot to get more comfortable.

"May I assist you, Milord?" Lisa asked moving quickly to Nicolas's side. She sank to her knees, leaning against the lounge so her full breasts were at his eye level. Her gaze slid appreciatively across his body.

Fire licked his loins.

She grinned seeing the effect she had on him.

"Little tease." He released a low-toned laugh and gave a yank on her leash. He loved seeing his collar around her slender neck.

"I'm no tease, Milord." She looked up through feathered lashes. "I'm all yours tonight."

Thud. His heart pounded as his cock pressed against his pants. How could a man feel anything but aroused being attended by this sexy blonde?

Unless, of course, the redhead across the room wanted the position of serving and pleasuring him. Something he fully intended to accomplish before the night was over.

Jana kept her distance as she stood quietly. Her intense expression gave him the feeling she was contemplating the theory of relativity instead of preparing for the sexual experience of a lifetime. Trent's presence had definitely thrown her for a loop.

Jana was amazing. Intelligent. Beautiful. She just needed to learn how to relax and enjoy herself.

Nicolas lay on his back awaiting Lisa's assistance. But she had other things on her mind. She stood facing him, raising one of her legs to gracefully straddle his booted feet. She eased down, bending one knee to rest on the lounge, as she lowered her hips, slowly, to touch the toe of his boot with the apex of her thighs. With a thrust of her pelvis she ran her scantly clothed pussy over one boot and then the other. With a graceful move she scooted backward, grasped his boot and tugged, tossing it aside, before she began to pull off the other. His socks followed in a slow sensual display of a strip tease as she flung

189

them over her shoulder. When she was finished cool air caressed his feet.

He couldn't wait to get out of his leather pants. Already his cock was filled with blood and throbbing.

Covertly, Lisa waved at her friend to follow suit. The subtle gesture didn't go unnoticed as Jana frowned. One step, then she hesitated as if she was thinking twice about following Lisa's lead.

Jana took a visible deep breath of courage, steeled her shoulders and moved to Trent's side.

"Master, may I assist you in removing your boots?" she spoke softly, her eyes cast to the floor. Her innocence was alluring. She was heart-stoppingly beautiful playing the submissive.

Nicolas's chest tightened. He held his breath. Thoughts of her bending to his desires and serving his needs sent more blood rushing to his balls, resulting in a throbbing ache.

Trent leaned back, tucking his hands behind his head as he lay on the lounge. "Ah, my beauty, it would please me immensely."

From the corner of Nicolas's eye he caught Lisa giving Jana instructions to turn around as her index finger made a circle several times.

Acknowledgement came with Jana's quick nod. Her chest rose and before his eyes she transformed from a diffident woman to a sensuous temptress. She dropped her eyelashes as she'd seen Lisa do. The hint of a grin sent chills up his spine, until he realized the smile was intended for Trent.

Suddenly it dawned on him. *Duh!* He wasn't the one receiving Jana's attention.

Well shit!

Nicolas felt a stab of jealousy in his chest as heat scorched his face. Then his jaw dropped as Jana presented them with her back. Gracefully, she straddled Trent's legs, kneeling upon the lounge, so his legs were between hers and he had a perfect view of her scantly-clothed ass.

She had a gorgeous ass. Firm, yet soft and round.

Nicolas's palms itched to touch her.

But it was Trent who bent forward and cupped her buttocks, his tanned fingers a striking difference lying against Jana's pale skin. Her back arched, which only served to lift her ass higher, spreading her cheeks wider. Long auburn tresses brushed across the back of Trent's hands.

Gently his friend kneaded her tender flesh, before maneuvering to kiss the small of her back. She trembled beneath his caress and the finger that traced her spine.

Nicolas couldn't help wondering what Jana was thinking. Did she enjoy Trent's touch? His kiss?

Dammit. This possessiveness was ridiculous. Especially with a woman he had become reacquainted with only a month ago. But it couldn't be helped.

Jana was his.

Soft fingertips smoothed across Nicolas's tense jaw. Like a magnet he followed their path upward until he gazed into Lisa's brown eyes. She was exquisite in the black corset crisscrossed with silver rhinestones that parted to expose the swell her breasts. The small scrap of material that hid her sex urged him to caress her thigh.

"Let me feed you, Milord." She draped over him so her chest dipped close to his mouth, her light musk caressed him, before she pressed her lips to his ear. "She'll be yours soon. For now, enjoy what I have to offer."

What the hell was wrong with him? By the seductive look in her eyes, Lisa was more than willing to see to his needs. If he admitted it, she was more sensuous than Jana, more open and carried less baggage than her friend.

He couldn't keep his mind off what was happening on the lounge next to him. Try as he might his gaze drifted. It was pure agony watching Trent slide his finger beneath the rhinestone straps of Jana's thong, listening to her small gasps of surprise as his friend's finger slipped further beyond the material.

"Enough! Quit fucking Master Trent's legs and see to his hunger or you'll be punished." That didn't quite come off as Nicolas had intended. His words revealed more emotion than he would have liked. He found it maddening that Jana simply sat still and allowed this stranger to do whatever he wanted.

Man, he was losing it. Wasn't Jana doing exactly what was expected of her? Submitting. Not to mention it was his fault they were in this position to begin with.

"Lord Nicolas, your redheaded pet *is* seeing to my hunger. My appetite is quite varied, my friend. At the moment I'm starving to feel the softness of her skin, everywhere."

So was Nicolas.

Fuck.

Jana didn't know whether to be thrilled or pissed. Nicolas was jealous. Yet, wasn't this what he wanted? Did he want her to flirt and entice his friend? It wasn't easy for her to accept what Master Trent's presence indicated. But then again, she had to realize this was a game to Lisa and Nicolas. She might have let feelings and desires cloud the situation, but they were firmly on the right path.

It was only sex. She reminded herself consistently as she let the stranger touch her in ways she had expected Nicolas to do tonight—wanted him to do tonight.

Jana inched her way off Master Trent's legs, feeling his fingers glide across her ass once more. What had Nicolas expected, placing her in a foursome? She had only attempted to please him, make him proud of her, and once again it blew up in her face.

The silly thought left her dumbfounded, not knowing why it really mattered or what she was supposed to do now. She felt stupid and inadequate. Given one task to remove a man's boots and she'd failed, while Lisa moved with such ease, turning Nicolas on like a light bulb, if the bulge in his pants could be used as a gauge.

She stroked Master Trent's loins with her gaze, thrilled with the rise that appeared between his thighs.

Look what I did! she silently boasted. *I'm not a complete loser.*

"Over here and kneel between us," Nicolas growled.

Talk about confusing. It wasn't her fault that Nicolas got a case of jealousy. He should have thought about that before he put her in this situation. She couldn't help the excitement coursing through her. Nicolas was jealous.

She swayed, sinking to her knees between the men's lounges, not an easy feat wearing three-inch heels. Master Trent rolled to his side and began to run his fingers through her hair.

"Silk. Pure silk." Trent grazed her bare shoulder with his knuckles, and then went back to stroking her hair.

"Feed me a strawberry," Nicolas barked.

Damn Nicolas. For two cents she'd cram one into his face. Instead she chose a strawberry slightly on the green side. When he opened his mouth to speak she popped it inside.

The minute he bit down his cheeks sank in, his lips puckered. His expression almost made Jana laugh. Then Nicolas's menacing frown stole the enjoyment from the moment.

"You've earned a punishment," he growled again, as he swallowed.

Well bully, bully. Jana was already getting tired of being pushed around like a second-class citizen. Her knees were hurting, becoming one with the hard marble floor she knelt on. She wouldn't be here if it weren't for him and now he was taking it out on her. Men could be idiots.

What an awkward position she was in. Two sexy men stared at her; Trent with sexual hunger, and Nicolas with a look like he could strangle her.

Dammit! I didn't do anything wrong. Well, besides the tart strawberry.

"Bind her, Lisa," Nicolas snarled. His dark sapphire eyes pinned Jana with a threat she didn't want to think about. "From the ceiling and floor," he added sending a chill up her spine.

She fought down the fear flowing like ice water through her veins. Nicolas's words rang in her ears. *Trust me. I won't hurt you or let anyone else hurt you tonight.* She took a deep breath.

Lisa's lips parted as she began to speak, but an upheld hand from Nicolas kept her quiet.

Jana hated being helpless. As Lisa assisted her to her feet, she prayed she could trust Nicolas. Lisa gathered Jana's leash in her hand and led her to the corner of the room where the foreboding chains hung. A sudden tremor shook Jana.

Lisa rubbed her cheek along Jana's as she released the leash and pressed her lips softly against Jana's skin. She said, "You know I've always fantasized about having two men?"

Lisa slid her palm up Jana's arms raising her wrists. Cold metal touched her skin and she jerked back, but Lisa held her firmly, securing her wrists together with a cuff connected to a chain hanging from the ceiling.

"You have?" Jana swallowed hard trying not to concentrate on what Lisa was doing, but failing miserably. *I don't know if I can do this.*

Her friend laid her soft cheek against hers again and she murmured, "Yeah. One to clean and one to cook."

Nervous laughter leaked from Jana's taut lips.

"Now don't you feel better?" Lisa's teasing smile turned warm as she jerked her head toward the men. "Look at them, Jana." Her voice dropped. "What would it feel like to have two powerful men want you? Caress you? Fuck you? They both want you. See the way they look at you, desire you. Relax. Enjoy. If at any time you want to quit, you only have to say your safe word. 'Red' is what you chose." She kissed Jana on the cheek again. "Trust me. Trust Nicolas. I do." Then, with her soft palms on Jana's body, Lisa slid down to her knees.

When Lisa's hands slipped between her legs to position them further apart, Jana's gaze shot downward.

Trust me, her friend mouthed again.

A chain rattled as Lisa reached for it, drawing it and a manacle across the floor, before securing the metal around Jana's ankle, and then the next one, until she was spread-eagle, an X of surrender. Jana felt vulnerable, but if she was truthful to herself, excited as well.

It was heady knowing two men wanted her. She could even feel the air of competition between them, but knew who would win in the end—or at least she prayed would win in the end.

Oh, God. She realized just how turned on she was when moisture dampened her thong. The tightening of her nipples as they drew to taut nubs confirmed the fact.

"Now remove her corset," Nicolas demanded.

Jana felt as if her eyes actually popped out of their sockets like a cartoon character. Dressed, she felt a reasonable amount of confidence. Naked, she would be totally exposed. She jerked her head up, pinning Nicolas with a hot glare.

Lisa braced herself against Jana's thigh as she rose. As she reached to unfasten the rhinestones, Nicolas said, "No. Reveal her slowly. Sensuously. Stand behind her so I can see her face as your hands move across her skin."

Inch by inch Nicolas stripped Jana's defenses away. She wasn't sure she liked this game anymore with a stranger in the mix. Jana had to admit when Lisa's soft touch splayed across her abdomen, a thrill went through her. She swallowed hard.

Jana didn't have time to think as Lisa pulled on the jewels and slowly they began to dislodge, slithering across Jana's chest, causing hundreds of goose bumps to rise. Only then did she look at Nicolas. His eyes were heavy-lidded, dark. The bulge between his legs moved and Jana couldn't help but wish it was him removing her clothing.

As the final rhinestone slipped from its loop, the satin corset parted, revealing the swells of her breasts. Slowly, Lisa's fingertips slipped the material across her aching nubs.

Jana gasped at how sensitive her nipples were to the cloth, how cool the air felt caressing her breasts and how aware she was of the collar around her neck and the dangling leash. Not to mention how surprisingly sensuous it felt to be bound and stripped in front of two men. Men with fire in their eyes—fire for her.

Something about the situation made Jana feel powerful. Sexy. Desired.

"Milord. I can't strip her completely since she's bound." Lisa soft voice floated over Jana's shoulder.

Nicolas growled, deep and low, revealing his frustration. "Then just push back the corset further, I want to see her breasts."

"What about her thong?" Lisa moved beside Jana, a sparkle lighting her eyes. Nicolas's spur-of-the-moment punishment hadn't been planned efficiently. He hadn't requested that Lisa disrobe Jana before securing her. By the tightness of Lisa's lips as she fought back a smile, Jana knew her friend was enjoying Nicolas's dilemma as much as she was.

"Leave it." A note of disappointment rose in his voice.

Jana realized that having her clothes ripped off would have been provocative—wild—like the brunette bound to the St. Andrew's cross earlier. A waste of money, but exciting. Just the thought elevated her breathing. Her nipples puckered, a rush of warm moisture dampened her panties.

With an intense expression, Nicolas rose and approached. He stood quietly before her, his gaze stroking her body as if he dragged a flame across it. Her nipples were so tight they ached. Her body felt like a furnace.

Then Nicolas said, "Baby, come to me."

Without delay Lisa moved from beside Jana and walked into Nicolas's waiting arms. Slowly he began to undress her, touching her friend gently as if she would break, almost reverently. His pride in Lisa was evident by the way he kissed her as the corset slipped off one shoulder and then the other. Large hands smoothed across her porcelain skin.

Lisa's soft sighs of delight as she was caressed and cherished made Jana envious. Was this what Lisa had felt when she had been bound and forced to watch Jana receive pleasure while Lisa's was withheld?

It didn't take long to strip Lisa naked. Trent joined Nicolas and both men began a sensuous attack, stroking and kissing Lisa's lips and body. Slowly, they took turns disrobing while the other caressed the woman between them. Lisa's head fell back on a moan. Her eyes closed. The blissful expression on her face made Jana pull against her bindings, wanting to join them, wanting to feel four strong hands move across her body.

As if each man knew what the other was thinking, they began to manipulate their positions, moving Lisa closer to the huge bed with each touch, each kiss. Their bodies slid up and down Lisa's, her steps appearing unconscious as if she would follow them anywhere they led. It was Trent whose knees came in contact with the bed first, pulling Lisa down upon him, while Nicolas reached for one of the small square packets sitting alongside a jar positioned on a nightstand off to the right. "Would you like to fuck Master Trent, baby?" he asked, handing her one of the packets containing a condom. He reached for another condom and sheathed his thick, hard cock, before grasping the jar and unscrewing the top.

"If it would please you, Milord." Lisa's response was breathy as she ripped open the shrink-wrap, extracted the latex, and then began to place it on Trent's erection, which nearly touched his navel. Her lithe body writhed seductively across his strong, muscular form as she leaned into his kiss.

"Straddle Master Trent. But don't take him in your body. Not just yet." Nicolas dipped his fingers into the jar, and then set it back on the nightstand. "Instead, rub your pussy along his cock." Jana heard Nicolas hiss as he applied the cool blue gel to his own jutting erection. His lips parted. His eyes shuttered as he began to stroke. Voice dropping an octave, he said, "And do not climax without my permission."

For the love of God. Both of them were going to fuck Lisa and make Jana watch. Her throat tightened. There were only three orifices on a woman for a man to invade. Since Nicolas's cock was slick with lubricant, she doubted that Lisa's mouth was going to be one of the openings invaded. The thought both alarmed Jana and excited her.

What would it feel like to have two men fill her body, sandwiched between them? She jerked against her bindings. *Damn these chains. Damn Nicolas for forcing me to stand helplessly watching, instead of participating.*

The thought took her back. Who would have guessed that she would even consider a four-way, much less a ménage with her best friend? But then who would have ever thought she'd have sex with a woman?

Just how did she get in this position?

Better yet, did she want out?

As her body went up in flames, she knew the answer was no. She wanted to be on the bed with Nicolas, Lisa, and even Trent.

Trent cupped Lisa's breasts. His fingers tugged, pulled and pinched, eliciting soft whimpers from her. She arched her back pressing her globes deeper into his palms as she continued to caress him with her juices sliding along his thick, hard shaft.

Nicolas reached for a tissue and wiped the excess gel off his palms before tossing the tissue aside. Then he moved behind Lisa, his strong hands smoothing over her hips as his hot gaze stroked her ass. The muscles in his back tensed. Then he looked over his shoulder and his eyes met Jana's. Raw heat burned in their depths.

"You have earned a reward for your good behavior, baby. I'm going to fuck your lovely ass, while Master Trent fucks your pussy," he said, never releasing the visible hold he had on Jana.

She held her breath.

Without breaking eye contact with Jana, he gripped his cock in one hand and slowly guided it to Lisa's tight rosebud. Trent followed his lead thrusting into Lisa's slit, again and again. She threw back her head and cried out in ecstasy.

Nicolas took care in entering Lisa. His movements were slow and cautious. Even though his attention appeared to be on Jana, she felt sure that he proceeded with thought to Lisa's comfort. Or perhaps it was to drag out Jana's punishment. Kill her with the knowledge that she wouldn't feel Nicolas's cock buried deep inside her.

With each of Lisa's moans, Jana felt the emptiness between her thighs grow. Then Nicolas began to move, slipping in and out between Lisa's slick cheeks. While he screwed her ass, he fucked Jana with his hot gaze. Fire licked across her skin, tightening her nipples to an unbearable ache. When his gaze dropped, caressing her neck, she couldn't help the loll of her head as it fell back, exposing her throat and giving him more access. Her breasts grew impossibly heavier as he stroked them with his eyes, moving across her belly, down and across the vee of her thighs covered by the black thong she wore. God, she couldn't believe that with a heated expression he set off small spasms to explode inside her pussy.

As the three people on the bed moved in unison, Jana suffered. Nicolas ensured it by holding her in his hot glare. Her mouth was dry. Her sex wet. She hungered for the feel of a man, one man in particular.

Jana saw Lisa's body quiver and heard her breath catch.

"Don't come until I give you permission," Nicolas growled through clenched teeth. The tendons and muscles in his arms bulged. His hips flexed, creating hollows in his ass cheeks just below the small of his back. Man, what she would give to smooth her hand over the area and touch it with her lips.

Jana was burning up inside. And just when she didn't think she could take any more Nicolas yelled, "Now! Come for me now."

Jana knew that he spoke to Lisa, but still spasms filtered through Jana's pussy as her climax rolled through her like a sudden storm. She jerked against the chains, setting them to rattle. Wave after wave of ecstasy coursed through her so that her body trembled and shook beneath Nicolas's aroused glare, which only intensified the effect.

His chest expanded and he released a groan torn from somewhere deep within. Fingers dug into Lisa's hips as he pumped several times and then stilled. His chest rose and set rapidly.

Amazing. As the last of the tremors subsided Jana was left bewildered, but strangely sated. This had never happened to her, an orgasm without even being touched. It must have been the fact that she was restrained, while watching three people fuck. Or was it the desire reflecting in Nicolas's eyes that made her feel she was the one between the two men and not Lisa.

Gaze still affixed to Jana's, Nicolas took one step back, withdrawing from Lisa's body. As he rolled off the condom and disposed of it in a trashcan next to the nightstand, he said, "You have earned another punishment."

Chapter Sixteen

Jana was extraordinary.

Nicolas couldn't believe that she had climaxed on his command without even touching her. He watched her blissful expression turn cold as he threatened her with punishment for disobedience. Although he had told Lisa she could come, he hadn't told Jana.

But Lord knew he had willed it.

She was beautiful, standing in the corner of Trent's playroom, her wrists bound together high above her head, her legs spread shackled to the floor. His collar around her slender neck, the leash dangling at her side was the picture of dominance. But it was the arousing image of the black corset spread wide baring her breasts, black panties and three-inch stilettos that turned him on. A selection of playthings behind her reminded him of the delicious things he could do to her.

Without a word he moved away from Lisa and Trent, who continued to kiss and fondle one another, and went to stand before Jana. "I didn't give you permission to climax."

"But—"

"Silence!" Her jaws snapped shut at his command. "You don't have permission to speak." A fire sparked in her blue eyes. He loved the fight she possessed within. She was a survivor.

He'd never want to crush her spirit or thoroughly control her. No. More than anything he only wanted her to understand her weaknesses and strengths—pain and pleasure—and to know that both were just a part of life and meant to be savored.

He moved behind her, out of her line of sight and she twisted her neck, trying to follow him, but failed. Her perfect ass tightened with tension and for a moment he stood there and caressed her with his gaze.

She was sleek and beautiful and all his.

From the wall, Nicolas selected a flogger made up of synthetic polyamide products similar to elastic. The light thongs could tickle lightly as well as leave a sting of enjoyment. As he ran the whip over his palm, felt the coolness against his skin, he caught the look of hesitation in Lisa's eyes as she drew to a sitting position next to Trent. Concern flashed across her face as Trent pulled her into the vee of his legs and began to stroke her breast. Jana must have connected with Lisa, because Lisa's frown faltered and her lips pulled into a smile. She mouthed something he couldn't quite make out. But he was sure it was words of assurance for her friend.

Moving closer to Jana's back, he stopped to where he could feel her body heat. Leaning next to her ear he whispered, "You've been a very bad girl, doll." She shivered, the tremor sending a sense of delight through his body. "Very bad." He let the thongs of the flogger tease the beginning swell of her ass. "Do you know what I do to bad girls?"

"No." Her voice was almost inaudible.

"No?" He firmed his response.

"No, Milord," she corrected.

He paused, building her anticipation, while he allowed the flogger to slip down her legs and sway across her calves. "Bad girls get punished."

With a flick of his wrist he lightly swatted her on the ass. This close to her he couldn't make the strike hurt, even if he had wanted to, but he could smell her sweet perfume and musky desire. His intentions were to tease and arouse her, not harm her. He took a step back and smoothed the thongs across her back, and then lightly shook them down her tense arms.

From over Jana's shoulder he could see Lisa still sitting between Trent's legs, her back pressed to his chest as his friend massaged her knees, working slowly up her thighs. Nicolas grinned, knowing exactly the path Trent was taking. Trent once told him there was nothing sweeter than the nectar between a woman's legs, and Nicolas definitely had to agree.

Just the thought of sampling Jana's juices right this moment was driving him crazy.

Dragging the flogger across her shoulder, he moved around her body until he faced her. Her eyes were large blue pools of anxiety that darkened when the elastic thongs slipped over one of her breasts. The nipple beaded and tiny bumps formed around the rosy areola. She gasped at the sensation of the straps as he continued to slide them back and forth over the taut nub. When she arched into the caress he drew his attention to her other nipple and began the torture anew.

He hadn't forgotten Lisa or Trent, but he figured that they could keep each other occupied until he was through with Jana—at least for tonight.

With ease he dragged the flogger across every inch of her body, down an arm, up a leg, over her abdomen, wanting her to get used to the feel of the rubber against her skin, to know that the instrument induced pleasure as well as pain. Occasionally he flicked his wrist so she felt the slight sting of the whip. Each time, he watched her reaction, looking for fear or discomfort. The thongs met her delicate skin, now pink from his attention, and her nostrils flared. She hadn't uttered a word, but her breathing had grown heavy. Her chest rose and fell, pushing her breasts up and down.

When her tongue slid sensuously between her lips drawing his attention to her mouth, he knew he had to taste her. Tossing the flogger aside, he cupped her face in his hands and pressed his lips to hers. Her body melted into his as he delved into her warmth, a sweet surrender that turned his kiss forceful as he drew her into his arms. She tugged against her restraints. Did she need to feel her arms around him, as he did?

What was it about this woman that turned him into such a romantic?

All he could think about was laying her upon the bed and making slow, passionate love to her. The thought was just a lost image in his head when he was joined by Lisa and Trent. As he released Jana's lips, Lisa captured them.

The blonde moved with such tenderness against Jana, pressing her body forward until her breasts met her friend's. Then she slowly moved, nipples stroking nipples. There was nothing invasive in her touch, only the need to calm her friend, ease her into the next experience.

The two women were beautiful in motion, leashes swaying. Their bodies were pieces of art to be cherished and adored. There was nothing more exciting than love between the female sex, especially Lisa and Jana because of the close bond they shared.

Before Trent moved behind Jana, he pressed a condom into Nicolas's palm. Already Trent had sheathed himself and laved his cock with gel. "Exquisite," he said with a smile. Then his friend began to place kisses behind her ear, down her slender neck, his hands caressing and training her to his touch.

Nicolas's hands were trembling as he tore open the packet and extracted the condom. Clearly Lisa and Trent expected Jana to be the recipient of the attention of all three of them. From Jana's heaving breathing, the wonder in her eyes, he knew she had been aroused watching him and Trent fuck Lisa. Did she want to feel two cocks inside her?

A possessiveness like he had never felt before swamped him.

This is ridiculous. He tried to brush off the heat that began to simmer lightly across his skin. *Do you really know Jana?*

Yes, a voice rang inside his head.

Nicolas had learned a lot about Jana through Lisa, and even more he had obtained himself over the past month. Like she was inquisitive. She probably did want to know how it felt to have two men make love to her. Would she enjoy the experience or try to analyze the possibility?

And why did he feel so possessive of her?

Nicolas rolled the latex over his erection, which hardened further when Jana released a soft whimper as Trent and Lisa caressed and kissed her body. The light whipping he had given her would make her sensitive to every touch.

He approached, reaching out to skim his knuckles across her soft cheek.

Jana was a fighter—a survivor. How else could she have forged ahead and made something of herself and grown into the lovely woman she had become?

Yes. Lisa had made sure he knew everything about her friend. Those special attributes about Jana that somehow the vixen knew would attract him.

Nicolas dipped his fingertips into her thong, grabbing the material and pulling. The snap of the string made Jana gasp as it loosened. The glistening rhinestones fell with a soft tinkling as they scattered about the floor. With a smooth brush of his hand, he tossed the scrap of material aside.

It was as if the scene had been choreographed. Lisa adjusted Jana's leash letting it hang over her shoulder, and then she moved out of his way so he could press his body to Jana's. With a bend of his knees, he wedged his cock between her thighs. With one thrust he buried himself, eliciting a cry from her kiss-swollen lips. Apparently, Trent began to massage her backdoor, because her eyes sprang wide.

"Trust me," Nicolas whispered in Jana's ear as his hips began to move. "Relax. The sensation will be something you have never felt before."

On the other side, Lisa leaned closer. "You can trust him, Jana." Her voice held an ethereal tone, airy and delicate, as if she were issuing a subliminal message. *Trust him.* Then she placed a hand on Nicolas's chest, pushing his and Jana's bodies slightly apart to wedge her head between them. Her tongue flicked out rapidly several times over Jana's taut nipple, before she took the nub deep into her mouth and began to suckle.

Heat flared across Jana's body. She was burning up. While Lisa's wet mouth laved her breast, Nicolas fucked her pussy, and Trent was covering the outside of her asshole with something wet and cold. When his finger slipped inside to further lube the taut hole, she startled.

Was she really going to experience two men in her body at once?

Excitement and fear made strange bedfellows. She couldn't think, not with the slow rhythm of Nicolas's hips moving as he slid in and out between her thighs. The warm breath that Lisa blew over Jana's wet nipple sent a shiver up her spine. If she wasn't mistaken, there were now two fingers in her virgin area. Then the sensation was gone and something bigger, harder nudged her entrance.

Her expression must have given away her lack of confidence, because Nicolas murmured, "Breathe with me, doll. Inhale." His chest rose, filling up with air.

Jana tried—she really did, but her ass was being stretched to impossible limits. The man behind her, invading her body, was no small man. She gulped down a breath as pain laced up her ass. "I can't do this," she whimpered.

A firm grasp on her chin brought her vision in line with Nicolas's. His hips had stilled. His firm erection buried deep inside her. Warmth filled his eyes. "You can. Jana, you are stronger than any woman I've ever met. There is nothing you can't do. There's a fine line between pain and pleasure. Walk it with me. Now breathe. I promise in the end it will be worth the momentary discomfort."

Lisa looked up at her. "Trust him, Jana," her friend coaxed. Then she dipped her head and latched on to Jana's breast once more.

Jana wasn't a coward, but more than that she wanted desperately to believe Nicolas, to trust him.

A deep gush of air filled her lungs as she focused on how Nicolas filled her void, both physically and mentally. Long, hard and thick, his cock again began to move in and out of her pussy. She was wet, moist with desire.

There was another moment of distress when Trent pushed past the tight rings inside her, and then he stood perfectly still, allowing her to adjust to his presence. It seemed like only a heartbeat before he began to move, and then nothing existed but the moment.

The incredible fullness was unbelievable. She was lost in sensation.

Desire so dark it almost turned Nicolas's blue eyes black stared back at her. He growled as his hips slapped against her pussy. His fingertips pressed firmly into the tender skin at her waist. Trent spooned her backside with his body. Lisa had moved around Nicolas, her blonde head dipping as she latched onto Jana's other nipple.

Pressure built low in Jana's belly. "Nicolas?" Her breathing was small gasps.

"Yes, doll. Come for me."

The fires of arousal grew out of control as they licked her cervix and filtered across her skin. Stars burst in her head. The dam broke, releasing an orgasm that shook her from head to toe. She threw back her head, resting it on Trent's shoulder and screamed. Her climax was so powerful she couldn't control the convulsions that shook her body.

The overwhelming sensation was the most exciting, exhilarating thing she had ever felt, especially when Lisa moved away and both men reached their pinnacles and sandwiched Jana between them to the point it took her breath away.

Chains rattled as she jerked against her restraints. She needed to grasp onto Nicolas, needed to feel his arms around her.

In a sandpapery voice he said, "Release her." As Lisa worked on the handcuffs, Nicolas drew their bodies together, his arms like tethers around her until it felt like they were one. Trent withdrew, leaving her with a void, but all she really needed was the completeness that Nicolas filled deep inside her. As Jana fell, she couldn't help clinging to Nicolas. She felt warm and protected in his arms. The realization was shocking, because she had never felt this way with anyone other than Lisa.

Jana had to admit that for once it felt good to lean on a man. Even if Lisa said there was nothing between her and Nicolas, Jana's feelings were growing. Hell, she had never gotten over her high school crush. But knowing and touching him had raised her desire to a whole new level—a dangerous level.

Couldn't she just enjoy the moment? Enjoy what the three of them had together? The thought nearly made her release her hold on Nicolas. When had she begun thinking of them as a threesome? This romantic triangle could only lead to disaster—wouldn't it?

She didn't have time to think before she was swept up in Nicolas's arms and pressed against his firm chest. "Do you want to call an end to the night? Or continue our play?"

Held in his strong arms, so close to his heat, it was nearly impossible to back down. Fact was she wanted more—needed to discover the fascination of this dark world with both Lisa and Nicolas. She sucked in her bottom lip, teasing it with her teeth.

Remember curiosity killed the cat, a small voice in the back of her head warned. The next thing she heard was her doctor's reassuring voice, *Face your fears.*

But there were so many. Loss of control, the mental and physical fear of being hurt, and opening herself to trust someone other than Lisa were only a few of her issues.

Although Jana's first impression of what was happening within the walls of Master Trent's home appeared to be abuse, it couldn't be. People walked freely about. What they did was consensual—a shifting of power as Lisa had explained.

Jana took a deep breath. *Continue* lingered on her tongue, but she found no voice.

How many years of therapy had it taken for her to understand what she had felt at the hands of her foster father had been humiliation and abuse?

What Jana had experienced tonight had been incredible and she wanted more.

"Continue." The single word was just a whisper, but won her a bright smile from Nicolas and a tender kiss as he set her on her feet. He helped her to wiggle out of the corset, tossing it on the floor alongside the rhinestones and what was left of her thong. With a sweep of his hands he cradled her in his arms and carried her to the bed.

Lisa disappeared briefly and when she returned she had a bowl in her hands and towels draped over her arm.

"Roll over," Nicolas said as he sat on the bed, making it groan beneath his weight.

She hesitated, wondering exactly what was planned as Trent and Lisa crawled onto the bed. The liquid in the bowl sloshed over the side wetting the bed as Lisa giggled.

"Relax, Jana," Lisa encouraged. "We're going to clean you up."

"Uh...I can do that," Jana insisted, scrambling to sit up only to be gently pushed back down and then rolled upon her belly.

Now this was awkward. Really awkward.

Nicolas leaned close and whispered, "Yes, but we want to do it for you. Let us take care of you."

The first wet cloth brushing across her back made Jana flinch. Moist and warm, it smoothed across her skin like a gentle breeze. When she felt her ass-cheeks spread wide she couldn't contain the squeal that surfaced. Then the cloth slid between her legs, cleansing her. They left no place untouched.

With a gentle push someone rolled her onto her back, the massage that followed left her feeling limp and relaxed.

"Shall we dine?" Nicolas asked. A twinkle sparked in the depths of his sapphire eyes as he rose from the bed.

Both she and Lisa followed, moving toward the table where the food was ready to serve.

"Not over there, girls," Jana heard Nicolas say as she and Lisa glanced over their shoulders in unison. Nicolas lay on his back on a cushiony carpet before the fireplace, his knees bent and spread wide. Master Trent approached and took a similar position except that his head rested about a foot away from Nicolas's feet. "We're ready."

Jana and Lisa slowly turned to face the men. From the bewildered look on Lisa's face she had no idea what they were supposed to do, which left Jana at a complete loss.

"Lisa, kneel between us facing me. I want your sweet ass above Trent's head. Jana, kneel at my head facing Lisa," Nicolas instructed. Both women did as commanded. "Now straddle our faces. We're hungry."

Oh. My. God. So, this was Nicolas's idea of dining. And Jana had a front row seat to watch it all.

As Jana moved into place, parting her thighs to reveal herself to Nicolas, the leash hanging from her collar grazed his chest. Then his arms wrapped around her thighs and urged her downward, which made her legs spread wider. All the while, she watched as Master Trent positioned Lisa, so he could go down on her while she went down on Nicolas's semi-erect cock.

Just the thought of the four of them linked in a quadruple ménage sent Jana's pulse racing, her heart thrashing against her chest. It was beyond anything she could imagine.

When Nicolas's warm, wet tongue slid across Jana's folds, she startled, releasing a whimper. Again, he caressed her slit, flicking her clit several times.

Lisa's eyes were heavy as Master Trent feasted upon her sex. Gently she kissed Nicolas's firming cock, ran her tongue along its ridge. Jana loved the way it jerked when Lisa licked the pearly bead of pre-come that squeezed from the small opening.

In her wildest dreams, Jana never thought of participating in such an act. She didn't know what came over her. She leaned forward, dropping to her palms and while Lisa laved one side of Nicolas's staff she performed the same on the other side. Together they began to give him head.

The growl that surfaced from Nicolas vibrated in Jana's pussy, sending the most delightful rays shooting inside her. When his strong hands grasped her hips, pulling her closer as he latched on to her clit and began to suck harder, Jana knew she had pleased him.

Lisa's smile met hers. And then their lips joined, tongues dipping and tasting. Pressure building between Jana's legs made her arms wobbly. She fought to stay upright. The result was shaky arms that barely held her up.

Another growl from the man between her legs broke their kiss and together they began to stroke his cock again with their mouths and tongues.

Nicolas's fingers found her breasts and began to knead, before pinching, pulling, and teasing her nipples. While he worked her body into a frenzy, his hips rose faster, his suction on her clit firmed, and then he bit down hard.

Jana screamed her release.

She was soaring higher and higher. Nicolas hadn't lied when he said he would take her to places she'd never been.

Nothing could have prepared her for the rush of adrenaline coursing through her body, awakening every nerve ending so that she swore the entire utility company for Arizona was housed in her shell. And then she was falling, drifting, coming back to earth.

As she opened her eyes she was just in time to see a fountain of come erupt from Nicolas's cock and squirt Lisa just above her right eye. Jana couldn't have stopped the laughter even if she had tried.

Wide-eyed and blinking, Lisa opened her mouth as the milky substance dripped over one eye, sliding down her cheek. She tentatively touched it, drawing back her hand. Then her gaze snapped to Jana. She didn't have time to respond. Lisa moved quickly, lunging to capture Jana in her arms. Intertwined they tipped to one side and rolled off the men onto the cool marble floor.

Wrestling, they giggled and grunted as Lisa attempted to wipe Nicolas's come in Jana's face.

Neither was aware of their audience and neither of them cared. Once again they were free-spirited girls enjoying each other and just having fun.

Breathlessly, Lisa released Jana, and then rolled upon her back. "God, I love you."

Jana crawled to her side, swiped her finger across Lisa's cheek and popped her finger into her mouth, tasting Nicolas. "I love you, too." Jana leaned forward and kissed Lisa squarely on the mouth. The first time she had taken the initiative.

When they parted Lisa's eyes were filled with moisture.

Jana's smile faltered. "What's wrong?" she asked.

"I just don't want this to end," Lisa choked through unshed tears.

"Oh, Lisa." Jana drew her friend into her arms. From behind them Jana heard Nicolas say, "You two didn't forget about us, did you?"

Ahhh...shit! Yes, Jana had. A flush of embarrassment flooded her cheeks as she released Lisa. What must the two men think of them? Two naked women rolling around the floor like children.

When she turned to face them she couldn't believe her eyes. Both men stood above her with rigid hard-ons.

Lisa was right. Nicolas *was* insatiable.

Chapter Seventeen

It had been two weeks since their romp at Trent's place. Life had settled back into its normal pace with the exception that each night, instead of one woman Nicolas had two, excluding the times Lisa had opted out of their ménage a trois due to working late and the occasional headache. From a male's point of view, he should have been happy, but things were getting awkward.

After placing his razor and aftershave in his carry-on, he zipped the bag before tossing it over his shoulder. Then he reached for his larger suitcase. He wasn't sure about their trip to Puerto Vallarta, a quaint city just due west of Guadalajara in Old Mexico. There was hesitancy in his steps as he made his way from the bedroom to the front door.

Lisa had grown even more distant and he just didn't understand why. Had he made her feel like the third wheel? After pulling the door shut, he inserted his key and locked it, before heading for his truck. The fact that it was getting harder and harder to share Jana with Lisa wasn't helping. He wanted Jana all to himself. Showing each woman the same amount of attention wasn't easy.

His luggage made a *thud* as he threw it in the bed of his truck. For a moment, he leaned against the vehicle.

When had Jana stolen his heart?

Dammit! He pushed away from the truck. He couldn't deny that the times he and Jana had spent alone together had been special to him. She was everything he had been looking for—that he hadn't even realized he'd been looking for.

With a tug, he opened the door and climbed in. He sorted through his keyring, found the right one and inserted it. As he turned the key the engine roared to life. The sounds of the garage door lifting, gears grinding rang in his head. Hands on the steering wheel, he paused again. He didn't want to hurt Lisa. And he had no chance with Jana without Lisa.

Jana would never jeopardize her friendship with Lisa for him. The bond between the women was that tight. Helluva position for him to be in.

He backed out of the garage, hit the automatic garage door button to close it again, and headed toward Lisa's house in Chandler.

Sitting at a red light—lost in thought—he startled at the loud, obnoxious sound of a horn blaring behind him. When Nicolas looked up he saw that the light was green and everyone around him was in motion, except for the angry people stuck behind him.

Shit! With a jerk his truck lunged forward. He ran his fingers through his hair. Man, he couldn't live like this. Something had to be done.

A perfect scenario would be for Jana to move in with him and they both keep Lisa as a friend. "Not gonna happen ol' boy, but you can dream," he said aloud. No, there wasn't a win-win solution in this triangle and he should have known that from the start. But he hadn't counted on falling for Jana.

Was he fucked or what? Or just hoping for something he couldn't have? He thrummed his fingers on the steering wheel.

Could that be it? Was he only attracted to Jana because he knew there was no way of obtaining her?

God. Could he be that superficial?

As he steered his truck into Lisa's driveway he reached for the strength to see this next week through. Some deep soul-searching would need to be done on his part.

Exactly what was it he wanted from Jana and from Lisa? What was he willing to give up? Was he willing to lose both women?

As he climbed out of his truck then jogged up the steps to the door, Nicolas wondered what his options were. Two from his point of view. Two women or none. Neither choice was acceptable as a long-term solution.

The front door of Lisa's house was unlocked, so quietly he let himself in. He could hear shuffling sounds coming from the hall. Then the telephone rang. Lisa ran past him without a hello, nearly tripping over the pink luggage sitting just off the hall. She was breathless as she reached the telephone sitting on the coffee table next to the couch.

"Hello. Yes. Yes. Oh my goodness. Yeah. Of course." She held onto the telephone and flinched with surprise when she turned around. "Nicolas. I didn't see you there."

Strange. How could she have missed him?

Lisa shook her head, her brows furrowed. "Well, it looks like I'm not going with you two." She slipped the telephone receiver back into its cradle.

"What?" Jana's voice came from down the hall.

Lisa gave an exasperated wave of her hands and raised her voice. "Susan at the center has had a family emergency. She was supposed to substitute for me while I was gone. With her going back to Texas there's no one to cover for me. I can't go."

Jana entered the living room, disappointment etched on her face. She released a heavy sigh and shrugged one shoulder. "Oh well. We can always go another time."

Lisa's eyes widened. "Hey. Just because I can't go doesn't mean the two of you have to cancel your trip. Go on. Enjoy yourselves."

Jana frowned. "No. Not without you."

Lisa turned to Nicolas. "Tell her this is ridiculous. No way am I going to ruin your vacation." Her gaze shot back to Jana. "Jana, you have to start work soon. This may be your only opportunity to get away. Nicolas had to jump through major hoops to get the week off from the restaurant. You guys have to go."

Nicolas looked from one woman to the other. A whole week alone with Jana—he had to be dreaming.

He attempted to hide his excitement. "Jana, Lisa's right. If she doesn't mind us going we might as well. Maybe she can join us later in the week if she can find another replacement."

Lisa wiped her palms down the front of her pants. "He's right!" There was too much animation in her voice, as she continued, "I'll start today. There has to be someone available who can take my place. My ticket is refundable, I'll reschedule as soon as I can. I'll probably be on the next plane out." Her grin lacked something.

"I don't know." Jana's gaze jumped from Lisa to Nicolas and then back to Lisa. "It feels strange going without you."

Lisa gathered Jana into her arms. "You're being silly. Heck, you guys will probably enjoy a little one-on-one, if you know what I mean."

Nicolas knew exactly what she meant and couldn't agree more. The solemn mood that had been riding him began to dissipate like a sour note on a brisk breeze. In fact, he was looking forward to the next week.

"Come on, doll. We'll keep the sheets warm until Lisa can join us." A delightful blush heated Jana's cheeks at his insinuation.

Insinuation! Hell, he might never let her leave the hotel room, much less the bed.

Jana scanned Lisa's face for any objections. "Lisa, is this really okay with you?"

Lisa gave her a shove toward Nicolas. "I wouldn't have it any other way. Now get your bags and get the hell out of here." She gave a carefree grin and waved them out the doorway.

As Jana climbed into Nicolas's truck, she couldn't believe that for the next week she would have Nicolas all to herself. Her excitement overwhelmed the guilt that simmered quietly in her belly.

Before Nicolas could shut the door she jutted a hand out stopping him. "Oh wait! I forgot my cosmetic bag."

He smiled, cupping her face in his warm hands. "Doll, you don't need makeup. You're naturally beautiful." He kissed her gently.

God, he was gorgeous. She loved the way his T-shirt stretched over his broad chest. And the way that errant lock of black hair drooped over one eye. She brushed it lightly away. "And you're full of shit. I'll be just a moment." She bounded from the truck.

As Jana entered she heard Lisa talking in the kitchen.

"Yeah. It worked. They're gone. Yeah. Yeah. I know. I'll be there in about thirty minutes. I love you, too."

Jana stood paralyzed for a moment. Who could Lisa be talking to? Was this convenient family emergency an excuse not to go with her and Nicolas? And who was Lisa telling she loved? A knot formed in Jana's throat as she moved down the hall and into the bedroom she'd been using ever since she arrived in Arizona. She stood for a moment and looked around the pale pink room.

Lisa didn't keep secrets from her. Did this have anything to do with her and Nicolas? Recently Lisa had been distant. She'd been working late and her headaches were coming more frequently. Or was that a lie, too?

"What are you still doing here?" Surprise rang in Lisa's voice. Jana spun around to face her friend's shocked expression.

Jana picked up the case sitting on her bed. "I-I forgot my cosmetic bag."

"I see." Lisa glanced nervously over her shoulder and then back to Jana. "I thought you left. I mean—you'd better get going. You don't want to miss your plane."

"Lisa, I don't feel right going without you." *Please, Lisa, don't lie to me.* Jana didn't know what she'd do if her trust in her friend faltered. She didn't have anyone else, except for Nicolas. The thought made her freeze, then she brought her attention back to Lisa. "Is there something wrong? Don't you want to go with us?"

"You silly goose." Lisa's laugh brushed off Jana's concern as foolish. "Of course I want to go. Who wouldn't? I just can't right now." She swiped her tongue quickly over her lips and swallowed. "Please understand, Jana. I just can't go right now."

There was nothing Jana could do. If Lisa couldn't—or wouldn't confide in her, Jana couldn't force the issue.

Something in Jana died, a heaviness that built in her chest and withered.

Perhaps Lisa had found someone new and just didn't know how to tell her and Nicolas.

Maybe Jana had already worn out her welcome.

Oh hell! She could stand here forever wondering what Lisa was hiding and what reason was behind it, but still it wouldn't get her anywhere. With no real options, she walked over to Lisa, gave her a kiss and then brushed by her as she left.

Nicolas was waiting just outside the truck with a big grin as he held open her door. At least one of the three was happy to be traveling to Puerto Vallarta.

The drive to the airport was slow going. Traffic moved at a snail's pace on Highway 101 and then on the 202. With each mile away from Lisa, Jana grew more anxious. She shifted in her seat.

What was Lisa up to?

"Is something wrong?" Nicolas asked, pulling off at the airport exit just as a small red car shot in front of them.

"No." She continued to stare into the mass of cars ahead. All the while she let Lisa's words, "I love you, too," thrum through her head. Her friend wanted both her and Nicolas gone.

But why?

"Are you okay with this?" She could feel Nicolas's eyes on her. She turned to face him forcing a smile on her face.

"Of course."

He focused back on the traffic. "Your eyes are saying one thing, while your words say another."

Damn Nicolas for being so insightful.

"I just hope everything is okay with Lisa."

"Why wouldn't it be?" he asked.

Now that was the question of the day, wasn't it?

Chapter Eighteen

The flight had been less than desirable, Nicolas thought as they moved through the airport and the front doors leading outside. Jana still had a green pallor to her skin as they dashed out into the rain to climb into their cab.

Who knew that sunny Mexico would be rainy Mexico? As he looked up at the angry clouds he prayed it wouldn't be like this the entire trip...or did he? A smile crept across his face thinking about spending an entire week in bed with Jana.

He glanced toward Jana. Worry lines furrowed her brows and she looked as if she would bite if someone bothered her.

"Bad sign," she murmured beneath her breath.

"Bad sign?" The muscles and tendons in his neck tightened.

"We shouldn't have come here without Lisa." She stared straight ahead as she had during the ride to the airport.

Dammit! He wasn't spending a week with Jana moping over Lisa. "You think Lisa could have rescheduled the weather?"

She glared at him, and then her expression softened. "I'm sorry. Do you want to head back to Arizona?"

"Hell, no! I want to spend the entire week wrapped in your arms, buried between your thighs, lost to this world." Nicolas caught the driver's eyes darting to the rearview mirror. With a grin on his weathered face he scanned up and down Jana's form. Then his vision went to Nicolas and the old man's brows bounced a couple of times.

She swallowed hard. "Oh."

Nicolas snorted as a blush of pink stained Jana's cheeks. "I'm sorry." The old man's gaze was still on Jana and the car was veering to the right. "Eyes on the road," Nicolas snapped. Manuel, the license on the visor identified, jerked his gaze and the car back to the road. "I probably shouldn't have said it like that."

"Or perhaps as loudly." There was a playful tone in her voice.

He scooted closer and drew her into his arms. "But it's true." Her womanly scent surrounded him like he was trapped in a balloon. She always gave him the impression her skin was on fire.

She tipped her chin up to receive his kiss. At first it was tentative, just a brush of their lips. Then he pulled her closer to prove to her exactly what he meant to happen. He tasted her, took command of her, and left no doubt in his mind or hers that he would have her as soon as they were settled in their hotel.

An interested snicker from the driver had him releasing her lips, but not her body. Mouth next to her ear, he murmured, "Jana, you're mine to do with as I wish for the next week. My sex slave. That was our agreement."

She sighed, "Yes," and cuddled up to him.

"If I demand you go down on me right now you would, because I command it." She stirred in his arms, but he didn't release her. "You agreed to this before we left." Well, it wasn't actually their agreement. It was made between him and Lisa and Jana a couple of nights after Trent's party. His friend had recommended the vacation to loosen Jana up and to train her more thoroughly. What Nicolas really wanted was just to get to know her better, to see how far he could take her in the game of submission.

She wiped her tongue along her lips. "I don't know if I could do that."

"But you would because you want to please me."

This time when she pulled away he released her. "Yes. I want to please you."

"Then unzip my pants and touch me." He loved the innocent expression in her eyes when they sprang wide and then darted toward the cabbie. After which, the most sensual smile filtered across her full lips.

Her fingernail scraped along the metal teeth of his zipper causing a grating sound that sent a shiver up his spine. Another swipe and she grasped the tab and drew it down so his cock pressed against his underwear, begging to be released. Next she unhooked his button. When her warm palm caressed him through the cotton he sucked in a breath. Slowly she inched his briefs down, all the while keeping her focus pinned to his crotch. Baring him, she clutched his erection in her small palm and began to stroke from balls to tip, tip to balls. As she slid up and down his cock, she rotated her hand, making circular motions that made him almost come off the seat.

Damn she was good.

His testicles drew up and an ache developed that pushed the borders of pain. His cock was hard as a rock. And all he could think about was ripping off her clothes and taking her right here, right now.

Eyes half-shuttered, she gazed up at him. She glanced at the driver whose foot must have released the gas pedal as they began to slow down. Once again Manuel's attention was focused on Jana and not his driving.

The cabbie was enjoying the show. Jana knew he watched. Did it turn her on? When she dropped her head between Nicolas's thighs, he knew both he and Manuel were in for the show of a lifetime.

She licked his shaft like it was an ice cream cone, long, wet swipes that had his hips coming off the seat. When she made several swirls around the crown, he thrust forward, wanting to feel her warm mouth engulfing him. One hand was fisted, the other he buried in her silky tresses, forcing himself not to push her down.

Breathlessly he waited to see what she would do on her own. Praying it was what his body was screaming for. He wanted to fuck her mouth so bad he could taste it.

Nicolas couldn't help glancing toward the driver, who was keeping a better eye on them than the road. Nicolas's chest expanded with the air that filled his lungs. This woman was his—all his.

To say he was not getting off from having an audience would be a bald-faced lie. But knowing what control he had over Jana was the ultimate high. He nearly lost it, his toes curling in his shoes when she took him to the back of her throat. There was nothing more beautiful than Jana's head bobbing between his legs.

He tangled both of his hands in her hair. He couldn't tear his eyes away from her as she sucked and nibbled and licked. The cheeks of his ass tightened. He could feel the draw of energy that pulled like a force of gravity when he was close to coming. It grew stronger and stronger. He held his breath. Then his vision went black. Stars burst brightly against the darkness as his seed lanced through his cock and filled Jana's precious mouth. To his surprise she sucked harder, swallowed, and continued until the last of his semen was spent.

Then she carefully tucked his cock back into his pants. Zipped and buttoned his jeans, before settling quietly beside him, staring forward as if nothing had happened.

Her cheeks were drawn tight as if she resisted the urge to smile. A sparkle twinkled in her blues eyes as she licked her lips.

There was a grin a mile wide on Manuel's face. And Nicolas's was bursting with excitement and pride. Jana had wanted to please him. So much so that she stepped out of her comfort zone and took him straight to heaven. This was one taxi ride he would never forget.

Probably one Manuel wouldn't forget soon, too.

Nothing was said as they pulled beneath the hotel's portico. The rain had stopped. The fresh clean scent surrounded them.

As they climbed out of the car, Manuel gathered one of Jana's hands into his own. He bent slightly and pressed a kiss to the back of her hand. "*Muchas gracias, señorita.*" Then the old man turned to Nicolas who started to hand him some money. Manuel shook his head, waving his hands. "*La casa paga. Que le vaya bien.*" Then he winked.

When Nicolas shrugged, unsure of what just happened, the porter holding their bags translated. "Your passage, uh...ride is on the house. And he wishes you well," he said to Nicolas.

With a jerk, Nicolas pulled her into his embrace. They began to laugh as they walked into the lobby.

Puerto Vallarta was a city brimming with joy and happiness on the surface. Desk clerks, guest service representatives and porters were all smiles as they checked Jana and Nicolas into their room and ushered them to the third floor.

The room was a suite and was okay as far as hotel rooms went, but the real beauty lay in the scenery. From the balcony they could see the ocean roll in to kiss the shore. The sunset was hidden behind a blanket of gray clouds, unlike the ones in the brochure Lisa had brought home once they'd decided to take the trip.

As Nicolas tipped the porter, Jana leaned against the railing and thought about her risqué performance in the taxi. What had come over her, she couldn't say. But the blissful look on Nicolas's face, as well as Manuel's, was worth it. Not that she would repeat that kind of performance at home. Being away in a foreign country made her feel freer—more daring.

"There's a fiesta on the beach tonight. Want to go?" Nicolas asked as he joined her. He placed his warm palms on her arms and only then did she notice the chill that had set in. With the cloud cover the temperature had dropped to the seventies, but it was the fact that her clothes were slightly damp that made it seem colder. "You need to change your clothes."

She glanced over her shoulder at him. Her eyes were bright and shiny. "A fiesta sounds wonderful. Do you think the weather will hold out?"

He turned her slowly around and drew her firmly against his chest. "If it doesn't we'll have our own fiesta right here." Then he captured her mouth.

Locked in his embrace, swept away by his caress, Jana didn't want this moment to end. Once more she found herself wanting something that belonged to Lisa.

Nicolas.

When the kiss broke, he whispered, "We don't have much time. The event begins in fifteen minutes. I'd rather take you to bed, but I don't want you to miss anything."

She pulled away and for a moment she didn't think he would let her go, but he did.

T-shirts and jeans would have been Jana's choice of attire, but for the trip she and Lisa had gone shopping. She never would have spent her money frivolously, but she didn't want to look like a poor urchin next to the exquisite appearance of her friend. So in her suitcase were sundresses, an assortment of bathing suits, various shirts and short sets, and a couple pairs of jeans because she couldn't help herself. Additionally, she had a few evening dresses for the nights.

As she rifled through her clothes, hanging some and placing others in the wardrobe drawers, Nicolas approached. "Wear something easy to get in and out of." He patted her sharply on the ass, making her jump.

Her choice was a short sundress, sandals, and a light cardigan just in case the evening became cooler. Evidently it met with Nicolas's approval as he smiled when she walked out of the bathroom.

The walk down to the beach was short. Masses of people seemed to be heading the same direction. As they approached, Jana could hear the tide rushing in. The night was alive with torches strung along the beach. Already a band played. A small Mexican woman pushed her way through the crowd. Dressed in a colorful skirt and peasant blouse, she held a big brown jug in one hand. Draped around her neck were numerous small jugs identical to the one she held. She smiled, showing a mouthful of teeth.

"*Señor y señorita.*" She placed the large jug at her feet. From her neck she extracted two small cups and looped one over Jana's head and then Nicolas's. Then she retrieved her jug and filled each cup. "Tequila. You will never be dry in Mexico."

Jana and Nicolas looked at each, tipped their cups, and slammed back the alcohol with a shudder. It was fiery hot going down, immediately warming Jana's blood.

The woman laughed as she quickly refilled their cups.

Nicolas raised his brows in question.

"Why not?" Jana said, and she sucked down the drink. Nicolas followed suit.

When she filled Jana's cup for the third time, Jana's gaze dropped down to the cup. "I don't know about this."

"Why don't we take a seat," Nicolas suggested, leading her away from the brown jug and the woman who seemed eager to get them shit-faced. Before they reached an open table with six out of eight seats vacant, he tipped his cup and dumped the tequila on the beach.

"Good idea." Jana happily emptied her cup too. "One more and the night would have been over for me."

"Don't tell me you're a lightweight?" he teased.

"No. But tequila is not a lightweight either."

As they sat down the entertainment began. Jugglers, flame eaters, dancers dressed in colorful costumes—it was a spectacular show of Mexican culture and fun. Jana found herself laughing and enjoying the company surrounding them. Two couples over the age of seventy shared the four bottles of wine Nicolas purchased.

The crack of thunder and release of Mother Nature's tears drove everyone from their seats and toward shelter. Quickly, Jana scanned the area, noting an unoccupied umbrella to their right. As she darted off a hand around her biceps halted her.

"No, this way," Nicolas said. Then the damn man proceeded to drag her further into the downpour toward the beach.

"Nicolas?" she squealed as the rain soaked her to the bone.

He smiled and that mischievous spark in his eyes flickered. "Look at it this way; we'll have the beach to ourselves."

Through a shower of rain they left the party-goers who were fleeing for shelter. When they were down the beach a distance he pulled her to a stop. "Let me take your sandals off." He reached down and grasped Jana's ankle, raising her foot and slipping off her sandal and then doing the same with the next one. He held them in one hand as he wrapped his other strong arm around her shoulders. His pace was casual, slow, as if a thousand raindrops made no difference in their stroll toward the ocean and into the darkness.

Nicolas held her tight and Jana could swear his embrace took away the damp chill, leaving her warm and feeling safe in his arms. She couldn't help snuggling closer, loving the feeling of closeness.

No one but the two of them existed at that moment.

By the time they reached the water that lapped the shoreline, the rain had eased into a drizzle. The ocean rushing in on a nearby rock caused a misty spray to rise, falling softly over them as he turned her into his arms. Sand shifted beneath their feet, water moving sensuously around their ankles.

"I want to make love to you on the beach." Nicolas's face was an array of light and dark shadows cast by the moon peeking from the clouds. "I want to bind your wrists and heart, render you helpless, while I capture your body..." he paused, "...and your soul."

With each of his words, Jana's pulse beat faster. It wasn't what he said but how he said it. There was almost an ache to his tone, as if he reached down deep to find the words he wanted to say. If she hadn't known that this was just a game between two people, she would have sworn he meant every word, felt every word from his heart.

It was silly, she knew, but she wanted it to be true—wanted to feel like she belonged to him—truly belonged to him, if only for a moment.

The first to go was her cardigan as he pushed it from her shoulders and off her arms. He tossed it aside, the waves tugging at a sleeve as if wanting to tease it further into the water. When his fingertips grazed her thighs, a tremor raced up her spine. Achingly slow, he raised her dress until he bared her body—she wasn't wearing panties or a bra. For a second she worried about being discovered, but she wanted Nicolas—now.

"Beautiful," he breathed, tossing her dress next to the cardigan and sandals. Without hesitation, he began to undress. It was a sensual striptease that had Jana's breasts heavy with desire and her nipples drawing into taut nubs of arousal. Moisture released between her thighs as he took his time to undo his khaki shorts and push them over his hips, down his legs, and then stepped out of them. From a pocket he extracted a condom and slipped it over his long, hard erection. Then he took her dress and smoothed it out over the sand.

Jana couldn't resist his masculine allure. She placed her palms on his chest, needing to feel his strength. Power and control pumped beneath her touch. Again, a nagging thought of being caught slipped into her head, but vanished quickly. A smile raised the corner of her lips. If anyone was as crazy as they were, they wouldn't be there to spy on two lovers. They'd make their own beautiful music.

Besides, she recalled the thrill she experienced knowing that the taxi driver watched as she went down on Nicolas.

Gently, Nicolas eased Jana onto her dress upon the sand, water foaming up around her feet, legs, and hips. Tiny bubbles teased and tickled as the sand shifted beneath and around her. The two shots of tequila she'd drunk earlier warmed her body. She could feel it relaxing her as he moved between her thighs, parting them further. He slipped the little brown cup from around her neck, untied the ribbon, before tossing the jug aside. Without a word he wrapped the strip of silk around her wrists and then pressed her arms above her head until her breasts rose invitingly, begging for his attention.

His touch was tender, almost tentative, as if he wanted to stretch the moment out to its fullest. Slowly, he dragged his palms down her forearms, across her biceps and then cupped her face. For seconds he simply stared at her, their eyes locked in a magical moment as the ocean sang and the rain began to lightly anoint them.

No foreplay. No warning. He simply leaned forward and, with a single thrust, drove his cock into her pussy. She arched, releasing a whimper as he moved deeper and deeper into her cradle. He was long and hard. Her body welcomed him.

As he filled her with an incredible sensation of oneness, the heavens lit up. It was a production like Jana had never seen. The electrical storm produced an orchestra of lightning that danced throughout the sky like fireworks in celebration of their joining. Being this close to the water, they should've been afraid of the storm, but nothing could have dragged her away from this precious moment.

Every stroke as he slid in and out of her body was meant to bind her closer to him—tie her to him so no man would ever be able to satisfy her.

Mine. He wanted to leave no doubt in her mind it was true.

The moonlight on her body, the way the lightning reflected off her eyes, made her look ethereal. As if he coupled with an angel instead of a mere woman.

She arched beneath him, a cry upon her lips. "*Nicolas.*"

Perfection was in the warmth that surrounded his erection. An ache began at the base, threatening to push onward. He willed himself to hold back his climax. Looping her legs into the bends of his elbows, he tilted his hips and ground against her clit, sending her back once again off the sand.

"*Ahhhh...*" She released a throaty moan. "*Ohhhh...*" And then her body clamped down on his cock with her orgasm, pulling him deeper into her cove, deeper into ecstasy.

He couldn't help the groan that ripped from his throat as sensation after sensation tore down his shaft. It took everything he had not to increase the pace, not to slam against her body. Instead he slowed his rhythm, wringing out every thrust so it was slow and sensual.

When both of them were spent, the warm water lapping at their bodies, he held her close. The thought of Lisa surfaced and he pushed it away. He had six more days to figure out how to make Jana his—all his.

Chapter Nineteen

Jana was happy walking arm in arm with Nicolas down the cobbled streets of Puerto Vallarta. This morning, Nicolas awoke her with a kiss. The sex that followed had filled her with such contentment. She sighed just thinking about the way he touched her tenderly, made her feel wanted—even loved.

It was late afternoon as they entered the outdoor restaurant situated between two three-story buildings connected by large wooden studs overhead. The arbor was draped with greenery and exotic flowers of rich reds, yellows, and blues releasing their sweet scent. Nicolas offered Jana a chair. Off in the distance, several Mexican women hand-washed their laundry in the small stream flowing across the dirt road. She watched the women at work. Quietly, Nicolas took the seat next to her, pulling the tablecloth askew as he sat. He straightened it and then turned his attention back to Jana.

It was like taking a step back to a much simpler time. She breathed in the scent of spicy Mexican food mingling with the not-so-pleasant smells of everyday life. Here people lived as they could afford. A couple of children played in the stream, splashing and laughing. There were no video games, no television, and no mall to hang out in.

Several macaws perched in the trees, flapping their vibrantly-colored wings that matched the hues of the flowers above her. Their screeches echoed over the lively music of three guitarists who floated around the restaurant entertaining the tourists.

"Are you having fun?" Nicolas asked as he placed his hand atop hers.

Jana couldn't forget Lisa's words or the fact that her friend had intentionally lied to her. "Yes, but—"

His hand slowly left hers as he sat back in his chair. "Yes, but you wish Lisa were here." Disappointment turned the corners of his mouth down.

Was she that transparent? Actually it wasn't really that. She was confused. Guilt and greed played havoc with her emotions all morning long. Lisa was pulling away. And Jana was finding it difficult to be sad about the happiness she had found with Nicolas when it was just the two of them. Each morning when she woke, Nicolas always cuddled with her, leaving Lisa off to the side alone. When they made love his attention was on her.

No wonder Lisa was beginning to pull away.

Before Jana could answer Nicolas, an elderly man holding the reins to a donkey appeared, strolling through the restaurant. There were no health inspectors to stop him. No signs that warned no animals allowed. In disbelief she watched the man and the burro climb the several flights of stairs to the building off to her left. Not once did the donkey hesitate, taking each step like he had done this a million times.

"Uh... Do you see what I see?" she asked, releasing a giggle. "Exactly what do you think he has in mind to do with that donkey?" When a mischievous smile hiked the corner of Nicolas's mouth she felt a heat of embarrassment flush across her face. "I didn't mean that." He continued to grin. "Nicolas, is sex always on your mind?"

"When I'm around you it is." His gaze fell to her low-cut halter top, caressing the swells of her breasts. The sting of arousal tightened her nipples. "Let's get out of here and I'll show you." He reached for her hand, dragging it beneath the table and placing it on the bulge between his legs. "See what you do to me?"

Thank God for the tablecloth hiding her hand.

Lust burned hot and bright in his eyes. He wanted her and the knowledge released a flood of desire. She wore no panties at Nicolas's request. When he slipped his hand beneath her skirt, easing his palm against her thigh to touch her sex, her eyes widened and her gaze darted around the room.

"You want me, too." His voice was low and hoarse as he inserted a finger and began to stroke.

"Nicolas!" She squeezed her thighs together, trapping his hand.

"I think it's time for you to address me as Milord."

"But—"

"Part your thighs, doll." She didn't make a move as his eyes narrowed and his voice firmed. "Spread your legs or you will be punished in front of all these people."

Jana didn't know what came over her, but she did as he commanded. Her heart pounded in her ears. As a waiter approached, she started to shift in her chair but a shake of Nicolas's head stilled her. He inserted another finger deep inside her, moving them at a slow rhythm in and out of her chamber.

"Are you ready to order?" the short waiter asked. He held a tablet and a pencil.

Nicolas continued to finger-fuck her as he casually addressed the waiter. "We'll start with two margaritas and we'll order after they arrive."

"*Gracias, señor. Señorita.*" He nodded and then turned to leave, but Nicolas wasn't going to let her off that easy.

"Sir, before you go." Nicolas flicked her clit and she jumped, drawing the waiter's attention. Jana fought down the heat she was sure was turning her neck and face as bright red as the birds across the way. "I noted the large baskets on the donkey's back." He pressed down on her clit and rubbed slowly.

The dark-haired man smiled. "Donkeys are still used for delivery in many parts of our city. José and Paco were probably making a grocery run for Juanita. She is blind and doesn't move too well any more."

Unconsciously, Jana's hips rose against Nicolas's hand. A flame was igniting and she was helpless to stop it.

"*Gracias.* Could you please send the musicians to our table?"

Jana was going to kill Nicolas.

"*Sí,*" the waiter said before taking his leave.

Nicolas faced her. He leaned forward and brushed a kiss across her pinched lips. "Admit it. Knowing that someone may be watching turns you on. If you lie you'll be punished."

"Yes," she murmured. *Yes. Yes. Yes.* She had never considered herself an exhibitionist, but it was damn hot having Nicolas stroke her pussy, not knowing who or when someone would notice. Fuck, the episode in the taxi had been hot, but this was even more thrilling. Another wave of desire released in his hand.

"Yes?" he asked.

"Yes, Milord," she corrected. As the walls of her cervix began to spasm he stilled his fingers, but left his hand cupping her. She shot him an agitated look and he returned it with a grin, as the musicians approached, strumming their guitars and singing a song in Spanish she had never heard before. The harmony of their voices, their passionate expressions told her it was a love song. It was like a sedative relaxing her. In fact she almost forgot about what was laying between her legs, except Nicolas took that moment to rekindle the fire.

The song ended. She clapped, thinking that when Nicolas did the same she'd lock her legs together at the knees. Instead he reached in his shorts pocket with his free hand and gave the taller of the musicians a five dollar tip, all the while pushing his fingers in and out of her hot, moist core.

The musicians played yet another song as Nicolas's and Jana's drinks were delivered. They placed their order while the donkey and man descended the stairs. Again the pair passed through the restaurant and disappeared around the corner.

Twice more Nicolas brought her close to climax then stopped, forcing her to ease back down without fulfillment. He was teasing her unmercifully. Jana could swear that the man two tables away who kept looking at her knew what Nicolas was doing. Funny thing was that it didn't matter. All she cared about was reaching an orgasm and soon.

As the waiter placed their cheese enchiladas before them, Nicolas pinched her clit, hard. She barely had time to muffle her cry as waves of ecstasy washed over her. Nicolas continued to stroke her slit, flick her clit as ripples of pleasure coursed through her. Fingers clutching the table, she gritted her teeth and tried to quiet the tremor that overtook her. It was the hardest thing she'd ever done. But it was also the most delicious thing she'd ever done.

Lunch finished, the waiter quietly removed the dishes from the table. Jana's scent lingered in the air. The subtle aroma bewitched Nicolas, threatening to tie him closer to her. Elbow on the table, he propped his chin on his palm and watched her laugh as several of the children wading in a stream began to play tag. Her eyes sparkled as a young mother held her baby to her face and smothered the infant with kisses.

Personally, Nicolas had never thought about children, but observing Jana, seeing how her face lit up while watching the kids, made him wonder if there was another part of life that he had overlooked. If they had a daughter together would she have Jana's dark red hair, or his mother's wavy ebony hair? Would a son take after him or would Jana's unknown past bring forth a surprise? He chuckled silently with his wanderings.

Then he rose from his seat and grasped her by the hand and tugged. "Come on, I want to buy you something."

She came to her feet, responding as he knew she would. "But, I don't need anything."

He pulled her into his arms and kissed her solidly on the lips. "Sometimes you just buy something for the hell of it, Jana. It doesn't have to serve a need—it serves a want. And I want to buy you something."

She shook her head as if saying, "Frivolous."

Nicolas threw down a handful of Mexican pesos, an equivalent of thirty US dollars to cover the check and tip and they were on their way.

Every street was lined with vendors. People from all over the world were haggling for a better deal. A hand-carved chess set caught Nicolas's eye and he tugged her toward the booth. There was a gray-haired woman in her mid-sixties counting out her money.

"Many of the crafts available here are made by local Indians," the woman explained. "Did you know that these chess sets and many of the other gifts from Puerto Vallarta are produced by using the same methods they've had for hundreds of years?"

"I didn't realize that," Jana said. Her gaze widened at the numerous selections.

The woman purchasing the chess set smiled, her eagle eye watching the salesman wrap her choice in paper and place each piece into a box. "I'm here with my daughter from California. The chess set is for my husband."

Jana scanned the store taking in the many wood carvings along the wall. "It's a lovely gift. I'm sure he will enjoy it."

"Are you buying one?" She accepted the now-sealed box the salesman handed her.

"Uh... Are you buying one?" Jana turned to Nicolas.

"Why not? Which one do you want?" he asked.

"I don't play chess," she responded.

He cocked a brow. "I do. I play chest *all* the time." His play on words was not lost on Jana or the older woman, who blushed prettily and then quickly said her good-byes. When the lady was out of sight, Jana's hand came out and playfully popped Nicolas on the arm.

He flinched, and then winked at her.

"That wasn't funny," she growled, even though her eyes danced with laughter.

"She thought it was." He grinned.

Jana shook her head.

"In fact, I'm in the mood for chest right now." He grasped her hand and they were off again, but this time he knew exactly where they were going. He had seen an alley around a couple of buildings and down the street. He was still hot and horny from finger-fucking Jana in public. His erection felt like it was about to burst, pressing against his shorts.

"Where are we going?" Jana stumbled as a cart pulled by a donkey caught her eye. He slowed his pace.

"I have to feel you around my cock or I'm going to explode."

"What?" Her eyes widened and she tugged on his hand.

"I'm going to fuck you in the next couple of minutes even if I have to throw you on the ground in the middle of a crowd."

Panic, or perhaps disbelief, spread across her face. "You're kidding." He raised a brow. "You're not. Okay." She quickly scanned the area. "Alley?"

"Alley," he agreed.

It wasn't the most romantic place. Garbage littered the ground and the smell had Jana wrinkling her nose. Nicolas was hurting, his cock pressing painfully against its constraints. He pulled her into a walled alcove and pressed her back against the brick building, his mouth finding hers.

Jana reached for his khaki shorts, popping the button loose. His zipper hissed on its descent. His aching erection pushed into her palms and she began to fondle him.

"No. I need to be inside you." He bit her earlobe. "Are you ready for me, doll? Wet? Hot? Horny?"

"Yes." She pushed down his shorts just below his butt cheeks and threw her arms around his neck.

He grabbed her ass and lifted her up. "Wrap your legs around me." She didn't hesitate. As she did, he slipped his cock into her pussy. "Shit. Jana, you're so hot." He thrust his hips once, twice. "So. Fucking. Hot." He pulled her down hard on him eliciting a whimper from her lips. "I'll never get enough of you."

She went wild in his arms, even biting his neck as he moved in and out of her slit. "Fuck me hard, Nicolas," she purred and he nearly lost it right there. Clenching his jaw, he tried to breathe, tried to hold on. But, when she said, "Oh, God," he exploded. Hot sensation shot down his shaft, filling her with his seed. Her orgasm clamped down around him and began to milk him, wringing out every spasm, until he felt weak in the knees and spent.

Her next words were, "Oh, shit!"

He nuzzled her neck loving the smell of sweet perfume on her skin. "What?" he murmured, relaxed and sated and wrapped in her arms.

"Tell me you're wearing a condom."

He froze. How the hell did he forget the condom? There were four of them in his pocket, but there wasn't one on his cock.

She went rigid in his arms, her legs unlocking from around him as her feet hit the ground. "Oh shit!" she repeated, but this time there was panic in her tone.

When he stepped away from Jana her eyes were closed. She leaned against the building as if she would fall if not for its support. Then she put her fingertips on her forehead. "It was just one time. What are the odds?"

Was she trying to convince him or herself? Clearly he had fucked up. "Jana?"

"Don't say it." She opened her misty eyes. "Just don't say it. I've heard enough sorrys to last me a lifetime." She rolled her eyes skyward. "It was as much my fault as yours." She took a deep weighted breath. "What are the odds? Right?" She pulled her skirt down around her thighs.

"Right," he said. *Fifty-fifty*, he voiced silently, drawing his shorts up and zipping them. For some reason he didn't feel scared, nor guilty. If she became pregnant with his child they would get married.

It was as simple as that.

Perhaps his problem of tying her to him had just been solved.

Chapter Twenty

Evening came and stars graced the heavens like tiny specks of light scattered about. Jana felt as if she were floating in a dream world, the ocean singing a soft lullaby to lull her further into her fantasy. Hand in hand, she and Nicolas walked on the beach, soft sand squishing between her toes as the tide swirled around her ankles. They had left their sandals and a blanket further up the beach beneath a palm tree.

It was a perfect ending to a perfect week that had gone by much too quickly. Tomorrow they would return to Arizona and the rat race of the real world. The intrusive thought morphed her happiness into a sudden melancholy, forcing a heavy breath from her lungs.

"Something wrong?" Nicolas asked, looking down at her.

"No," she lied, refusing to meet his eyes. "It's just so beautiful...so peaceful. I hate to leave." Honesty hung in her last words. Many things had been missing from her life, serenity being one of them. She had no idea that such peacefulness existed, until now. From the corner of her eye, she glanced at Nicolas. Emotion squeezed her chest. "Thank you."

He pulled her to a stop, stepping in front of her. Strong, warm hands cupped her face. He stared into her eyes before leaning in to brush a feather-light kiss upon her lips. "No. Thank you." His palms moved to stroke up and down her arms.

"It's been years since I've taken a vacation and I can't think of anyone I'd rather spend my time with than you."

How Jana wished that were true. Lisa hadn't found a replacement. Nicolas had been stuck with her all week long. She turned in his arms, his length spooning her back as she gazed out over the water. Shadows and moonlight bounced across the surface. The slight scent of fish and salt mingled in the air. In the distance muted music played and laughter rose.

"I guess a family-owned business poses more difficulties than most jobs?"

His arms tightened around her as he laid his cheek against hers. "Yeah. Trying to keep things running can be challenging. But I love to cook. It's in my blood." His fondness expressed a passion beyond her comprehension.

What would it feel like to care about something as he did? She wondered.

"Did your mother teach you to cook?"

"Grandmother and mother. I always seemed to be drawn to the kitchen. Mom said, 'The kitchen is the heartbeat of a family.' Most decisions in our family were made around a big pot of spaghetti sauce and, of course, freshly baked garlic bread." Every time Nicolas spoke of his mother his features softened, and there was an inherent quality in his voice. Love.

"I wouldn't know anything about family."

Nicolas spun her around, holding her so he could gaze into her eyes. "Those days are gone."

A snort pushed from her lips. "Those days never existed, Nicolas."

Jana pulled from his arms and strolled deeper into the water, allowing it to splash up her legs and dampen the hem of her jeans shorts. A cool breeze off the water caressed her belly, exposed by her crop-top shirt.

"I'm sorry."

She turned sharply facing him. "Don't be." Her tone dropped, harsher than she had intended. "You can't miss something you've never had."

Who was she kidding?

But strangely, somewhere between the time she arrived in Arizona and this moment her past *had* taken a backseat to her future.

She wanted to laugh aloud. Who would have thought that Jana Ryan would actually be thinking of a *real* future?

"Jana—"

"Nicolas, don't you see? I may not have been born to a family, or inherited one through a foster home, but I can make one of my own. Marriage. Children."

Holy shit! Is that me talking? Damned if Dr. Tate wasn't right. *The world is at my fingertips.* She could make her life anything she wanted—well, almost anything.

Water slapped against Nicolas's legs, never touching the hem of his khaki shorts as he moved toward her. Gently he placed a finger beneath her chin, lifting until their eyes met. The black silk shirt he wore made him almost fade into the night.

"Is that what you want, doll? Marriage? Children?" he asked.

She couldn't read his expression in the dim moonlight, and it wasn't important. She knew he didn't want the same things she did. The triangle between Lisa and them was proof.

"Yes." Her response was breathless, knowing that each word would wedge between them. Drive Nicolas away. But she didn't hold back. There was no future between them—there couldn't be. "Yes. I do want those things. I want a man to love me and children to hold in my arms and protect."

And she wanted one last night with Nicolas. When they returned home her new life would truly begin—a life without Nicolas Marchetti. The thought was bittersweet.

His hand dropped from beneath her chin. Her gaze followed the nervous bounce of his Adam's apple as he swallowed. "What if you're already pregnant?"

Oh. My. God. He's right. Jana's pulse sped. Did Nicolas worry she would try to trap him in a relationship? She stared at him a moment longer, expecting to see an expression of accusation or regret.

And what would Lisa say?

It took every ounce of strength Jana had to dismiss his comment as if it were insignificant. "I'm not worried about it." Truth was, until now she had never imagined herself being a parent, much less a single parent. The idea of a life growing inside her sent a shiver up her back.

Nicolas's baby.

"Are you cold?" he asked, pulling her into his arms.

"A little." She buried her face in his shoulder and inhaled his masculine scent. He smelled good. In his arms she felt safe, something she hadn't experienced in so long. She couldn't bear the thought that this was their last night together.

"Jana, if you're pregnant—"

"I'm not." She didn't want to hear him make a promise he couldn't keep. "Don't worry about it."

"But—"

Jana captured Nicolas's objection in a kiss he could only describe as hungry. Arms wrapped tightly around his neck, she held him close as she devoured his mouth. Without hesitation he swept her up into his arms and blindly moved up the beach where their sandals were and a blanket was spread.

Their kiss broke briefly as he laid her upon the soft blanket and then followed her down, lying beside her. Her chest rose and fell, the gentle swells of her breasts peeking beneath her shirt. With a brush of his hand, he eased the material up, baring her globes.

"Beautiful," he whispered, before dipping his head and drawing her nipple into his warm, wet mouth. Her back came off the ground as she arched into his touch, weaving her fingers through his hair to hold him to her chest. The diamond-hard bud slid over his tongue as he teased, suckled, and then bit, scraping his teeth across the sensitive skin.

She gasped. "*Nicolas.*" His name was breathless upon her lips. "Fuck me. Make me remember tonight, forever." There was something desperate in her request. But he didn't have time to analyze it as her delicate fingers slipped beneath his shorts and briefs, cupping his balls and massaging tenderly.

As he moved from one nipple to the next, he quickly pulled her shirt over her head and tossed it aside. His hips undulated against her hand.

"I want you naked," she moaned, extracting her hand to fumble with the button of his shorts.

She didn't have to ask twice. He released his hold on her breast, and then jerked his T-shirt over his head. In seconds he was relieved of his clothing. The only thing left was to make her equally naked. She was already a step ahead of him as her hips rose, and she forced the offensive material down and off her legs.

There was nothing as exquisite as her dark silhouette framed by the gray moon and billowy ocean. When had he gotten so lucky to have met a woman like Jana?

He rolled to his back. "Ride me, doll. I want to watch you fuck me."

Like a cat she crawled toward him, slinky and sexy. When she straddled him, easing her wet slit across his engorged cock his pulse quickened. Instead of taking him deep, she rocked her hips anointing him with her slick juices.

Nicolas grasped her hips, moving her faster, harder, against him. "Doll, you feel so good." Then she leaned forward, tilted her hips and before he knew it he was buried deep inside her warm body. A deep throaty groan slid from between his clenched teeth. "You're so wet. Tight."

He raised her hips until only the crown of his cock parted her folds, then he eased her down, watching himself disappear into her depths. Over and over, he rivaled at how she fit him perfectly.

Her rhythm broke and she stilled, placing her palms against his chest. "Nicolas?"

"Yes?" he moaned low.

Breathing labored, she said, "Condom."

"Shit!" His eyelids slid closed. He'd almost done it again. Was it subconscious? Did he want to tie Jana to him no matter the cost?

As she slid off him, he reached for his shorts and extracted a foil package.

"Here let me do it." She took the package from him. Put a corner of it in her mouth and ripped it open, and extracted the thin protective sheath. Cool and wet, she slid the rubber over his throbbing cock.

Damn he hated the barrier between them. Frustrated, he guided Jana upon her back, and with a single thrust, parted her folds. As she reached for him, he caught her wrists and pinned them above her head.

Then he fucked her hard and fast, pounding between her thighs.

"Yes," she cried out. "Harder."

His nostrils flared. Blood rushed to his testicles, drawing them tight against his body. There was no way he could stop his climax as it thundered down his shaft and exploded.

Jana cried out. Her pussy contracted and clenched around him, holding him tightly. She writhed beneath him, whimpering as spasm after spasm continued to milk him. After his release, the tip of his cock always became sensitive, so sensitive that every movement she made drove him closer to the point where pleasure and pain met. He needed her to stop squirming—prayed she wouldn't.

When Jana lay quietly beneath him, he rolled over and pulled her into his embrace. The blissful sigh she released made him smile. But his happiness was short-lived.

The night was slipping away much too quickly. Tomorrow when they woke, their time together would be over. The reality of their situation waited for them in Arizona.

After this week there was no way he could go on hiding his feelings for Jana. He cared deeply for Lisa, but Jana held his heart in her hands. Jana was the woman he wanted to spend the rest of his life with.

The bond between the women was strong, stronger with the physical intimacy they now shared. The question of the day was whether Jana's desire for marriage and family was stronger than her need for Lisa. And would he lose Jana if he gave her an ultimatum to choose between him and Lisa?

Chapter Twenty-One

As the hundred-degree weather in Phoenix, Arizona blazed across Jana's face, she felt a flood of disappointment. Life went on and her brief escape from reality was over. Watching Nicolas loading their luggage into the back of his truck, she thought of Lisa. It was one excuse after another why her friend couldn't or wouldn't join them in Puerto Vallarta. The last time Jana had called her there had been no answer and it had been nearly midnight.

A moment of optimism surfaced. Maybe Lisa had found another man. Maybe there was a chance for Nicolas and Jana to become a couple. But as quickly as the idea rose, it vanished.

Who was she kidding?

What woman in her right mind would give up Nicolas? Not to mention, what man would take one woman when he could have two in his bed?

Jana couldn't push away the additional feelings she had developed over the last week for Nicolas. He had opened up something in her she had never known existed—the need for a man in her life. She needed to feel loved and wanted. And she wanted more than ever for that man to be Nicolas.

"Glad to be home?" Nicolas asked as he held open the truck door. Unlike when they departed for Old Mexico, the airport's parking garage was nearly empty. Yet, the smell of oil and gas was strong.

No. Staying in Puerta Vallarta with Nicolas would have been her first choice. Still, she placed a false smile on her face and looked into his eyes. "Yes."

He drew her into his embrace, an expression of hope on his face. "I'm not buying that. Tell me to take you away and we'll jump on another plane to anywhere in the world you want to go. Tell me that you love me and I'll never let you go." He squeezed her tight. There was an ache in his voice, something she had never heard before.

Jana's heart lurched against her ribcage with a thud.

If only that were true.

Her emotions were too raw to take his teasing banter as a joke. Yet, she shored up her shoulders, giggled and playfully pushed out of his arms. "Get serious, Nicolas. We both have to be at work next week. Besides, what about Lisa?"

His soft expression hardened. He moved aside and allowed her to climb inside the truck. The slamming of the door startled her and she jumped. When Nicolas crawled in beside her, he was frowning.

The silent ride to Lisa's house set Jana on edge. Nicolas never once glanced her way. She knew because she would have caught him as her gaze continued to stray in his direction. He acted mad. Surely he was just kidding when he offered to take her away again. When he asked her to tell him she loved him.

Love? What did she know about love anyway?

As they pulled down Lisa's street Jana's old home came into view. The sadness and fear it usually conjured didn't appear. She felt stronger. Nicolas and Lisa had given her that gift. She now had the strength to face her·demons and to realize that the past was just that—the past. Their support had helped get her to this point. Her foster father could never hurt her again.

Jana's gaze slipped further down the street toward Lisa's house. There was a strange car parked in the drive. For a moment Jana panicked, wondering what to do.

What if Lisa had a man in her bed?

Then she saw Cathy, Lisa's mother, exit the house, Joe following behind her. A ray of happiness filtered through Jana. She hadn't seen them for five years.

Their heads were low as Joe opened the passenger door to the Cadillac and stepped aside, allowing Cathy to get in. Nicolas pulled his truck beside them. Instead of the shared happiness Jana felt for seeing them again, they glanced nervously toward each other with dread in their eyes.

Jana couldn't help bounding from the truck, not waiting for Nicolas, and throwing herself in Joe's arms.

"Jana." Lisa's father had aged significantly since Jana last saw him. With an iron-tight grip, he wrapped his arms around her. "*Jana*," he repeated and she thought she heard a tear in his voice.

He had missed her. Her mood lifted as if she floated on a cloud.

Cathy climbed out of the car and the first thing Jana noticed was that she'd been crying. Her swollen eyes and pink nose were a dead giveaway.

Jana eased out of Joe's embrace. "What's wrong? Where's Lisa?" The big man turned away from her, refusing to look her in the eyes.

Cathy swallowed hard.

The safe, secure shell that Jana had felt only seconds ago began to crack. It rang in her ears and she could almost feel it shattering around her feet.

The sad expression on Cathy's face made something twist in Jana's belly. "Is Lisa okay?" she whispered the words, afraid of the answer.

Cathy came to her arms opened wide. "Jana, dear." But before she reached Jana, a river of tears began to fall. Her body shook as she held Jana as tightly as Joe had. "Lisa is in the hospital," Cathy choked.

Jana's grip tightened. Her knees felt rubbery. She was afraid she would fall if it wasn't for Cathy's hold.

"Hospital?" Fear stuck in Jana's throat as they parted. "What happened?"

A sorrowful expression etched wrinkles deeper into Cathy's forehead. Her tongue flicked out over her dry lips. "She asked us not to say anything. She wants to tell you herself. She's expecting you."

Jana's hand gripped Cathy's arm. "No. Tell me now. What's wrong? Is she okay?"

From behind her Nicolas's arms snaked around her waist. His warmth as he pulled her back to his chest did nothing to chase away the cold that drove straight to her bones.

"Release her, Jana." When she didn't comply he pried her fingers off of Cathy's arm, which now sported Jana's fingerprints. "I'll take you to the hospital. Which one?" he asked.

"Banner Desert Samaritan Hospital off of Dobson," Joe replied, as he took his now sobbing wife into his arms. "We'll follow shortly." He cradled Cathy and began to stroke her head buried against his shoulder. "Hush, sweetheart. Hush."

"Jana?" Jana heard Nicolas say her name. There was no use in responding, because she couldn't. It was as if her body and mind had begun to shut down to survival mode. She knew the feeling well, but this time she felt completely alone.

Like a zombie Jana allowed Nicolas to lead her to the truck. The bewildered and lost look on her face squeezed his heart. She was afraid for Lisa, as he was, and there was nothing he could do.

Lisa's parents were devastated. Something was clearly wrong. But if Lisa could talk, if she was conscious, then it couldn't be all that bad. Could it?

His truck purred to life. He shifted into gear and headed back toward town.

Miles were left behind as Jana leaned against the truck door and turned her head to stare out the window. She was eerily silent and strangely apathetic, at least on the exterior. She was a hard woman to understand.

No outburst.

No tears.

He glanced in her direction. Had he ever once seen her cry? No. Her eyes had misted on occasion, but never tears. Never a loss of control.

This can't be good, he told himself. His mother once told him that tears were a woman's release. The key to what was important to them. They signaled joy as well as pain and agony.

The only movement that showed any sign of nervousness was when she flexed her fingers and then drew them into a tight fist. Then he could see tension gather along the tendons in her arms, up her neck, and her jaw.

As they pulled into a parking space at the hospital she turned to look at him, opened her mouth as if to speak, and then shut it and glanced away. He turned off the engine and expected her to spring from the truck. Instead she remained motionless staring straight ahead.

"I can't do this," she mumbled.

After climbing out of the vehicle, he moved around the truck and opened her door. He stood quietly and waited.

"I can't," she whispered so softly he barely heard her.

"Whatever is going on, Jana, I'm sure Lisa needs you." He paused. "And you need her." His hand reached out to her. "Let's go inside."

Jana tugged her brows together, as if thinking hard about refusing him. Then she placed her hand in his. He pulled her into the shelter of his body, while she clutched her palms tightly together and remained quiet.

Even when they stopped at the information desk and discovered that Lisa was located in the hospice wing of the hospital she remained quiet.

Hospice? A chill raced up his spine. That could mean only one thing and it wasn't good. Hospice handled only terminally ill patients. He glanced at Jana. Had she made the connection?

The elevator ride to the fourth floor was solemn. When the doors opened, nausea washed over him and for a moment he thought he'd be sick.

Only the terminally ill resided on this floor—no recovery— no hope was in this wing of the hospital.

It was probably just his imagination, but it smelled of death as they exited the elevator.

Room 420 was to the right and the door was closed. When he placed his hand on the doorknob, he looked down at Jana. She'd grown pale and her chest rose and fell rapidly.

A door had never looked more ominous than the one before Jana. She was afraid to touch it, afraid to walk onward as Nicolas opened it. But more importantly she was afraid not to.

Holding her breath, she took one step and then another until she was inside. Lisa's blonde head was turned away, but when she heard their footsteps she rolled over to face them.

"How was Mexico?" Lisa smiled, but it didn't reach her eyes. She looked weary, troubled, but not exactly how Jana had expected. There was no oxygen mask, no intravenous tubes. Lisa just lay there wrapped in her silky pink lingerie, a white sheet and blanket pulled up to her waist.

Jana wanted to scream, *How was Mexico?* But she stood silently, waiting—just waiting.

It was Nicolas who spoke next, "Boy, did you miss a wonderful trip." As if everything were normal, he approached Lisa, leaned over her and pressed his lips to hers. Then he cupped her hand in his. "What's going on here, baby?" He sat down at her side, the bed creaking beneath his weight.

Nicolas looked calm, so in control that Jana would have given anything just to have an ounce of his courage at that moment, because she had none. She didn't want to know what was going on. She just wanted to take Lisa home. Wanted to pretend her best friend wasn't lying in a hospital bed. And she wanted to forget what she knew about hospice.

"Jana." Lisa patted the bed on the other side of her.

As if lead suddenly filled her legs, Jana found it difficult to move. Every step was an ordeal, coupled with her breathing, which had taken that moment to stop. Jana felt like she might faint.

Lisa held out her hand and Jana accepted it, sitting on the other side of the bed from Nicolas. "What a homecoming." Her friend's laugh was uneasy. Moisture built in her eyes and for a moment Jana thought Lisa would cry, but she swallowed and pushed back the unshed tears. She took a deep breath and said, "I have ovarian cancer."

Silence followed her statement.

Jana couldn't think clearly. Had Lisa just said she had cancer?

Nicolas brushed a lock of hair from Lisa's face.

Lisa bit her bottom lip. With a gasp, she inhaled a shaky breath. "I've known for a while. But it looks like time is running out for me."

This wasn't happening. Jana refused to accept what she was hearing. Her friend was sick—terminally ill.

Nicolas slowly rose to his feet. "Lisa, what are you saying?"

For a moment she simply looked at him, then she looked away. "I'm dying." Lisa's words were surreal.

Jana jerked her head from side to side, trying to chase away the threads of fog that wound around her mind like tentacles. It wasn't real. She closed her eyes and prayed that when she opened them this would all be a hallucination.

Lisa's voice then Nicolas's, but Jana couldn't hear what they said, their speech mere mumbles to her. When she opened her eyes, Nicolas's lips parted, but he said nothing.

Lisa seemed to know what Nicolas's next question would be. "I'm in the last stage. Soon." Lisa sniffled and rubbed her nose. She fought to hold back the tears, blinking her eyes and swallowing hard, but it was no use. They fell, releasing the hopelessness Jana felt as she jerked to her feet.

"No," Jana's knees buckled slightly, but she regained her footing as she began to pace. "No. No. No." She trembled as her voice rose in pitch. "We'll find another doctor." The room began to spin. She held out her hands to catch herself, and then drew them tightly around her.

Any moment she'd wake beside Nicolas and they would be back in Mexico, waiting for Lisa to join them. This couldn't be real.

Lisa said she would never leave me.

Lisa tried to smile through her emotion. "That's why I didn't go to Puerto Vallarta with you two. Mom and Dad took me to another specialist." She tilted her head and shrugged. "He was my last chance." Sucking in her bottom lip, she bit down hard enough to leave an imprint when she released it. "He can't do anything for me. No one can." Tears fell in streams. A none-too-delicate snort slipped out as she tried to rein in her control. "My head hurts all the time now. I'm forgetting things, my equilibrium is gone, and my mood swings are increasing." The low-toned laugh she released was drowned by her emotion. She swallowed hard again, the tears still flowing. "Morphine is the only thing that curbed the pain these last few days."

Jana held up her hand. She didn't want to hear any more. The need to flee was strong, building like an undercurrent, demanding that she run far and away like she had after graduation. She spun around, staring at the door as if it were beckoning her. Before she could lunge forward she was wrapped in Nicolas's embrace.

She struggled, making whimpering sounds that made him hold her tighter. Her breasts rose rapidly with each tight breath.

"Let me go."

"Lisa needs you now. Hold it together," he whispered close to her ear.

Damn Nicolas for reminding her that Lisa was the victim here. Lisa was the one dying, although it felt like Jana was withering inside.

"You can do this. We'll do it together. You...Lisa...and me," he promised, releasing her. She gazed into his eyes, wanting to believe him, needing to trust him that her world wasn't falling apart. But despair like she had never known closed in on her, attacking, an invisible force that dropped her to her knees.

She gasped, but she couldn't inhale—couldn't breathe.

The thrumming in her ears grew louder.

The lights were dimming, fading.

No sounds penetrated.

All feelings and sensations were going numb.

She was falling...

As she slipped deeper, Jana was surrounded by a nothingness that threatened to swallow her up. She didn't have the strength to fight it. Instead, she welcomed it.

Take me.

There was a peace she had never known, a vacuum that carried her further away.

From somewhere in the dark she heard her name. It was only a whisper, but it pulled at her like a magnet, drawing her toward a light in the opposite direction.

"Jana." The deep voice was firm, demanding her obedience, but she fought it. She didn't want to go where it led.

For the first time in her life it was safe here in the dark.

For a moment she stared at the light. It was cold and held pain and loneliness.

"Jana." This time the voice was feminine—softer and desperate to be heard, pleading to draw her back into the light.

As the two voices joined together, interweaving and wrapping around her like chains, they took a unified front, closing in on Jana and taking away her ability to struggle, her ability to escape.

A strong ammonia smell jerked her toward the light as if it ripped her through time and space. Sensations and consciousness flooded back in a wave of nausea that hit with such an impact for a moment Jana thought she would vomit.

Like a fish out of water she gasped for air, trying to suck oxygen into her starved lungs as fast as possible, only to hear voices telling her to slow down—take it easy.

Her body ached. Her vision was a shimmer of light and dark shadows as familiar faces came into focus.

Nicolas cradled her in his embrace. Cathy, Joe and a nurse she had never seen before hovered above. From the bed where Lisa lay, her tear-streaked face appeared ragged with concern.

"She's back," Jana heard the nurse say.

Chapter Twenty-Two

Night had fallen and the hospital room was dark. Nicolas shifted in his chair beside Lisa's bed. Her form lay silently between a mass of sheets and blankets, her breathing so shallow it was almost unrecognizable. The morphine had put her out like a light. Had it been four hours ago? After Jana's episode, Lisa had had one of her own.

Her pain and agony had taken his breath away, left him feeling helpless as the memory resurfaced of how she had grabbed her head and thrashed upon the bed. He pinched his nose to hold back the emotion that slammed against his eyelids. God, he had never seen anyone in such pain. It twisted the beauty from her face. Thank God, she was in only a moment of distress, before the nurse quickly relieved Lisa's suffering with a shot of morphine. But it had been long enough to clear Jana's mind and let her know Lisa needed her.

Jana's own anguish would have to wait.

As well as his own.

He inhaled deeply and caught a hint of the medicinal smell common in hospitals, more predominant in the wings of the institution where patients were receiving medicines and other attention. Lisa had requested no care to prolong her life—just something to ease the pain—morphine. The brave woman wanted to die with her pride intact.

Memories of his mother surfaced. The situation with Lisa was opening up old wounds. Only a year ago he had lost his mother. Would she be proud of him for what he had accomplished with the restaurant? Or ashamed of the triangle affair he was involved in? The thought brought him back to Jana.

Nicolas had been thankful when Jana had finally fallen asleep on the green vinyl recliner sitting in the corner. He couldn't stand the hollow, drawn look in her eyes. Empty. Lost.

She groaned and shifted, crying out Lisa's name.

He ran his trembling fingers through his hair then glanced across the room in Lisa's direction. He had tried to take Jana home but she wouldn't leave Lisa's side. Besides, Cathy and Joe were staying at the house and Jana said that she would feel awkward going back there. She couldn't bear watching Lisa's parents' sorrow, she'd told him. Cathy and Joe were losing their only child and it was tearing them up inside.

Nicolas stood and stretched. Every muscle, every tendon drawn tight. When had he lost control of the situation, or had he ever really had control? He was the strong one. Yet at the moment he felt anything but strong.

Lisa was dying.

Jana would be lost without her.

Uneasiness prickled and tightened his skin, spreading rapidly across his arms. The sensation made him feel trapped within his own flesh.

He could lose them both.

The realization made his breath catch. With each second that ticked, he felt a cramp in his chest that made breathing difficult. He covered his face with his hands, fingertips pressing against the ache behind his eyelids.

Nicolas willed himself to pull it together. He pinched the bridge of his nose. Lisa and Jana needed him. His eyes opened.

Through a part in the curtains he saw the moon's reflection. He stood and walked over to the window, looking toward the heavens and wondering what the future held.

Mexico seemed like only a dream. The past two months he had spent with Lisa even more distant.

"*Nicolas*," Jana whimpered in her sleep.

He turned and gazed at the woman he had fallen in love with, and then toward Lisa, the catalyst who had brought them together. Lisa had been the lodestone in the triangle. She had been the core of their relationship.

For a moment he selfishly wondered if what Jana and he had built between them was strong enough to withstand the loss of their anchor.

Lisa.

His footsteps were lethargic as he moved toward the bed. He leaned over and gently kissed Lisa's cheek, feeling her warmth. She smelled different. Not able to put his finger on it, he pushed the thought aside. In a slow motion he drew his knuckles along her jaw line tracing the contour of her face, memorizing the wrinkle in her nose when she smiled, the laughter in her brown eyes when she was happy.

A void filled him as he released a heavy sigh that rattled through his body. He was going to miss her touch, her kiss and her effervescent personality. Her death would be like snuffing out the brilliant spark of a flame.

Unconsciously his fingertips smoothed down her arm, cupping her hand and bringing it to his cheek.

Jana watched in silence Nicolas's tenderness as he caressed Lisa while she slept. No matter how hard Lisa and Nicolas had pretended their relationship was only physical, obviously it wasn't. He cared for her deeply. It was in the softness of his lips against her skin. His hand smoothed lightly across her, he appeared as if he were worshipping her with his touch. The room was dim, but if she could have seen his face—his eyes, she knew there would be love.

She looked away. The precious moment wasn't meant for anyone else's eyes.

Emotion rose in her throat, sour and raw, threatening to choke her. She swallowed hard, fighting it down.

She was losing her best friend. Someone she loved more than life itself.

As the third wheel, Jana had stolen valuable time away from Lisa and Nicolas. But she would never regret what she had found with them. She had never felt so loved and a part of something beautiful when she was with them. She would always be thankful for the strength they had given her to face her demons.

But how she was going to live without Lisa, she had no idea.

Lying in the dark, nothing seemed real. Several feet away were the two most important people in her life. She didn't know exactly when Nicolas had become just as important to her as Lisa, but her feelings were strong for him.

She trusted him.

She heard Nicolas's footsteps walk away from the bed. She glanced in his direction, their gazes meeting.

"You're awake," he said as he began to approach her.

She nodded, watching the shadows flicker across his handsome features.

Without a word he came to her, extended his hand and helped her to her feet. Immediately, she was pulled into his arms. He held her tightly, almost to the point of restricting her breathing as her ribs pressed against her lungs.

His actions touched her and she couldn't help but respond by wrapping her arms around him. For what seemed like forever they stood in the silence and just held each other, taking what comfort each offered.

Then Lisa moaned and they drifted apart, moving toward the bed as if drawn by an invisible force.

Lisa's eyes were heavy, her eyelids slightly shuttered. She tried to swallow, but seemed unable to complete the task as if it were monumental. Both of her hands rose an inch off the bed, and then dropped. Jana and Nicolas parted, each taking a different side of the bed to be near her and to cup her hands in theirs.

"I—" The word simply disappeared from Lisa's parched lips. Moisture swelled in the corner of her eyes. One tear rolled down her cheek, landing upon the bed. "—love you..."

She took one last ragged breath. As she exhaled, Jana felt Lisa's body shake.

And then she slipped away.

Lisa was gone.

Chapter Twenty-Three

Slowly, Jana pulled her car into the median, awaiting a left turn. A beat-up truck zoomed by way too close, the gust of air rocking her vehicle and giving her a claustrophobic feeling. From the other direction a van passed, continuing the sway and tossing her about. It was surreal. Almost as if she weren't surrounded by tons of metal, but instead a feather on the wind being whipped from one side to the next, bending to the unforeseen force. The sense of security she should have felt behind the wheel just wasn't there.

She felt raw and exposed.

A rush of anger flooded across her face, clearing her head. She clenched the steering wheel.

You said you'd never leave me. She struck the steering wheel hard with the palm of her hands. *Damn you for lying. Damn you for dying.*

A horn blaring made Jana startle. She'd pushed on the gas pedal without even looking both ways as she'd pulled into traffic, barely dodging an oncoming car. When she was safely across the street she drove slowly toward the cemetery.

Lisa's parents were waiting for Jana at the house, but she hadn't been able to go back—not just yet.

After the funeral today, Jana had slipped away, alone. She drove around for a while, but she ended up in the same place as before. The cemetery. She parked her car and got out. There were a few people lingering around other graves. They didn't pay her any heed, wrapped in their own grief and sorrow.

A breeze sent her auburn hair flowing around her face. The wind carried a heavy scent of flowers, Lisa's flowers.

"Lisa," Jana whispered, looking at the pile of flowers heaped upon the fresh mound of dirt. It was selfish to want her friend back, but there you have it. Jana was selfish.

It was the knowledge that she would never see Lisa's face, hear the laughter in her voice, or feel her soft touch, that was tearing Jana up inside. She pressed her palm to her mouth.

She wouldn't cry.

Not knowing how long she stood there alone, Jana was startled when a gentle hand touched her shoulder. Before he even slid his arm around her shoulders and drew her close, she knew it was Nicolas. His subtle aftershave smelled familiar and comfortable, unlike the scenery around her.

How did he know she'd be here? Or had he come for his own reasons?

"I came to take you home," he said, as if reading her mind.

"Home?" The word came out with a short burst of laughter. "I don't have a home, Nicolas. I never have." She didn't look at him, just continued staring at the numerous flower arrangements. Everyone had loved Lisa.

His arm tightened around her. "You do with me."

She closed her eyes. If only it were true. She took a moment to catch her bearings. "You're being kind. Thank you. But I'm a big girl. It's time for me to act like it." Her shoulders drooped.

"I'd better go see Cathy and Joe. Their plane will be leaving shortly."

She tried to wiggle out of Nicolas's embrace, but he spun her around in his arms. "Jana..." Moisture filled his eyes, but no tears fell. He trembled, and then he cleared his throat. "Let me take you to the house."

Jana still wasn't ready. She was running away again. Perhaps not physically, but in her mind she was trying to stay one step in front of the loneliness that hunted her. And it was relentless in its pursuit. With each minute that passed she felt it gaining strength, moving closer. With no weapons to fight it, she knew it was only a matter of time before she lost the battle.

"I need this time alone. I need to think," she said. He released her and she moved quickly toward her car. With a jerk she opened the door, slipped inside, before shutting the door with a *clunk*. Nicolas remained behind, staring at Lisa's grave. When she pulled out of the cemetery, he still hadn't moved.

Jana didn't want to go back to Lisa's house, but she had nowhere else to go. She hadn't packed and neither of Lisa's parents had said anything about when they expected her out. Thankfully, traffic seemed to stay away from her this time as if everyone knew she was unstable. The road was hers. No red lights stopped her, no one blocked her way as she traveled down one street and then another.

This time, when Jana passed her childhood home there were no hurtful feelings, no bad memories clouding her thoughts. Nothing proved to be worse than losing her friend.

As she steered her car into Lisa's driveway everything looked normal. She shifted the car into park, and then gazed across the grounds and at the Spanish-style home she loved. There were no signs that Lisa was gone—never coming back. No evidence that Jana's life had changed forever.

Jana closed her eyes and prayed for the strength to get her through the next couple of minutes. She squared her shoulders, took a deep cleansing breath and climbed out of the car.

Cathy and Joe were sitting on the couch waiting for her when she stepped inside.

"Sit down, Jana," Cathy said, "next to us." Joe scooted away from his wife, making room for Jana. When she sat, the older woman hugged her. There were no tears in her eyes. She had cried enough already to refill Saguaro Lake and then some after Jana had told her the news of her daughter's passing.

From the coffee table Joe picked up a manila folder and placed it in Jana's hands. The big man's sorrow stabbed through Jana like a knife. He inhaled a ragged breath. Opened his mouth to speak, but he couldn't. He just shook his head and turned his gaze away.

Cathy forced a smile. "Lisa signed the house over to you." Jana's eyes widened. "She wanted you to have it. Joe and I do, too."

"I can't take your home," Jana insisted. The envelope in her hands began to shake as she pushed it toward Cathy.

She gave it a shove back in Jana's direction. "You can and you will. Joe and I have always thought of you as our daughter, too. You're the only one we have left." Tears moistened Cathy's eyes with each word. "Please accept Lisa's gift."

Jana didn't know what to say about the house, about Cathy's heartfelt comments.

Joe took Jana into his arms. "Lisa loved you. We love you." Then he abruptly released her. "C'mon, Cathy, we need to leave." He pushed himself to his feet. His features were strained and tight.

As Cathy rose, she said, "There's a letter in there from Lisa. She wanted to make sure we gave it to you after the funeral."

A letter?

"Now give me a hug. We plan on visiting at least once a year, perhaps twice. Joe and I expect to see you at Christmastime." Jana rose and stepped into Cathy's warm embrace. For the first time in her life she felt a mother's love. "Thank you," Cathy whispered.

"For what?" Jana asked, confused.

"For being the sister we could never give Lisa." Cathy hugged her tighter and then released her. "Joe. I'm ready." She turned and together, hand–in–hand, they walked out the open door.

Jana watched Cathy and Joe leave, saddened by their departure, but relieved that she was now alone. The silence in the house was deafening. She scanned the room, not knowing if she could live here. Not without Lisa. Every room was filled with her friend's memories.

The envelope that was clutched between her fingers slipped out of her hand and landed softly on the floor. She'd forgotten she still carried it. She knelt and picked it up. Her fingers were all thumbs as she retrieved the letter and sank into a chair as she opened it.

At the top of the letter the date August 29th was written in Lisa's handwriting and then the following words:

My dearest Jana,

You can't know how many times I began this letter, tore it up, and then started again. I struggled to find the right words to express how I cherished our friendship. Hunted for the words to express what your love has meant to me. I found none that could accurately reflect my feelings, because you are my sister, the true half of my soul forever.

Jana's hands shook, tears misting her eyes as she read on.

I can hear you cursing me for leaving you. But that is only in the physical sense. I kept my promise, Jana. I'm in your heart as you are in mine. Can you feel me?

A blanket of warmth fell over Jana's shoulders like a cloak. For a moment she closed her eyes and Lisa was sitting beside her. When she opened them she was alone, but the sensation that Lisa was close remained.

I'll be with you always in a memory or thought, until it's time we meet again. But for now hold onto the love you have found with Nicolas. Find strength in his arms. Let him into your heart as you have me. Be happy and live your life to the fullest—for both of us.

Lisa

Clutching the letter to her chest, Jana gazed around the living room, and then rose.

Blindly, she moved through the house, needing to hear Lisa laugh, praying to hear her light breathing as she moved down the hall. When she stood before Lisa's bedroom door, she pushed it open. The light, powdery musk her friend had worn caressed her as she stepped inside. On the nightstand was a picture of Jana and Lisa and Mickey Mouse taken the last time she had visited Disneyland in California. To the left the closet door was wedged open. She went to shut it and instead walked in.

She skimmed her fingers across one outfit and then another. When she came to Lisa's favorite blue shirt Jana buried her nose in it, inhaling her friend's scent. It fell from the hanger and into her hands.

A moment of nothingness lingered. A silence that echoed the void she felt deep inside her. Then a wave of sorrow thundered through her, violently shaking her body.

It hurt to breathe.

Her chest felt heavy.

"Lisa," she cried out, as the wall holding back her tears burst. She threw back her head and released a bloodcurdling scream, before she fell to her knees, the letter and shirt pressed to her breasts.

And for the first time in years, Jana cried.

Quietly, Nicolas stood in Lisa's driveway. He had spoken briefly to Lisa's parents before they left. They weren't sure exactly how Jana was, but recommended that he give her some time alone. Evidently Lisa had left her a good-bye letter.

With wide strides he paced up and down the hard concrete. When he felt like he was about to explode with impatience he went to the front door and opened it.

Jana's screech sent Nicolas racing through the house. When he reached Lisa's bedroom he came to an abrupt halt. From where he stood he saw Jana in the closet. For half a second he watched as she knelt staring at the ceiling. Tears streamed down her cheeks, one and then another, each rolling faster than the next. She swayed back and forth. Her face a twisted mass of anguish, her pain so raw he felt it rip through his soul like a knife.

In a heartbeat he was by her side and down on his knees. He cradled her firmly and rocked her in his arms.

She released something in her hands, while her fingers twisted in his shirt. He heard the seams of his shirt give, ripping, beneath her struggle as she clung to him desperately.

Each breath was a short, fast intake that shook her as if she was breaking apart from the inside out. "I can't live without her."

He held her closer. "But you will," he murmured in her ear. She had to. He wasn't going to let her go. No matter what she chose to do he would be there to ensure he was a part of her plans.

For what seemed like forever he simply held her while she cried. When she finally began to calm, just a few sniffles remained. He stood and then lifted her into his arms. A shirt he had remembered seeing Lisa wear before, along with a letter, lay on the closet floor.

In several long strides he made it to the bed and began to lay Jana down when she said, "No. Not here. Not in Lisa's bed." Moisture filled her eyes. "I smell her, Nicolas." A tear dropped, and then another. Her expression grew tight. "She's everywhere," Jana whispered.

"Okay, honey." He kissed her softly as he moved out of the bedroom, carrying Jana down the hall into her own bedroom. Gently, he laid her down on the bed.

Then he crawled beside her and snuggled close.

"Sleep," he said.

"I don't know if I can."

He stroked her hair, ran his palm across her back. "You should try."

She was silent for a while, and then she said, "I hurt." Her voice cracked.

"I know, honey." He kissed her forehead, ran his hands along her back.

She began to cry softly. "I feel so alone."

"But you're not, Jana. I'm here." Why couldn't she see that he was here for her? He loved her.

"That's kind of you."

He jerked away from her and stared directly in her misty eyes. "I'm not being kind. I love you, Jana." His tone lowered. "I've loved you for some time."

She shook her head. "What?"

He cupped her face. "I love you."

"But Lisa—"

He released an exasperated sigh. "I cared for Lisa. There's an emptiness inside me when I think about her. But it's you I love. You, I want to share the rest of my life with. And you I want to have babies with." She was looking at him like he'd gone crazy. And maybe he had. Nothing made sense anymore, except that he couldn't lose Jana.

"Let me hold you," he whispered. "Let me take away your pain if only for a moment. Please."

She didn't say anything, just moved into his embrace.

Tears rolled softly from her eyes, dampening his shirt. After a while she grew quiet. And later still she finally fell off to sleep wrapped in his arms.

Chapter Twenty-Four

It was a new day, but somehow it didn't feel like it. Nicolas threw his arm over his eyes as he lay on his back. Jana had tossed and turned and even cried out in her sleep all night long. But at least she had slept. In fact, she was still sleeping and it was late afternoon. He had gotten up several times during the morning, each time returning to be with Jana.

He didn't want her to wake up alone.

The rustling of sheets drew his attention. She stirred, kicking off the sheet around her legs. "What time is it?" Her voice was drowsy, almost as if she were sporting a hangover.

He rolled to his side, cupping his head with the palm of his hand. "One twenty."

Her eyes were puffy. Her dress was wrinkled and pulled up, barely covering her ass. He had thought of undressing her, making her more comfortable, but he didn't want to disturb her slumber. He still had on the pants and now-ripped shirt he had worn to the funeral.

She blinked the sleep from her eyes, then rubbed them, releasing a sigh. "Really?"

He leaned over and brushed her hair back behind her ear. "Really. You've been out like a light."

She scanned his face, as though a multitude of thoughts rushed through her head. If only he could hear them. "You didn't have to stay with me," she said, her tone a little nasal.

His knuckles smoothed across her cheek. "I want you to know I'm here if you need me."

The muscles in her throat tightened as she swallowed, hard. "Thank you, but—"

He placed his finger against her lips. "Don't shut me out, Jana." His pulse jumped. Should he declare his love again? Tell her how much he needed her?

She closed her eyes and pressed her face to his hand. "Oh, Nicolas." For a moment there was silence, then her eyelids rose. "I have no idea where I belong."

His hands closed around her biceps. "Here. Right here with me. We belong together. Let me take care of you...love you."

After all she had been through yesterday, all he could think of was branding her his, of making sure she knew how he felt before she made any decisions that would tear them apart.

"Jana, you don't have to love me—just pretend. Pretend it's *me* you want to hold. *Me* you want to make love to."

He was trembling.

Dammit! He couldn't believe he'd lost control. Maybe it was the fact that he hadn't slept, worried that Jana would wake and slip away into the night. Or maybe it was simply because he didn't want to live without her by his side.

But when she reached for the buttons of his shirt and began to undo them, his heart crashed against his chest.

He placed his hand over hers. "Jana, this isn't what I meant." She didn't say anything, just continued to undress him, as one after another button came loose. Then she pushed his shirt from his shoulders. "Are you sure you want this, right now?"

She swallowed, an expression of pain washed across her face. "I feel dead inside." She trembled fighting for control. "I need you to make me feel alive. Please, make love to me." She reached for him and began to unfasten his belt.

He grasped the hem of the black dress she wore and moved it slowly up her body. She stopped briefly to lift her arms and let him drag the gown over her head. She wore a strapless black bra, a slip and panties beneath. A faint hint of her perfume teased his nose as he revealed her breasts, tossing the bra aside.

In moments they were both naked and in each other's arms.

Jana was lost in a river of emotions. Last night his declaration of love had taken her by surprise. The unshed tears ringing in his voice made her reach for him—to comfort him.

His touch was tender, as if he thought she might shatter into a million pieces. Yet he left no part of her body untouched, except for one place. His hands caressed and smoothed up her arms, dipping into the hollows of her shoulder blades, up her neck where he began to place light kisses in the paths of his palms. He kneaded her breasts, licked and suckled, then moved down her body slowly.

He loved her.

With slow, wet kisses he trailed a path along the inside of her thighs. She parted her legs further, but each time he drew close to the place that wept to be caressed he moved away. Then he slid his body along hers until they were eye to eye, chest to chest. Their gazes locked.

The silence broke when he murmured, "I love you." His warm expression said he didn't expect an answer. But she did love him. She just couldn't say it. Not now.

With a shift of his hips he thrust his cock forward, parting her slit and filling her completely. She released a cry of fulfillment that had her arching off the bed and pushing into him, needing to take him deeper. Rocking gently, he drove in and out, in and out, until her body burned with the need to climax. Like a small fire building, he stoked her desire higher and higher. Each stroke calculated to drive her slowly out of her mind. When he shifted his hips, placing pressure on her clit, her arms clamped around him and she screamed. White-hot sensation tore through her body making her quiver until the last spasm disappeared.

Nicolas drove hard between her legs forcing her body to slide on the sleek comforter, her head bumping the headboard with a thump. He released a groan that was deep and hoarse and then he collapsed atop her.

Jana listened to his rapid breathing slow and then he moved off her. He kissed her softly on the forehead, gathering her into his arms and against his warm body. It was calming, soothing. In the afterglow of their loving she drifted off to sleep.

Chapter Twenty-Five

Jana woke in the middle of the night wrapped in Nicolas's arms. The steady beat of his heart played beneath her ear pressed to his chest. The dark, curly hair next to her nose tickled, and she rubbed it. The room was dark, the house quiet. The comforter lay on the floor. Only a single sheet was draped over their hips. Nicolas must have awakened during the night and covered them.

She lay silently and thought about the last two days. It seemed like a dream. In less than forty-eight hours she had buried her best friend and had a man profess his love.

Nicolas loved her.

Through the tinge of insecurity that nagged somewhere deep in her head, she couldn't help but feel the joy of knowing someone loved her—really loved her.

She wasn't alone and it was all because of Lisa.

Jana looked about the room. Shadows of her past in Lisa's childhood bedroom brought back memories. What she and Lisa shared. How they loved. Lisa's last words spoken in a letter. Jana couldn't believe she had left the letter lying on the closet floor.

Carefully, she extracted herself from Nicolas's embrace and attempted to crawl off the bed, but still it squeaked as she moved. Nicolas groaned and turned over, but he didn't wake.

She crept into the hall and then the bedroom closet where the letter lay. She blindly felt for the light switch. When light flooded the small area, Jana blinked her eyes, trying to focus as she bent and picked up both Lisa's shirt and the crumpled letter. Her heart ached as she read the letter again, but this time something jumped out at her.

The timing was clearly off. It didn't make sense. The date August 29th didn't fit.

Jana hadn't even arrived back in Arizona until the first week of September. Lost in her thoughts, she flinched when a shadow fell over her.

"What are you doing in here?" Nicolas asked as he rubbed his watery eyes. He frowned at the light, and then squinted. "Come back to bed." He extended her his hand, and then paused. "What do you have there?"

"Lisa's letter."

"Oh." He paused as if unsure of what to do. "Do you want to talk about it?"

"It doesn't make sense," she said, moving toward the door. He stepped back and let her pass.

She heard the light switch snap and then it went dark again. As she walked into the hallway, she folded the letter. The bedroom was dusky as she moved toward the bed, setting the letter on the nightstand.

"What doesn't make sense?" he asked, coming up from behind her and pressing his body against hers. He was so warm. His arms were strong and comforting as they folded around her.

"She wrote this letter a week before I even came to Arizona." She stood in the dimly lit room and tried to make sense of what she knew.

"Lisa said she'd known about her illness for some time," Nicolas said as he guided her toward the bed. "Get in, I want to hold you."

Jana slipped into bed. Nicolas followed her, drawing her against his heat.

She rolled onto her back, frustrated because she couldn't get past that nagging sensation consuming her thoughts. "Yes, but you and I hadn't met."

"Why does that matter?" he asked. His palm was gentle as he stroked her belly.

"She mentioned us—you and me."

Nicolas kissed her softly on the cheek. "You must have misunderstood her."

"No," she said firmly.

She felt his sigh as he pushed into a sitting position. "Let me see the letter."

Jana leaned over the bed and flipped on the nightstand lamp. Light flooded the room as she reached for Lisa's letter and then handed it to Nicolas.

He paused as if asking permission. "Go ahead," she said.

It took only a couple of seconds for him to read what Lisa had written. Then a smile slid over his face.

"That little devil." There was laughter in his voice.

Now Jana was really confused. She found nothing in the letter to laugh about. "What?"

"Can't you see what she did?" He handed the letter back to Jana. "Lisa set us up."

Jana frowned. *What the hell is he talking about?*

"She played matchmaker. Baited us, and then she reeled me in hook, line and sinker. I fell for you hard." He leaned against the headboard. "It all makes sense now. She made sure I knew everything about you before you arrived. She had me panting and drooling, before I even met you." The way he stroked Jana with his gaze, she knew he told her the truth.

"You mean all of this, the threesome, was simply to get us together?" Jana looked at the letter in disbelief.

"Lisa and I knew we weren't compatible. Hell, we knew it from the start. From day one I heard about you. The things you'd accomplished. Your strength. Your red hair." He reached out and flipped a lock between his fingers. "Come here." She went into his arms. "Have I ever told you I love your red hair?" He kissed her softly on the lips.

Her pulse jumped.

"Can't you see? Lisa loved you so much she couldn't bear leaving you alone. She wanted to make sure you were happy before her time ran out. I was simply the tool in Lisa's eyes." He pressed his lips on her forehead. "I feel so used," he teased.

Bittersweet emotion bubbled up inside Jana. If Nicolas was right, then Lisa's love was truly unselfish. Even when Lisa discovered she was dying, she'd thought of Jana. "My God, the elaborate schemes."

Nicolas huffed. "Don't kid yourself. That woman enjoyed sex. You gave her more than you will ever know. Each time she looked at you with love in her eyes I grew envious at not being in your circle. She was happy, Jana. Happy with both of us."

It was too much for Jana to comprehend. Lisa had known about her feelings for Nicolas when she was just a teenager. It was unbelievable that Lisa would go through such an elaborate scheme to see Jana's dreams come true. And then that blanket of warmth she had felt once before in the closet surrounded her.

This *was* what Lisa had wanted, for Nicolas and Jana to be together. She could feel it deep inside.

"I have an idea." Nicolas stroked her belly once again. "We can name our first daughter Lisa."

"What?" Jana's voice squeaked.

"Uh...I forgot the condom, again." His sheepish expression made her shake her head.

"What am I going to do with you?" she asked.

"Take me to bed and never let me go," he responded as he laid her down and pressed his length against hers. "Love me, Jana. You'll never regret it. I'll make sure you don't."

Jana moved into his arms. "I do love you," she said. And with all her heart she meant it.

And at that moment Jana understood. Lisa's gift was her unselfish love and Nicolas.

About the Author

A taste of the erotic, a measure of daring and a hint of laughter describe Mackenzie McKade's novels. She sizzles the pages with scorching sex, fantasy and deep emotion that will touch you and keep you immersed until the end. Whether her stories are contemporaries, futuristics or fantasies, this Arizona native thrives on giving you the ultimate erotic adventure.

When not traveling through her vivid imagination, she's spending time with three beautiful daughters, two devilishly handsome grandsons, and the man of her dreams. She loves to write, enjoys reading, and can't wait 'til summer. Boating and jet skiing are top on her list of activities. Add to that laughter and if mischief is in order—Mackenzie's your gal!

To learn more about Mackenzie McKade, please visit www.mackenziemckade.com. Send an email to Mackenzie at mackenzie@mackenziemckade.com or sign onto her Yahoo! group to join in the fun with other readers and authors as well as Mackenzie!

http://groups.yahoo.com/group/wicked_writers/

Look for these titles

Now Available
Six Feet Under
Fallon's Revenge
Beginnings: A Warrior's Witch
Bound for the Holidays

Coming Soon:
Take Me
Lost But Not Forgotten
Second Chance Christmas

Vengeance is what she sought...eternal love is what she found.

Fallon's Revenge
© *2006 Mackenzie McKade*

Young and inexperienced, Fallon McGregor is an immortal with one thing on her mind. Revenge. She'll do anything to destroy the demon that killed her daughter and made Fallon his flesh and blood slave. One step ahead of her tormentor, she knows her luck is running out. She needs to discover the mysteries of the dark—and fast. When she meets Adrian Trask she gets more than she bargains for in tight jeans and a Stetson.

Adrian will share his ancient blood and knowledge with Fallon, but he wants something in return...her heart and her promise to stay with him forever.

But Fallon doesn't have forever. Once her nemesis is destroyed she will seek her own death. Tormented, she must choose between a promise made and the love of one man.

Available now in ebook and print from Samhain Publishing.

Don't get mad...get sexy!

The Reinvention of Chastity
© *2007 Eve Vaughn*

Plain Jane paralegal Chastity Bryant has had a raving crush on her boss Sebastian Rossi since meeting him. Always willing to jump at his beck and call, Chastity's world comes crashing in on her one morning when she overhears him laughing about her less than exciting life. To top it off, he freely admits that he's used her crush to his advantage!

After a pep talk from her friends, they devise a plan to teach the arrogant Sebastian a lesson. Armed with a new look and a new attitude, Chastity sets out to seduce her hunky boss and bring him to his knees.

Sebastian Rossi has always been able to depend on two things in life: his successful law practice and his dependable employee, Chastity. But his whole world is turned upside down when she walks into his office looking like she just stepped off the cover of a magazine. Now, all he can think about is her. He doesn't know what brought about the change, but one thing is certain, he'll stop at nothing to possess her.

Things are going according to plan for Chastity, but the only thing she hadn't counted on was falling in love.

Available now in ebook from Samhain Publishing.

Enjoy the following excerpt from
The Reinvention of Chastity...

It was official.

Sebastian wanted Chastity Bryant. He'd reached his boiling point and could no longer deny what had begun from the moment she stepped into his office with her glamorous new look two months ago.

It grew more difficult with each passing day to watch her stroll around the office looking drop-dead gorgeous. It wasn't just her looks either. Chastity now exuded a confidence that hadn't been there before, and he found it sexy as hell. He couldn't get a proper night's sleep from thoughts of her. He'd wake up in the middle of the night, body drenched with sweat after dreaming about burying himself between silky, chocolate thighs.

Whenever she walked past him, he couldn't tear his eyes away from her slow, rhythmic movements that seemed to scream, "jump me". He'd already lost count of how many times his dick got hard with just the mere mention of her name. Sebastian wanted to run his hands over her body just to see if that rich, dark skin of hers was as soft as it looked.

Once, he'd caught her nibbling on her bottom lip and he literally had to stop himself from grabbing her and tasting it for himself. Sebastian would sit at his desk for hours trying to concentrate on his work when all he could think about was stripping Chastity's clothes off, one article at a time—tasting every delectable inch of her.

Tossing his pen aside, he stood up in frustration. It was already past twelve. He might as well grab something to eat since he wasn't getting any work done. On his way out of the office he knew he'd pass by Chastity's desk.

His plan to keep walking without looking her way went down the tubes when he spied Jeremy leaning over her desk. Chastity gave his friend the big smile she used to give him. Her eyes twinkled with apparent amusement at whatever Jeremy was saying. The deep dimples in her cheeks gave her a look of sweet innocence.

Since her makeover, Chastity had taken to wearing low cut tops and today was no exception. The sexy décolletage on display was enough to set his pulse racing. His fingers itched to trace the tops of those generous mounds. She wore her hair pulled back into a ponytail tied with a pink satin ribbon. Although he preferred her hair flowing around her shoulders, she looked lovely.

An irrational burst of envy soared through his body, making him clench his fists. Unable to help himself, he walked over to them. "What are you two grinning about over here?" Sebastian cursed inwardly. He didn't mean for his voice to sound so harsh.

They looked up at him, Jeremy eyeing him with mild curiosity and Chastity looking slightly resentful, as though he'd intruded on a private conversation. Jeremy straightened up, an easy smile splitting his face. "What's up, Seb?"

"I was on my way to lunch actually."

The blond frowned. "I thought you had a business lunch with one of your clients."

"They had to reschedule," he lied. He wasn't about to admit that he canceled his appointment because his head was in his pants. "You didn't answer my question."

Jeremy frowned. "What question?"

Sebastian hated repeating himself, especially over something as trivial as this. "What were you two grinning about?"

"Just small talk. Chastity and I were on our way to lunch as well."

Sebastian's blood thundered. He wanted to knock Jeremy on his ass. He remembered his friend telling him of his interest in Chastity, but that didn't stop the green-eyed monster from rearing its head. A demon must have possessed him because he couldn't help saying, "Since we're all headed for lunch, let's all go together." His eyes never left Chastity's face.

Her lips tightened slightly before she turned her head away. She didn't seem pleased.

Tough.

"We were only going to the Gallery Mall, nothing fancy," Jeremy said, almost as if to put him off.

"I don't need anything fancy. You don't mind my tagging along, do you?" Sebastian knew very well that he was putting them in a position where they couldn't refuse without looking like a couple of jerks. The look on Jeremy's face spoke volumes. Chastity's face, however, was unreadable and he wondered what was going on in that beautiful head of hers. "Do you mind, Chastity?"

She looked up at Jeremy with a smile, not bothering to answer Sebastian's question. "I'm going to the restroom before we go."

Jeremy smiled back. "No problem. Take your time."

Both men watched her retreating figure, her curvaceous bottom swaying from side to side with each step she took. God, he wanted her. When she was out of earshot, Jeremy turned on him, blue eyes blazing. "What the hell was that about?"

"What do you mean? I thought you said you didn't mind my joining you two."

"You know damn well I couldn't say otherwise."

"Why couldn't you? I would have."

"Don't play dumb with me, Romeo."

Sebastian shrugged. "Who's playing dumb? Haven't we had lunch together on numerous occasions?"

"Not with Chastity."

"Okay, fine. What's wrong with a little friendly competition?"

For a second, it looked like Jeremy wanted to deck him before his face relaxed into a smile. "You're a son of a bitch."

Sebastian laughed. "And don't you forget it."

"She's going to see right through this new interest you have in her. You never gave two flying fucks about her before this sudden change."

"Neither did you."

"Okay, so we're both bastards."

Sebastian cocked an eyebrow and held out his hand. "May the better bastard win?" Even as they shook hands, Sebastian guaranteed himself the victory.

The three of them decided to have a meal at a small tavern not too far from the office instead of trekking all the way downtown to the Gallery Mall. When shown to a booth, Jeremy slid in next to Chastity and Sebastian took the seat directly across from her. That was fine with him. This way, he could face her, and she'd have no choice but to look at him as well. He wouldn't allow her to ignore him, if he had any say in the matter.

The look of agitation on her pretty face told him that he was getting to her as well. Good. He wanted her to be as aware of him as he was of her.

"I think the Cobb salad looks good. Have you eaten here before, Jeremy?" she asked, turning to the blond. Sebastian knew exactly what Chastity was up to, but if she wanted to play games, she'd soon learn just how competitive he could be.

Fixing his gaze on his prey, he said, "Chastity, why don't you try the Oysters Casino. A nice little aphrodisiac, don't you think?"

She only spared him a brief glance before her eyes darted away again. She fluttered thick lashes at Jeremy as if he were some kind of rock star. "I'm not really in the mood for anything heavy. What do you think, Jeremy?"

"Hmm, I think I'll have a hamburger and fries. Probably not the healthiest choice, but I'll just have to hit the gym a little harder tonight."

"I think I'm going to stick to the salad. My ass is big enough as it is." She closed the menu with a sigh.

Jeremy grinned at her wolfishly. "At the risk of sounding like a lecher, I think your ass is just fine."

Chastity giggled, dimples popping out. Before Sebastian realized what was going on, his lunch mates fell into a deep conversation, completely excluding him. His fury grew with each passing second. By the time the waitress took their orders, he was ready to strangle them both. He knew what Jeremy was up to, but what was up with Chastity's cold shoulder act? No woman had ever treated him like this before and it was driving him bananas. He hated being ignored, especially when it was by someone he wanted so damn much.

GREAT
cheap
FUN

Discover eBooks!
THE FASTEST WAY TO GET THE HOTTEST NAMES

Get your favorite authors on your favorite reader, long before they're
out in print! Ebooks from Samhain go wherever you go, and work with
whatever you carry—Palm, PDF, Mobi, and more.

Samhain
publishing ltd

WWW.SAMHAINPUBLISHING.COM